THE PREDATOR™

KT-467-188

THE PREDATOR™

BY CHRISTOPHER GOLDEN AND MARK MORRIS

BASED ON THE SCREENPLAY WRITTEN BY
FRED DEKKER & SHANE BLACK

BASED ON THE CHARACTERS CREATED BY
JIM THOMAS & JOHN THOMAS

TITAN BOOKS

THE PREDATOR
Print edition ISBN: 9781785658051
E-book edition ISBN: 9781785658068

Published by Titan Books
A division of Titan Publishing Group Ltd
144 Southwark Street, London SE1 0UP

First edition: September 2018
10 9 8 7 6 5 4 3 2 1

This is a work of fiction. Names, characters, places, and incidents either are the
product of the author's imagination or are used fictitiously, and any resemblance to
actual persons, living or dead, business establishments, events, or locales is entirely
coincidental. The publisher does not have any control over and does not assume
responsibility for author or third-party websites or their content.

TM & © 2018 Twentieth Century Fox Film Corporation.
All rights reserved.

No part of this publication may be reproduced, stored in a retrieval system, or
transmitted, in any form or by any means without prior written permission of the
publisher, nor be otherwise circulated in any form of binding or cover other than
that in which it is published and without a similar condition being imposed on the
subsequent purchaser.

A CIP catalogue record for this title is available from the British Library.

Printed and bound by CPI Group UK Ltd, Croydon, CR0 4YY

Did you enjoy this book?
We love to hear from our readers. Please email us at
readerfeedback@titanmail.com or write to us at
Reader Feedback at the above address.

www.titanbooks.com

For my son, Daniel, who is going to love this film.
CG

For my kids, David and Polly, who love monster movies.
MM

0

Space.

Cold. Silent. A billion twinkling stars. You can't imagine the serenity out here. The peace and quiet, the way it seems as if you might drift forever on this dark, glittering ocean. It might go on for eternity, an infinite horizon of invisible tides and unknown energies. You could surrender yourself and sail into this beautiful dream. Stars fall and comets burn in the distance, suns blink out, planets are born, and the Hubble Space Telescope watches it all with mechanical indifference.

Until there's a ripple in the void.

Close your eyes and you can see what I mean. The heat rising off a distant highway—the way the air shimmers above the blacktop—it's like that. Then the velvet black curls and folds and something emerges at speed that would make the air scream, if there were any air out here. The gleaming spacecraft is smoking, the hull scorched and dented, shedding scales off its hull as its pilot tries to get it under control.

The Hubble's in the way. The ship shears through it, both spacecraft and telescope now vomiting debris. Sparking and hissing, the ship's been through hell, and when it hits the outer limits of Earth's atmosphere there's a *whump* of resistance, like someone's awkward dad just did a belly flop into the swimming pool.

Oxygen stokes the sparks into flames.

Far below—but closer with every second—the ice caps are melting. On board instruments show an atmosphere getting hotter and more toxic by the day, only the pilot's not looking at *those* instruments.

He's at the helm. Smoke fogs the inside of the craft. Sparks pop and lights flicker but he doesn't flinch, focused entirely on the control panel. His talons dance across it, trying to keep control—trying to navigate this craft so it doesn't hit the ground at the same velocity it had when it sliced through spacetime, or smashed through the invisible wall of Earth's atmosphere. The pilot does not want to die.

Urgently, he taps a new sequence into the control panel. A slot opens on the console and even he—even this creature—hesitates a moment before he retrieves the device from within. In his language, or the crude version of his language you might be able to pronounce, it's called the *Kujhad*. The pilot snaps it into the gauntlet he wears on his wrist with a loud click that echoes in the smoke-filled cockpit of the shuddering spacecraft.

He rises. The pilot is no fool. The odds of the ship making it to the surface without tearing itself apart or exploding on impact do not favor his survival. He taps one final command into his control panel, initiating the escape sequence. As locks disengage on the primary escape pod, the control panel erupts in a fresh shower of sparks. But the pilot is already gone, heading toward the pod bay, moving more swiftly than his size should allow.

Seconds pass.

Outside the ship, a hiss and pop as the escape pod is jettisoned from the main body of the careening spacecraft. The pod bursts out in a blossom of flames, far from a clean exit, striking its edges against the ship as it tumbles away, trailing smoke, spinning in a descent as uncontrolled as that of the larger vessel.

The pilot will do his best to survive. It's one of the things his kind does best. They survive... and they hunt.

On board the ship he's vacated, sparks continue to fly. Smoke billows. Lights flicker, the control panel glitches, and then a sudden, savage burst of electric flame erupts—a power surge.

The lights fail. The ship slices across the night sky, trailing smoke in the darkness, until it fades out of sight above America's southern border.

All is peaceful again.

Cold. Silent.

But not for long.

1

MONTERREY, MEXICO

When a branch broke with a sharp snap beneath McKenna's boot, he gritted his teeth and immediately froze. Then, gradually, he relaxed, letting out his breath in a long, slow exhalation.

What was he worried about? Did he truly think such an inconsequential sound would betray his presence? Here in the depths of the jungle? Because what surrounded him could pretty much be termed a *cacophony*. Insects clicked and chirruped at ground level, exotic birds and monkeys chattered and screeched in the thick green canopy of trees overhead, and even the undergrowth in which he was crouched rustled all around him as unseen creatures went about their business.

No, short of standing up and belting out a rendition of 'The Star-Spangled Banner' at the top of his lungs, he thought he was pretty much okay as far as concealing the sounds of his own, mostly stealthy movements were concerned.

Not that that made his mission all that much easier.

Far from it.

Ignoring the sun beating down on the shoulders of his thick camouflage jacket, and the trickles of sweat that ran out of his hair and down the sides of his grease-blackened face, he adjusted his rifle on his shoulder, settling it into a slightly more comfortable position. Through its scope his gaze remained fixed on the incongruous sight of the gleaming black SUV parked at the side of the thin dirt highway that cut a groove through the teeming vegetation. He watched the men inside the SUV. Hunched, dark shapes. Just sitting there, as still as mannequins.

He'd been here for close on thirty minutes now, but he was prepared to wait a lot longer if need be. Quinn McKenna was a captain in the US Army Rangers. A professional sniper. Thirty-six years old, at the peak of physical fitness, he could shoot a man dead without his pulse rate showing even the slightest blip of reaction. He was as cool as a snake. As patient as a sphinx. Here, in the heat of the jungle, with the enemy in range, he was very much in his element.

The slight hissing in his Bluetooth headset was abruptly silenced and the clipped voice of Haines came through, tinny but clear.

"Piggy One, copy. You got eyes on the hostages?"

McKenna's reply was a murmur. "Negative."

The third member of his unit, Dupree, his Louisiana tang prominent, said, "Twenty bucks says they don't show."

McKenna smiled. "You yardbirds actually want to bet money on whether a drug cartel has executed the hostages?"

"Abso-fucking-lutely," said Dupree with conviction.

"I believe that was implied," murmured Haines.

McKenna's smile stretched into a grin. Sometimes the only way to cope with this job was to maintain a sense of humor—albeit of the graveyard variety. "Okay, just checking. I'm in for twenty."

He heard the rumble of an engine off to his left and swiveled the rifle to track the approach of a new vehicle. At first, he saw nothing but a swirling cloud of dust, then within it the glint of reflected sunlight on glass and chrome. Seconds later another SUV, as black and highly polished as the first, shimmered from the heat haze, as if beamed down from the USS *Enterprise*. Aware of movement to his right, McKenna swiveled again, and saw three men emerge from the parked vehicle armed with rifles, their movements languid, their weapons held casually, pointing at the ground. One of them—plump face, dark moustache, white, short-sleeved Guayabera shirt—was instantly recognizable. This was Gutierrez. Murderer. Drug lord. McKenna's target.

The second SUV jolted to a halt a meter or so behind Gutierrez's vehicle and two big, sweaty guys got out the back, one on each side. The guy closest to McKenna turned and reached into the vehicle and hauled out a young woman. A sack had been pulled over her head and cinched at the neck. The woman, her hands tied in front of her, stumbled as the hired goon pushed her toward Gutierrez and his men, but she made no sound. Not so the second hostage, a kid this time, similarly hooded and tied, who was yanked from the vehicle like a sack of potatoes and tossed onto the dusty ground. He landed in a sprawl of limbs, skinning his bony knees, yelping in pain. One of Gutierrez's men laughed.

McKenna watched without emotion—or at least, he kept his emotions tightly coiled inside him. The instant Gutierrez had stepped from the vehicle, McKenna had tilted his rifle a fraction so that the drug lord's head was positioned precisely in the center of his crosshairs. Aware as he was of the plight of the hostages, he remained utterly still, his heartbeat slow and steady in his chest, his breathing shallow, his finger poised on the trigger of his weapon.

Barely moving his lips, he spoke quietly into his headset. "I got a woman and a kid, target in the reticle, no crosswind. I'm not waiting, 10-50 out."

All in all, it was a pretty shitty time for an earthquake.

At least, that was what McKenna assumed it was at first. The instant he had finished speaking he became aware of a deep bass rumble, as if the world was about to split in two, and the ground beneath his feet started to shake. Then several things happened in very quick succession.

First, a flock of birds exploded from the canopy of trees overhead, screeching in fright. Something huge and dark appeared in the sky to McKenna's right (in his peripheral vision it looked like a boulder the size of an entire neighborhood) and sheared the top off a radio tower jutting above the trees in the middle distance, causing a mass of debris to fly off in all directions. On the ground, Gutierrez, his men, and the hired goons shouted and pointed their weapons, raising their faces to the approaching projectile as its vast black shadow rushed across the ground toward them.

Through all of this, McKenna, after a quick glance to his right, remained motionless, cool, focused on his job.

Readjusting his aim, which had wavered only slightly, he calmly shot Gutierrez through the head, taking him out of the equation. Even before the drug lord hit the ground like a dead weight, McKenna was swiveling, re-sighting, and finally taking in the details of the projectile heading toward him.

He was expecting to see a comet, or a meteor, or whatever such things were called—a lump of rock, at any rate, trailing a tail of fire.

Instead, he experienced a split second of awe, wonder, astonishment, as he realized the thing hurtling toward him was not a piece of space debris at all, but something... manufactured. A craft of some kind.

A *spaceship*.

He had time only to register that it looked like nothing he had ever seen before—hell, that it looked utterly and completely *alien*—and then he was up and running for his life. Thanks to his job, McKenna knew a little about course vectors and velocity, but he didn't need to be an expert to calculate that the craft—the *spaceship*—was going to pass right over the heads of the group gathered around the two SUVs (and even now, the goons were piling into the vehicles and hauling ass, leaving their bewildered hostages and the corpse of their leader behind) and crash down pretty much right where he had established his vantage point.

His only hope was the fact that to *reach* his vantage point he had had to scale the hillside of a steep jungle valley, hauling himself up via tree trunks and vines and the sinewy stalks of fleshy green plants. With luck, if he could reach the valley, the thing behind him, which even now was screaming like all the souls in Hell, would hit the ground, bounce right up over the top of the valley, and slide to a halt somewhere on the far side.

There were a lot of ifs and buts to cover for that to happen, but ifs and buts were pretty much all McKenna could rely on right now. That, and his ability to keep running, as the jungle did its best to hold him back, leaves and branches lashing at his body as he hurtled through them, vines snagging at his ankles, eager to trip him up.

Then, just when it seemed the screaming of the engines behind him would blot out his senses and the world with it, the ground disappeared beneath McKenna's feet. One second it was there, and the next he was pedaling air, like Wile E. Coyote in those old Road Runner cartoons.

Still holding his rifle in a death-like grip, he plunged downward, toward an array of branches and leaves and stalks and vines and rocks—*oh shit, rocks*. He tried to gauge his fall, to keep his body compact, but there wasn't a whole lot he could do to influence gravity, and within seconds he was tumbling end over end, only vaguely aware of the pummeling he was taking as he bounced and rolled and cartwheeled down the slope.

He had been knocked cold only twice before—once when boxing during his army training, and once in a bar fight when a redneck had got in on his blind side and hit him upside the head with a pool cue. Whatever it was that bashed him in the side of the skull now felt a little like that pool cue—a sudden, hard flash of impact, and then…

Nothing.

It was impossible to gauge how long he was out for, but

when he came to he did so suddenly, his eyes snapping open. His survival training, drummed into him so intrinsically it was as natural to him as breathing, kicked in, his senses instantly assimilating information.

He was covered in dirt, most likely from the avalanche of jungle debris created by the impact of the alien craft, which he could see had reduced the tree line way above his head to so much splintered matchwood. At some point it had started raining, heavy droplets splashing into his face and pattering on his fatigues like searching fingers.

His head was throbbing, and when he touched it his fingertips came away thinly smeared with blood, but aside from a few bumps and bruises he seemed to be okay.

His hands were empty. Where was his gun? Then, sitting up, he saw it lying in a clump of vegetation only a few meters away. He scrambled across to it, and snatched it up, and immediately felt better.

Were his comms still working? He touched his headset, which was miraculously still in position and apparently undamaged.

"Piggy One," he said. "Do you read? Over."

Nothing but static—so maybe it wasn't undamaged, after all.

He clambered tentatively to his feet—and gasped.

As he had calculated (*hoped*), the alien craft, the UFO, had hit the tree line at the top of the valley, bounced like one of those Dambuster bombs from World War Two, and come down on the far side of the valley, trailing a slipstream of debris behind it. But it hadn't *just* come down. It had effectively punched a tunnel through the jungle, pulverizing trees as it went and leaving a smoking, blackened trail behind it.

Shouldering his rifle, McKenna headed up the far side of the valley, and a few minutes later he was standing on the edge of the charred trail. Investigating UFOs was not exactly part of his mission remit, but how could he ignore something like this? Besides, he had to find his men. Haines and Dupree were out there somewhere, and chances were they'd have followed their instincts and, like him, converged on the UFO crash site. And okay, so this wasn't strictly US soil, but as an Army Ranger, not to mention a citizen of the world, he still felt a responsibility to maintain national security if such an opportunity should present itself.

Or in this case, judging by the evidence, *global* security.

The blackened vegetation crunched beneath his feet as he moved forward, his senses attuned, his eyes darting every which way, alert for anything. It took him a good five minutes of walking before he reached the thing he'd glimpsed hurtling toward him out of the sky, and when he did he allowed himself a moment— just a moment—to goggle in wonder at a craft that was *definitely* not of this earth.

Damaged as it was, he could see that the angles were all wrong, and that the materials used were… weird. Swamped in plant matter, it looked more like some amphibious or insectile creature, broken-backed, hissing and spitting and steaming, than it did a vehicle capable of flight (*space flight?*).

He approached cautiously, rifle up, finger on the trigger, scope trained unerringly on the open hatch, which was sticking straight up in the air like a gossamer wing, vast and dislocated. Beyond the opening, for now, he could see only darkness. He moved closer, stalking like a big cat toward its prey, the rain now pelting down around him, the sound like a million scurrying insects.

Closer still. He noticed something glimmering on the ground near his right boot, and glanced down. Frowned.

Liquid of some sort. Thick enough not to have been washed away by the rain. It was fluorescent, glowing bright green. Hell, what was that stuff? Rocket fuel? Radioactive waste? Alien goop?

Before he could decide, his eye was snagged by something else, lying a little closer to the craft, half-concealed by vegetation. It appeared to be a glove of some kind, or perhaps a shackle.

His mind rushed through possibilities. Impressive as the crashed vessel was, it was small, compact. Could it be an escape pod, perhaps something that had been attached to a larger craft? And the shackle—could its owner have been a prisoner? Or an escaping slave?

As he took another cautious step closer, however, McKenna saw that the thing was not a shackle, but a gauntlet, vaguely resembling the kind of thing a knight of old might have worn, but far more sophisticated, far more *alien*. Maybe it had belonged to a warrior of some sort? But why was it lying here? Had its owner discarded it? Had it been jarred loose?

Then he saw the face.

It was staring up at him from the ground, close to the gauntlet. Heavy browed, eyes slanted and glaring, but otherwise featureless. McKenna's heart jolted. For a split second he thought he'd stepped into a trap; that the craft's occupant had dug a pit for itself and was crouched within it, ready to spring out…

But no. Even as he swung his rifle around, McKenna realized that the face was not a face, but a mask, half-buried in ash and pulped vegetation. He glanced around, then stepped closer, probing at the gauntlet and mask with the barrel of his rifle, half-afraid they might have been booby-trapped.

When nothing happened, he knelt down, brushed away the muck from around the mask and picked it up. It was heavy, made of some dense grayish-green metal. He stared at it for a moment, into its eye sockets, empty but somehow malevolent. Stuffing the mask into his pack, he tried his comms again.

"Piggy One, Piggy Two. Do you copy? Over."

Nothing but the hiss of static. He sighed. "Fuck this."

He picked up the gauntlet, and was about to add that to his pack too when he paused. For a moment, he hefted it in his hand, and then, curiosity getting the better of him, slipped it onto his forearm. Immediately it attached itself with a sharp *snik* of meshing attachments, then, to his alarm and fascination, adjusted itself, scale-like plates sliding over one another, until it was encasing his arm snugly but not uncomfortably.

So engrossed was he in his new toy that for a moment he forgot where he was. It was only when he heard a sound behind him—the slither of something heavy on the rain-sodden ground—that he jerked upright and spun round, water droplets flying from his hair, gun leveled, finger already squeezing the trigger.

A figure, combat fatigues dark with rain. A white face wearing a stunned expression, staring not at him but at the smoking wreck of the craft behind him.

"Dupree!" spat McKenna, jerking his finger from the trigger. "Jesus!"

Dupree, on the far side of the impact crater, failed to respond, didn't even look at him.

"Where's Haines?" McKenna barked. And then, when Dupree still said nothing, he instilled every ounce of authority that he could muster into his voice. *"Vinnie! Where's Haines?"*

Only now did Dupree's slack-jawed gaze drift toward his superior. He blinked. "Dunno. Comm's not working."

McKenna hefted his pack and rifle, suddenly businesslike. "We gotta head for the extraction point."

Dupree nodded, then faltered again. "The fuck *is* that, Cap?"

McKenna glanced at the pod, shrugged. "Above our pay grade."

The stunned expression on Dupree's face was slowly fading, and he was beginning to look more like his old self. Shifting his gaze to McKenna's arm, he cocked an eyebrow, the question unspoken.

All at once McKenna felt embarrassed. "Evidence," he said.

Dupree nodded slowly. "Evidence, right. Because…?"

The two compadres grinned at each other, then spoke in unison: "No one's gonna believe us."

McKenna chuckled. Dupree grinned, but all at once something seemed to occur to him, and he looked around in puzzlement.

"Er… Cap? I'm… uh…" He raised his hands, palms tilted toward the sky. "I'm not getting rained on."

McKenna stared. It was true. Rain was falling to either side of Dupree, but not on Dupree himself. He looked up into the tree that was partly sheltering his comrade, but which should still have been allowing *some* rain to get through—which *had*, in fact, been allowing rain through until a few moments ago.

Was there something up there? Something dark and large among the leaves and branches?

Calmly he said, "Walk away from the tree, Dupree."

Dupree half-turned, squinting upward, following his Captain's gaze. "Why, is there…?"

At which point all hell broke loose.

With a sudden splintering crash of branches, and a shower of leaves, something fell from the tree. McKenna swung his rifle up as Dupree leaped out of the way and spun round to face it. At first the falling object was too swift to focus on, but a couple of meters from the ground it came to an abrupt halt, the vine it was suspended from snapping like a whip. It swung to and fro, arms outstretched, great red wings spread. For a dizzy, disorienting moment, McKenna thought that what he was looking at was a demon, or at least some kind of giant alien bat. Then Dupree made a kind of sobbing sound, a stifled cry of rage and horror and fear all rolled into one, and McKenna's vision readjusted, the thing coming into sudden sharp focus.

The reality was far, far worse than the fantasy had been.

Dangling from a vine above their heads, swaying like a side of meat, was Haines. He had been gutted, his intestines hanging in gray-purple loops, his chest and stomach slashed open so brutally that the two sides of his mutilated flesh hung in drooling flaps on either side of him. His face was a bulging-eyed rictus of terror and agony, blood running down the sides of it and through his hair, to drip and pool on the ground beneath.

"Jesus Christ," McKenna muttered. Then he pointed his rifle up into the trees and unloaded, shredding leaves and branches, not stopping until the entire clip had been exhausted.

Even then, even when the trigger clicked empty, he was not done. He switched to his handgun, firing bullets up into the trees, shooting at nothing, Dupree doing the same beside him.

When the answering fire came, it was so unexpected, so devastating, that McKenna experienced it in little more than a series of flash images. First there was lightning, or what seemed like lightning—a bolt of blistering fire that hurtled down at an angle from the trees overhead. Then Dupree, beside him, was pierced by the light. It impaled him like a skewer, his limbs flying outward in an X, his sizzling guts flying out of the hole in his back and hitting the ground like wet barbecue. McKenna had barely registered this when he himself was flying backward through the air, hurled ten feet or more, as if he weighed nothing. He only had time to wonder if he was dead and just didn't know it yet when he crashed down into a pit, into darkness.

Alice down the rabbit hole, he thought wildly.

He came down, sprawling, on a hard surface. His body skidded backward and then he hit his head—*wham!*—on something solid, unyielding. For a moment he saw stars, but even when he blinked them away he realized he was still seeing them. Then he looked round, and a prickle of awe and dread passed through his body as he realized where he was.

He was inside the crashed escape pod! He must have flown through the air and come straight down through the open hatch like a basketball into a hoop.

Surrounding him were all kinds of weird alien instrument panels, that even now were flashing to life, as though aware of his presence among them. He saw jagged symbols scrolling across screens, multiple readings for who knew what. It was fascinating and terrifying in equal measure, but he didn't have the time or knowhow to make sense of any of it. He had a more pressing matter to attend to—the enemy. The thing that had opened up Haines like he was a can of beans and eviscerated Dupree with an alien lightning bolt.

Looking out through the open hatch, McKenna at first thought his eyes were deceiving him. Beyond the edge of the impact crater the jungle seemed to be moving, shifting, as though it were alive. Then he realized there was something moving *across* the jungle, a vaguely man-shaped blur, but *tall*—seven feet, at least. It seemed to be made of liquid glass; through it, McKenna could see trees, leaves, shafts of light. But it was jerky, coalescing then breaking up, constantly resetting.

Elusive though this strange new enemy was, at least McKenna had something to aim at. He reached instinctively for a weapon, but neither his rifle nor his handgun was any longer in his possession. He must have lost them when he was blasted through the air.

All he had to defend himself with was the wrist gauntlet, with its two curved and jagged-toothed blades curving up and outwards over the back of his hand like claws. As the glassy thing moved again in the jungle, he jerked his arm up instinctively, ready to engage in hand-to-hand combat if necessary, and as he did so the gauntlet inadvertently clunked against the side of the pod opening.

The result was spectacular.

With a missile-like *whoooosh!* the gauntlet discharged a bolt of light, of *energy*, which shot up and over the edge of the impact crater and into the jungle beyond. Although McKenna hadn't exactly aimed the gauntlet, he'd been pointing it in the general direction of the glassy figure, and now he saw the shifting, liquid-like collage collapse downward as the bolt of energy—nothing but a wild shot—hit it and deflected away, striking the still-swinging body of Haines and not only pulping him like a melon, but also blowing apart the tree he was dangling from.

The figure, which McKenna now realized must look as it did because it was encased in a cloaking device, let out a hideous cry of rage and pain, and dropped to the ground, writhing in apparent agony. It was still close enough to the tree from which Haines had been hanging for the contents of the soldier's exploding corpse to spatter over it, drenching it in blood and viscera. As McKenna watched, the figure stopped writhing and slowly straightened up, raising its head to glare in his direction.

For the first time he saw its face, and his mouth dropped open.

Masked in blood, the thing was a living nightmare.

Trying to make sense of something so alien was almost impossible, but what McKenna's brain was telling him was that the creature was part shark, part crab, and part warthog all rolled into one. It was all tusks and spines and glaring eyes, and as it opened its mouth and bellowed at him a second time, mandibles stretched out on both sides of its face, it revealed teeth as long and sharp as steak knives.

McKenna was afraid of no man, but this was something different. His fight or flight instinct kicking in, and coming down heavily on the side of flight, he scrambled up and out of the pod and began running, legs pumping, arms swinging. Turning his back on the creature, he ran across the churned, blackened ground of the impact crater and all but dived into the jungle beyond, hoping to lose himself in the luxuriant foliage. He thrashed through bushes and leaves and veered around the trunks of trees, like a charging quarterback evading tackles, oblivious to whether the thing was behind him, giving chase. He had no weapons aside from the gauntlet, but at least he hadn't lost his pack, which bounced against his body as he ran with the weight of the alien mask inside it. All he could hear were his own panting breaths and the slap of wet leaves as he raced through them. But suddenly, overriding that, he became aware of another sound, somewhere overhead, a low, bass thumping, a steadily increasing *whup-whup-whup*.

The creature? Tracking him through the treetops? But no. It was something more mundane. Something he recognized.

He looked up, already knowing what he would see.

A helicopter, like a giant black dragonfly, vectoring in overhead. Salvation perhaps, but McKenna trusted his instincts, and on this occasion his instincts told him that the helicopter was not good news.

Focused on the chopper, his foot turned on a patch of uneven ground and he staggered, dropping to his knees. All at once he felt jittery, exhausted, his adrenaline almost spent—it had been a trying day. He glanced behind him. No sign of the creature. But what if it had got its cloaking device working again? ...or was creeping up on him even now? Desperately he examined the wrist gauntlet, his only potential weapon. There were various blocky little buttons all over it. Maybe it would be a good idea to familiarize himself with a few of them, see how they worked. Tentatively, he stabbed at one, and to his astonishment a tiny metal ball popped into being as if from nowhere, and glowed for a moment.

Then McKenna vanished, abruptly and completely. He was still physically aware of himself—of his weight, his aching muscles, his pumping heart—but he could no longer see himself. For a moment, he was alarmed—and then he realized that the benefits of being invisible right now far outweighed the negatives.

Gathering himself, taking a deep breath, he slipped as quietly as he could into the surrounding jungle.

The team of black-clad mercenaries who emerged from the helicopter looked to have all been cut from the same mold. Buzz cuts, faces carved from granite, muscles upon muscles, armed to the teeth.

By contrast, the man who stepped out behind them

looked like the nicest guy in the world. Around forty, slim, wide smile, skin like dark velvet, expensive haircut, CIA agent Will Traeger made his black hoodie and nylon jacket look like an Armani suit. Perhaps the only flaw in his personal picture was that he was popping tabs of Nicorette gum as though they were Tic Tacs. As his feet touched down on the dusty ground of the jungle dirt road, he removed his aviator sunglasses, exposing soft brown eyes that only further enhanced his handsome face.

"Gentlemen," he said, his voice a soothing burr, "heads up. Our enemies are large, they have ray guns, and fucking up your day is their vacation. Hit fast and hit hard." He held up a finger. "And remember… they're invisible standing still. When they move, look for the shimmer. Now, roll out."

As the mercs dispersed into the jungle, their guns like toys in their huge hands, a piercing shriek, like a war cry, ululated out of the jungle, seeming to come from everywhere.

The man who had emerged from the helicopter behind Traeger, handsome in his own way, but with the ability to blend into the background when needed, quailed at the sound. Traeger, however, merely raised his head as if sniffing the air, then replaced his aviator sunglasses, apparently unperturbed. Beckoning his aide toward him, he said, "I want the passenger. I want the pod. If it ain't from here—"

Traeger's aide, whose name was Sapir, finished his sentence for him. "You want it."

Traeger nodded, the jungle reflected in the lenses over his eyes. "I want it."

2

When he saw the battered, bullet-pocked sign, McKenna thought he might actually get home alive. Or whatever passed for home these days. He didn't live with Emily anymore, didn't see his boy Rory nearly as much as he ought to. Part of that had to do with serving in the field, but part had to do with him never having a goddamn clue how to be the husband Emily needed or the father Rory deserved.

McKenna knew his own faults. He just didn't whine about them.

He staggered, breath rasping, legs shaking. He felt like he'd run twenty miles, and maybe he had, but he damn well didn't have two hundred more in him. He shifted the pack on his back and stared at the run-down Mexican town splayed out ahead of him. Calling it a town was being charitable—the place looked more like a row of horse stables in the middle of nowhere—but he spotted one structure with a faded Coca-Cola sign and the words Cantina Rojo.

Bingo.

With a nervous glance over his shoulder, he dry-washed as much of the camo paint off his face as he could manage. He didn't have time to make himself pretty. Truth was, he didn't know how much time he had. There were going to be a lot of questions waiting for him, a lot of people who wanted to know what he'd seen—and maybe didn't want him to have seen it in the first place—people who would want to assign blame. When soldiers died—

Damn it. My brothers.

When soldiers died, everyone wanted to assign blame, to make sure the fingers were pointing at anyone but themselves.

But this? This was a whole different brand of FUBAR.

Still catching his breath, McKenna ran across what passed for a street and entered the cantina. Overhead, a ceiling fan rotated so lazily it might have been nothing more than the breeze making it turn. If it accomplished anything other than redistributing the heat, he couldn't tell. Sweat trickled down the small of his back. *Fucking Mexico*, he thought. McKenna had always known he'd die dirty and sweaty.

He reconned the room. A handful of customers, moving slow with the heat, happy to be in the shade. No one in the cantina set off his interior alarm bells, no cops, no military.

"*Fuera*," he said to the room, as he made a beeline to the bar.

The bartender came out from behind the bar, his gaze shifting past McKenna. Although his face stayed impassive, it was a studied sort of impassive, and McKenna didn't have to ask why. He heard the creak of a floorboard and knew at least one of the customers—probably more than one, since courage usually came in groups—had taken exception to his presence.

The corner of his mouth lifted in something like a smirk. He stared at the bartender.

"Want to know my favorite cereal?" he asked.

The bartender frowned. "*Que?*"

McKenna spun, spotted the two assholes coming for him. He moved with intuition that had been trained into him, smashed into him, burned into him. It felt good, after what he'd seen, to fall back into the rhythm of a simple bar fight, to glide into the motion of fists and kicks, to strike hard, to break bone.

"Snap," he said.

A thrust. "Crackle."

A kick. "Pop."

He knew the line was lost on the bartender and didn't care. "That's a hint," he said.

On the floor, the two men who'd attacked him groaned, but they were done. McKenna slammed his backpack down on top of the bar, then unzipped a pouch and pulled out a greasy wad of Mexican currency. The bartender arched an eyebrow as McKenna held out the cash.

"I need you to mail this from the embassy. *El consulado, sí? Muy importante.* Go!"

The bartender stared into McKenna's eyes, then gave an abrupt nod, grabbed the backpack and turned to go. As he did so, McKenna said, "Buddy?"

The bartender looked back.

"If you don't do what I ask, I'll find you. You don't want me to do that."

Without another word, the bartender vanished through the door behind the bar. McKenna tried not to think about the odds on whether he'd scared the guy too much, not enough, or just the right amount. Fear could be a weapon and a great motivator, but like any weapon, you had to know precisely how to use it.

Alone in the bar now (the guys he'd vanquished had crawled away at some point during his exchange with the bartender), McKenna leaned forward, grabbed himself a glass and a bottle of tequila, and poured himself a shot. Neither the glass nor the bottle was particularly clean, but what the hell? He raised his glass to the flies buzzing lazily around the ceiling fan, and was about to knock it back when he heard sirens, approaching fast.

He sighed. He wasn't surprised they'd found him, but he wondered how they'd done it so quickly.

As the sirens reached a crescendo and were accompanied by the sounds of several vehicles screeching to a halt outside, he reached into the right-hand pocket of his grimy combats and extracted a tiny, silvery sphere— the alien cloaking device. He held it between his thumb and forefinger as he rolled his head back on his shoulders, hearing his neck muscles crackle, then dropped it almost absently into his tequila.

He picked up the glass and upended it over his mouth, swallowing its entire contents in one gulp, as the door to the bar crashed open behind him.

3

Lawrence A. Gordon Middle School might have been the *Home of the Warriors*, like the sign out front said (a new, albeit temporary sign beneath bore the legend *HALLOWEEN HAUNT 10/25—WELCOME PARENTS & STDS*), but Rory didn't care much for the school's sports teams. At twelve years old, he was a scholastic warrior. A classroom warrior.

Not at lunchtime, though.

At lunchtime, Rory was a warrior of the chessboard.

Mr. Moore, his science teacher, ate lunch at his desk. The room stayed quiet, because Chess Club was in session. There were five games going on simultaneously, all of them taking place on the lab tables. Rory could have played—could have beaten any of the kids in the club—but instead he threaded through the room with his crust-free peanut butter sandwich in one hand while he studied each of the ongoing games in turn. In his mind, he worked both ends of all five games, had a strategy for each of the ten players that would have guaranteed them victory.

Only nobody ever asked.

Mr. Moore glanced up at him and sighed. A lot of times, the science teacher seemed like he wanted to talk to Rory, as if some great, weighty question burned at the tip of his tongue—or maybe some piece of wisdom that would reveal Mr. Moore as a more thoughtful, more intelligent, more sympathetic teacher than Rory's experience had thus far led him to believe. The man studied him sometimes, not in a creepy way, but more like one of the Chess Club kids on the losing side of a game, as if Mr. Moore looked at Rory and saw a puzzle that he thought he could solve if he could just find that one missing piece.

That was one of the oddest things about being on the autism spectrum. Rory didn't feel like he was missing a piece of anything, didn't feel like his puzzle hadn't been solved. He felt whole. He just felt like Rory.

Neuro-diverse, Rory thought, glancing again at Mr. Moore, catching him looking again. It was a pleasant tag doctors liked to put on kids and adults like him. The opposite of neuro-typical. But what was typical? Rory was what a lot of people still called an Asperger's kid, even though technically Asperger's had been erased as a specific diagnosis and was now just one slice in the larger pie of Autism Spectrum Disorder.

Once his mom had said she thought neuro-typical people were like cavemen, and kids like Rory were the future of humanity. He liked that idea, but he had a feeling someone like Mr. Moore would frown in even deeper puzzlement—and maybe a little uneasiness—if he said it in class. Sometimes he had a hard time imagining how Typicals thought, but he'd pondered this subject a lot.

He took a bite of his sandwich as he stepped up beside the board where Helen Jemisin and Ethan Hill were playing. Helen had been kicking Ethan's ass, but now she reached for her queen.

"I wouldn't—" Rory started to say.

Ethan scowled at him, but Helen arched a curious eyebrow and glanced up.

Which was when the world started to scream.

A minute before Helen Jemisin picked up her queen, two kids, Derek and E.J., the former wearing the mean and cunning look that would most likely carry him through life, the latter so slack-jawed and sleepy-eyed he might as well have had the word "Goon" tattooed on his forehead, had been standing in a deserted school corridor beside a fire alarm.

Glancing left and right, Derek had said, "Go on, I dare you."

E.J. had blinked. "Why don't you?"

"Because I dared *you* first."

E.J. considered the irrefutable logic of this. Then he shrugged and curled his meaty right hand into a fist.

Rory clapped his hands over his ears as the other kids stood up from their desks. The alarm blared over and over, a rhythmic shrieking assault on his brain. Mr. Moore went to the door, forgetting Rory as he ushered the other kids into the corridor. Maybe he looked back and maybe he didn't, but by then Rory had slid to the floor behind one of the lab tables and curled into a fetal ball with his fingers in his ears. He squeezed his eyes shut, all thoughts leaving him. Only the sound remained, tearing into his head, an intimate assault of pure noise.

He forced himself to open his eyes.

E.J. and Derek passed by, out in the corridor. The instant he spotted them, Rory stopped breathing, thinking maybe he could make himself invisible. For half a second he thought he had succeeded, but then Derek came to a halt, grabbing E.J.'s arm. Wolfish smiles split their faces as they stepped into the room.

Rory flinched. He knew, then, who had set off the fire alarm. He couldn't prove it, of course, but he knew it as surely as he knew his own name, and that Helen Jemisin had been three moves from beating Ethan Hill in that chess match.

"Hey, E.J.," Derek crowed. "You hungry?"

They strode across the science lab as if they hardly even knew Rory was there, ignoring him while at the same time completely focused on his presence. Their performance was bad theater and he wanted no part of it, but they'd never given him a choice before and they weren't going to start now.

"Hell, yeah!" E.J. replied. "You know what I'm hungry for?"

Rory tensed, knowing what was coming. He could have said the next three words with them, they'd said it so many times, these shitty kids who thought they were so clever. *An Ass Burger.*

"An Ass Burger!" E.J. exclaimed.

Rory was half convinced the jerks thought Asperger's was really spelled that way.

E.J. kicked him. Rory tucked into a tighter ball, trying to defend himself. He'd been kicked before, been bruised but never bloodied. These guys were dumb as a box of rocks, but smart enough not to do visible damage. Stupid to the bone, but they had a bully's wisdom.

"Mmm," Derek echoed. "That sounds delicious. A big, juicy Ass Burger!"

He gave a kick of his own. Rory grunted and promised himself he wouldn't cry. He didn't understand why bullies behaved like this, didn't understand hardly anything about why people chose to do the things they did, but he knew enough to realize that crying would only make them happy *and* make them kick him even harder. His therapist said it was difficult for him to translate and learn typical behavior, but he'd learned that much.

Both boys moved in to kick him again, but the alarm cut off abruptly and the lab fell into silence. They knew it was over. Students would be coming back, and so would teachers. They would get caught. They seemed displeased at being interrupted so soon and looked around. Sneering, the boys went from chess game to chess game and knocked over every piece on every board, as if Rory had been playing in all of them. In a way he had, but they couldn't know that, and he wouldn't tell them.

The assholes traded a laughing high-five and marched proudly from the room.

Rory rose, taking stock of his body. He stretched a little. There would be some bruising, but those kicks hadn't broken anything. Compared to other assaults, this one had been mercifully short.

He exhaled and let himself glance across the room, taking in each of the chessboards in turn, quickly making a mental inventory. Then he nodded—it could be done.

One by one, as fast as he could—hoping to avoid discovery by Mr. Moore—Rory McKenna put every chess piece back on every board, exactly the way they'd been before the fire alarm. It was simple, and deeply satisfying. Chaos and disorder troubled him deeply and the only thing that alleviated those feelings was to restore order.

To set things right.

On the walk home, the Ortegas' dog, Bugsy, tried to murder Rory again. Growling and snapping, the dog raced through its yard and would have torn Rory's throat out if not for the picket fence. At least, that was how Rory saw it. He didn't like dogs, and he especially didn't like ugly dogs that looked like storybook monsters. Mom said pit bulls were just like other dogs, that they'd gotten a bad reputation, but Rory still gave Bugsy a wide berth as he made his way home.

When he entered the house, the first thing he noticed was the silence. He could always feel it when his mother wasn't there—her absence was tangible, and he sometimes wondered if that was what it might be like if he ever met a ghost. Did ghosts give off the feeling of their absence, like a hole in the world? Of course, Rory knew ghosts weren't real, but sometimes he thought about them and it freaked him out anyway.

The front door slammed behind him. One of his mom's paintings jumped a bit on the wall and he hesitated, wanting to make sure it didn't fall. He supposed it was a good painting—he liked it, anyway.

In the kitchen, he dumped his backpack on the floor and then paused when he noticed a damp spot on the wall. Snatching a paper towel off the roll, he blotted the spot, erasing the bit of disorder that had irritated him. Then he went to the refrigerator, upon which hung a note from his mother. *Spent 1.5 hours cleaning house*, she'd written. *If you mess it up, I will cut you. XOXO Mom.*

Rory opened the fridge and surveyed its contents, debating what he wanted for a snack.

The doorbell interrupted his pondering, so he shut the fridge and went out into the foyer. When he opened the door, a postal worker smiled at him. The man had a handcart with the United States Postal Service logo on the side. Rory wondered how many letters it could carry, if there were only letters and not packages or catalogues or magazines. He wondered if someone could hide inside the handcart, or if a dog might hide inside, if the dog was particularly determined to kill and eat a middle school kid in his neighborhood. For half a second, he studied the handcart for any sign that Bugsy might be hiding inside.

"Quinn McKenna live here?" the postal worker asked.

Rory blinked.

The postal worker gave a lopsided smile. "Didn't mean to stump you. How's this: is Quinn McKenna your mom or your dad?"

"Dad," Rory replied.

"Now we're getting somewhere."

The guy upended the handcart and an avalanche of letters and bills and boxes poured out onto the floor of the foyer. Rory jumped back, staring at the pile of stuff spreading out across the floor. He glanced at the postal worker, wondering if the man had lost his marbles. *Lost his marbles* was a phrase his mother sometimes used to describe people who behaved in a way that seemed illogical or somehow outrageous to her. She'd often said she worried that Rory's dad had lost his marbles. She had never said it about Rory.

This postal worker, though—Rory felt sure his mother would have an opinion about this guy.

"His PO box payments are past due. Sorry," the man said. He didn't shrug, but Rory could hear the shrug in his voice. "Guess he's... not around much, huh?"

Rory gave a small nod. The postal worker's attention had already turned to one parcel, a big box that had been stamped and rubber-stamped and scraped and taped. Rory spotted the words *consulate* and *Monterrey, Mexico*, and thought: Mexico?

"That's my dad's handwriting," he said, mostly to himself.

"Embassy stamps," the postal worker said, studying the box like it was a cadaver and he was a TV detective. "He do some kind of government work?"

"MOS 11B3VW3," Rory replied, pronouncing each letter and number with emphasis.

The postal worker stared at him the way so many people stared at him. Rory had come to recognize the dumbfounded expression of the eternally confused.

"Military designation," the boy said. He paused a moment, but saw that the man still didn't understand. "He kills people."

The postal worker cocked his head and gave Rory an odd look. "You have a nice day, okay?"

Rory watched as the man went down the front walk, and then he closed the door. Frowning, he turned to regard the parcel from Mexico. After a moment, he picked up the box. It wasn't very heavy—not like it had been packed full of books—but it wasn't light, either. Why would his father have mailed this box to himself, and what was he doing in Mexico? More importantly, what was in it?

He wondered if it might be a present. His father always said he was going to bring Rory a surprise the next time he went out of town, but he always forgot. Maybe this time he had decided to mail something home, so he wouldn't forget.

Rory shook the box, his curiosity growing.

He told himself he wouldn't open it. Not without asking his father first.

But, of course, if it *was* a present, then it had been meant for him in the first place, hadn't it?

4

Casey Brackett sometimes wondered why she did this to herself. On a beautiful day when she had no classes to teach, she could have done anything with her time. Her mother would have told her to find a boyfriend, because her mother had grown up as part of a generation that believed a woman needed a man in her life for security or a solid foundation or something. Casey didn't mind the occasional man, but her mother's attitude drove her nuts. She didn't need a boyfriend... although she wouldn't have minded an outing now and then with a circle of friends.

She didn't have a circle. Laid out on a graph, her friends would have been more of a connect-the-dots. There were days this felt unfortunate, but when she was being honest with herself, Casey had to admit it was her own doing. After all, she didn't really like people very much. Which was why, on this beautiful day, she was sat on a bench in a dog park just outside Johns Hopkins, Maryland, red-penciling papers from college students who were never as smart as she wanted them to be. She went through a lot of red pencils.

The papers were on her lap, the red pencil in her right hand. In her left, she held a braid of leashes belonging to her stupid, beautiful, goofy dogs. They were ordinarily very well behaved, which often lulled her into thinking that she could bring them down to the dog park and get some correcting done. Then one or more of them would start acting like a lunatic or begging for her attention, and she'd remember how she'd promised herself the last time that she wouldn't fool herself like this again.

But it was a gorgeous day—and she did need to get her correcting done.

The eruption of urgent barking sounded like Casey herself, the day she'd reamed out the sacker at the grocery store for putting a jug of orange juice into a bag on top of a fresh loaf of bread. She knew that bark the same way a mother knew her baby's cry, and her head snapped up in irritation.

"Summer! Stop it!" she snapped. "That's not yours. Does it look like it's yours?"

The dog barked twice at the toy she'd been trying to steal, and then darted away, but not without casting a rueful glance at Casey. She could be trouble, that one. Sometimes she would gather up the unattended toys at the dog park and piss on them, to claim them for herself. Marking her stolen territory like a furry conqueror with a fetish. Then there was the time she'd bitten the handsome firefighter who'd been working up his nerve to ask for Casey's number. She'd given the guy her number for all the wrong reasons, thinking he'd call to make her pay for whatever shots or stitches he might need, but he'd never called. She'd been both relieved and disappointed.

As her red pencil hovered over the paper on top of the stack on her lap, a jogger ran by with his own dog on a leash. The guy slowed down. Even in her peripheral vision, Casey saw the way he craned his neck to get a better look at her.

Fantastic, she thought.

The rubbernecker backtracked, dog in tow, and jogged in place beside her. She wondered if he had any idea how much of a cliché he was in that moment, or if he would care.

"How's it goin'?" he said, toweling his neck.

Another dog yelp came from across the park. Casey glanced over, rolling her eyes. "Teddy! Knock it off! You can *see* she doesn't like that!"

The dog bolted across the park toward her, tearing up grass as he ran. Sometimes she thought the big stinker misbehaved just so she would admonish him. He rushed over and put his muzzle onto her lap, rustling her papers. Casey smiled, caressing one of his floppy ears, knowing it would calm him down. Teddy was a scoundrel, but sweet nonetheless.

The jogger stood watching this exchange, apparently unaware how intrusive it was.

"Seen you around here," he said, extending his hand. "Doug Amaturo." He scratched the ears of his well-groomed, designer dog, as if to mimic her interaction with Teddy. "This is Barkolepsy. She has a… sleeping thing. She's a lab—"

"Labradoodle," Casey said, frowning as she studied the dog. "Hypoallergenic cross between a poodle and a Labrador."

Gathering her papers, she stood up abruptly and began to walk. The guy—Doug—trailed after her persistently.

"Right. That's right," he said, eager to please. "Are you a breeder?"

Casey shook her head, hating that the guy had diverted the conversation to his dog, the oldest trick in the book, and it had worked.

"Science professor," she said. "Berkeley."

He tried not to look intimidated. "What do you teach?"

Casey heaved a breath, wondering why men did this. Why push it so far that she would have to be blunt with him? Was Doug Amaturo really that oblivious, or did he think persistence would break down the walls of her disinterest? Would his approach have been different if he'd first spotted her teaching her self-defense students or practicing at the shooting range?

"Evolutionary biology," she said. "The science of how creatures change. Adapt."

Doug nodded thoughtfully. "You mean, like… how a man changes when he meets an attractive woman?"

Casey grinned. Someone who knew her well would have known to take a few steps back at the sight of that grin.

"It's funny, you know? Darwin thought it was about agility, intelligence… but nowadays? You just have to be a rich, fat, white guy."

"I…" Doug started, and then he blinked, as if realizing for the first time that maybe his presumed charms were not working on her. "What?"

"Now, drop a CEO into the Serengeti? Only question is, what color animal shits him out twenty-four hours later? The Serengeti, probably be a jackal... reddish tan. Jackals? Eat fuckin' anything."

Doug visibly gulped. She saw his Adam's apple bob as he swallowed.

"Um, I don't wanna hold you up, so..." he murmured, and then he bolted, labradoodle hurrying to keep pace with him.

Casey watched him go, reaching into her jacket to fish out a silver flask. She opened it and took a swig.

"Doctor Brackett?"

Casey turned to see three men in dark business suits regarding her. They stood tall, not exactly ready for a fight, but ready for trouble. Immediately she thought of federal agents. Or somebody's expensive bodyguards. Then she spotted the fancy sedan idling at the curb and the government license plate on the back, and she knew her first guess had been on the mark.

"I understand you enjoy stargazing," said the agent who'd spoken.

Casey flinched. Her thoughts flickered. She'd heard the words before, but never expected to hear them again.

"My men will take care of your dogs," the lead agent said. "Would you come with me, please?"

Rattled, and hating to show it, she let them take her paperwork and the leashes she'd been holding, and then allowed them to lead her to the sedan.

Moments later, she was climbing into the back of the car, glancing out the window at her dogs as the car pulled away.

"Dog person, huh?" the agent said.

Casey took a breath, trying to settle down. "They don't judge you. They don't lie. No hidden agendas. Love you or tear your throat out. I kind of have to respect that."

The agent handed her a file. "How are you with *higher* forms of life?"

"I wasn't aware there *were* any," she replied, trying to keep her shit together.

The file bore the eagle-and-shield insignia of the Central Intelligence Agency. Casey opened it and studied the top sheet:

Classified: Project: Stargazer

Memorandum for Cleared Personnel

Subject: Class 4 Incursion—Monterrey, Mexico

Casey frowned. Her throat went dry as she flipped through the file. An eight-by-ten photo of someone named Quinn McKenna was the first in a series of photos. She saw a debris field and her heart raced with excitement. The next photo showed what appeared to be a spacecraft, not very large, surely not capable of interstellar travel. Some kind of sub-transport vessel, ship to ship? Ship to surface?

Then she flipped to the next photo and her heart froze in her chest. She sucked in a sharp breath, unable to process for a few seconds. This was a satellite photo, shot through the upper limbs of trees. No spacecraft debris in this photo. No charred spacecraft.

The picture was blurry, but she knew what she was looking at.

A humanoid figure. Whatever had been inside that spacecraft.

Casey Brackett forgot all about her dogs.

5

VETERAN'S ADMINISTRATION
CHATTANOOGA, TENNESSEE

There were no windows, unless you counted the one-way mirror on the far wall, and McKenna didn't. It amused him to think that anyone still bothered with such antiquated interview techniques. Anyone who'd seen a movie or television show in the past fifty years would know that someone lurked unseen beyond that reflective surface, watching in silence, evaluating both the person being interviewed and those doing the interviewing.

The floor and walls trembled, and McKenna could both hear and feel the rumble of thunder outside. The storm had already been going on when he'd been brought into this room, but in the past few minutes the thunder had grown much stronger. He couldn't hear the rain or see the lightning, but he imagined they must both be ferocious. A shame. He loved to see lightning burning inside storm clouds, and to watch it lance down from the sky. As a boy, he'd fallen in love with mythology—tales from various pantheons—and when he heard thunder roll or saw lightning flash, he still thought of Zeus and Thor and Hephaestus and so many others.

But the room had no windows, so he had to focus on these assholes instead.

"Tell me about the mission," said the man in the ugly tie, who sat across from him at the table.

McKenna, now wearing an orange jumpsuit, stared at him, and then glanced at the two other people in the room. One of them, he guessed, was a psychologist of some kind. The other was the polygraph tech, who had hooked McKenna up to the machine with the detachment of a gravedigger.

They'd already been through all the baseline questions, asking him his name and date of birth, that sort of thing, to establish what the machine would do when he lied versus when he told the truth. The tech reminded him of another tech, years earlier. McKenna's wife had been sixteen weeks pregnant and he'd taken her for an ultrasound. They'd been debating whether they wanted to know the sex when the tech glanced up, face flat and emotionless, and said at the moment she was just looking for a heartbeat. The callous bitch hadn't found one.

McKenna laced his hands together and leaned forward. "It was a rescue op. Couple of DEA agents had their covers blown. They were being taken to the head of the cartel."

He couldn't help feeling he was going through the motions here. He knew all of this would be in the file that these guys would have read before coming into the room. The US government had spent many hours and a vast amount of money trying to punch holes in the drug cartels, but had still never gotten serious enough to do any lasting damage. The cartels were like the legendary Hydra—cut off one head and two more would grow in its place. The truth was, too much money was on the table, and too much cash found its way into the pockets of government officials and corporate overlords in Mexico, the US, Central America, and South America for the problem to ever go away.

"I see," Ugly Tie said primly. "You were instructed to kill him?"

McKenna controlled himself with an effort. "No, I was instructed to offer him a selection of donuts."

The psychologist stared at him. Adjusted the ugly tie.

McKenna indicated the blood pressure cuff on his arm. "What's with the polygraph? I thought this was a psych eval."

"We need to know if you pose a threat."

"I'm a sniper. Isn't posing a threat kind of the fucking point?" He left off the word *dumbass*, but it was definitely implied.

"I meant to the general public… to yourself," Ugly Tie replied.

McKenna sighed.

Behind the one-way glass, Traeger stood with his arms crossed. From the moment he'd confronted McKenna, he had known the guy was going to be a problem. Quinn

McKenna had the same hardass quality that Traeger had seen in hundreds of military men, but the guy also had a brain. Not to say that the average soldier or sailor or Marine was a moron, but most of them had been trained to follow orders and that tended to carve grooves into their behavior patterns. They didn't usually study the shadows or the angles too deeply.

McKenna, though… this son of a bitch was a born questioner of authority. How he had survived this long in the Rangers was a mystery. He'd done what he had been told for years, but his records showed several insubordination incidents, all of them minor. McKenna followed orders—that hadn't ever been a problem—but he always wanted to understand *why* he was doing so.

In the darkness, the readout from the polygraph flickered on a screen. Traeger stood with his aide, Sapir, and studied the screen closely.

"He's good," Traeger said with a chuckle.

But the quiet laugh wasn't amusement. It was irritation. Sapir sensed that and handed Traeger a bowl of Nicorette. Traeger had been chewing the damn things non-stop and he took one now, almost without thinking about it.

"He was tortured in Kandahar," Sapir said. "Didn't break once."

"What does he want, a medal?" Traeger sneered.

"Actually, uh…"

"I know, I know. Silver Star. That's why we have to tread lightly. We can't just bury him behind the woodshed."

He popped the nicotine gum into his mouth and started chewing.

"Uh, I think you're supposed to park that in the corner of your—" Sapir began.

Traeger shot him a withering glance. "You say something?"

Sapir kept silent. Traeger kept chewing vigorously, waiting for the nicotine rush. He needed it.

McKenna was bored. He rolled his eyes. "Look, I get it," he said. "Mexico. Someone doesn't want any witnesses."

Ugly Tie looked startled. "Excuse me?"

McKenna looked him in the eye, and then fixed each of the other guys in the room with a brief but meaningful stare. "You're not here to find out if I'm crazy. You're here to make sure the label sticks."

Making an effort to regain control of the situation, Ugly Tie arched an eyebrow. "You think you're being railroaded. Is that it?"

"I can see the tracks on the floor," McKenna replied. The tone in the bastard's voice confirmed it all. Sounding paranoid would only help their case if they wanted to discredit him. He sighed. "By the way, I don't really see tracks on the floor. Relax. Jesus."

Undeterred, the asshole went on. "You spend most of your time now in country. Estranged from your wife and son. Alone."

Ugly Tie glanced at the polygraph. McKenna didn't have to look to know the needle would be flickering now. He could feel his anger boiling.

"You feel like a stranger on your own planet, don't you, Captain?"

McKenna tilted his head, studying the man. "Like an *alien*, you mean?"

It felt like every molecule in the room had stopped moving. Even the polygraph tech seemed to hold his breath.

"Is that what you wanted?" McKenna asked. "Do I get a cookie now?"

The psychologist stared at him half in triumph, half as if he was a wild beast that might spring forward at any second. McKenna didn't think he'd be getting any cookies.

6

The MP escorting McKenna out of the administration building was either stupid or impatient. He followed too closely, gave McKenna the occasional bump or shove, and muttered under his breath. Under other circumstances— if McKenna felt sure of his surroundings or feared he might be killed—he'd have been able to take the MP out in the blink of an eye. The guy might be decent enough at guarding someone in a cage or watching the front gate, but escorting prisoners was not his strong suit. Fortunately for him, McKenna had no interest in fighting actual US military personnel unless he had no other choice.

Outside, a colorless, hulking bus idled in front of the building. It looked like a prison bus, but without the associated markings. A second MP waited at the bus. As McKenna approached, the MP stepped up inside and waited for the new prisoner to climb aboard. When McKenna stepped onto the bus, MP number two opened the cage that separated the driver from the prisoners locked in back. McKenna shuffled in and paused to regard the five figures scattered around the shadowed benches. Although out of uniform, a moment's consideration told him they were all military, either vets or currently serving.

Well, not currently, he thought, considering they were all locked in the same cage he'd been thrown into. The men were clad in civilian clothes, but something about their demeanors suggested they hadn't been arrested as a group. A scruffy guy in a baseball cap fanned out a deck of cards and manipulated them like a stage magician, despite the manacles cuffing his wrists. A goateed bald guy glanced up at McKenna, a manic glimmer in his eyes. A guy toward the back of the cage wore a bomber jacket, which seemed appropriate, because something about his brooding presence resembled a ticking time bomb. Beside him was a long-haired Jon Snow-looking son of a bitch with a gang tat on his neck and a gold crucifix dangling at his throat.

They were hard men without a doubt, and yet for all that, McKenna sensed an air of mischief about them. He dropped into the nearest seat, next to the fifth man, a powerful-looking guy who wore the same heavy manacles as the rest of them.

The bus started to move.

As it did so, the big man beside McKenna seemed to stir. Leaning toward McKenna, he asked mildly, "Got a smoke?"

McKenna regarded him. "Pretty sure they don't allow that on the bus."

"Don't allow blowjobs either, but if Katy Perry walks in, I'm gonna ask."

McKenna settled in. The bus rumbled, and the men seemed content to worry later about where it might bring them. He scanned the group again, pausing to watch the scruffy magician work his sleight of hand with the cards. As someone who'd never been able to reliably pull off a card trick, McKenna felt confident in thinking the guy was talented. Not fucking Houdini, or he'd have escaped from the bus, but when it came to prestidigitation, he had the chops.

He wondered how long these guys had been lumped together, where they were being transported to and from. All of them were apparently psych cases of one sort or another, so his being thrown in with them began to make sense. Traeger and his fake VA doctors were trying to make it seem like McKenna was a nutjob in order to discredit anything he might say.

But what the hell? He'd been in worse company.

He extended his hand toward the big guy beside him. "McKenna. You?"

Manacles clanking, the man shook. "Nebraska Williams."

"That your real name?"

Williams paused a moment, wincing slightly. Then with a wry smile he admitted, "Name's Gaylord."

McKenna nodded gravely. "Good call, then."

"You do your psych eval yet?" Williams asked.

"Yup."

Nebraska eyed him up and down. "You crazy?"

McKenna didn't know how to answer that—not when he'd just met these men. "Yup," he said. "How'd *you* snag a ticket on this shitmobile?"

The big man gave an impassive shrug. "Put a bullet in the CO."

That gave McKenna pause. Even on a bus full of loonies, the idea that Nebraska Williams had shot his commanding officer unsettled him. This wasn't a guy with PTSD or who'd started seeing enemies that weren't there. This was a whole other level.

"Any particular reason?"

Another shrug. "He was an asshole."

A warm breeze drifted in through the slightly open windows. McKenna was no coward, but he decided his best option right now would be to sit very still and try to avoid irritating his fellow passengers.

The bus rumbled on.

7

Casey Brackett held her breath as the pilot guided the HH-60 Pave Hawk helicopter over a dam and what appeared to be a sleek, modern water reclamation plant. The structure perched on the edge of a cliff, and Casey tensed as the helicopter descended toward a marked landing pad beside a waterfall. It looked like something out of a James Bond movie, conspicuous in its attempt to seem innocuous, at least in her current mindset.

She'd never ridden in a helicopter before, and the moment the chopper touched down, she promised herself she'd do her best to avoid it in the future. Dr. Casey Brackett wasn't the type to shy away from risky behavior, but there was risk and then there was buzzing thousands of feet above the ground in a tin can with whirling blades overhead as gusts of wind tried to blow you from the sky.

One of the security men who'd been riding with her jumped out ahead of her, then another. They turned to assist her, but there was no sense of gallantry in these men, only practicality. She'd studied them throughout the flight and had concluded that they weren't regular military. Her father and grandfather had been military men—she'd been around them all her life, even lived on bases as a child—and she knew the difference. These guys were black ops, or even mercenaries. They wore no insignias denoting rank, no name tags, and they didn't joke around the way the military men she'd known always did. These men were all business. She tried to tell herself that was a good thing.

Agent Church, who'd so far acted as spokesman for the group that had requisitioned her services, climbed out of the helicopter behind her and strode toward what appeared to be an outbuilding, a structure the size of somebody's backyard shed. The guards went along with them, and Casey gazed around, wondering just how much of what she was seeing might be a façade.

At the shed, Church handed her a clipboard. "Non-disclosure agreement."

"I signed that when they recruited me, two years ago," she replied.

"It's a rider," Church explained. "New information's come to light in the last day."

A shiver went through Casey. Of course, there was new information—without it, they never would have brought her here—but still, she felt her heart racing.

"I'm in the middle of nowhere surrounded by armed mercenaries," she said. "Do I have a choice?"

Church gave her a terse smile. "There's always a choice."

She didn't like the sound of that. She also noticed that he hadn't challenged her identification of the guards as mercenaries, which meant she was right. Not only were they not regular military, but they weren't CIA either, or anything else truly official. She felt uncomfortably like she was about to take an almighty leap into the unknown.

Taking a breath, she signed on the clipboard. The code box outside the shed emitted a hollow *click* and heavy doors slid open to reveal a small, compact room—some kind of security checkpoint. A technician stood at a workstation laden with scanners, cameras, printers, and other instruments. On the far wall was a Big Red Button that drew her eye instantly.

The tech stepped forward and used one of the instruments to scan Casey's retinas, then another to record her handprints. As soon as the tech confirmed that she was clear, Church slammed his hand down on the Big Red Button. The whole room shuddered, and Casey heard a hydraulic whine coming from every wall as the entire chamber jerked and then began to descend.

Her eyes went wide. The interior of the shed was an elevator.

"Is it your imagination?" the tech asked in a deep, spooky voice. "Or is this haunted room actually *stretching*?"

Agent Church shook his head at the *Haunted Mansion* reference. "Every fucking time."

Moments later the elevator door slid open and Church ushered Casey into a sprawling underground complex, brightly lit and ultra-modern. Technicians bustled about like bees inside a hive, some of them wearing lab coats and scrubs. None of them seemed to take any notice of their arrival and for a moment Casey felt as invisible as a ghost. Then she spotted a bespectacled man headed straight for them as if they were his personal responsibility. The guy had big eyes and a set of gleaming teeth that she thought might give him a grin that could be joyful or terrifying, depending on his mood.

"Ah, there you are," he said. "I'm Doctor Shawn Keyes. Thanks for coming."

He shook Casey's hand and ushered her deeper into the hive, keeping up a stream of chatter. "I'm told you pretty much wrote the book on evolutionary biology."

"Four, actually," Casey said, before realizing how much that sounded like bragging. "Um… books…"

She glanced to her left, and halted in her tracks, staring in stunned amazement at a plexiglass display case. Or, more accurately, at what was behind the plexiglass. A large helmet, loaded with tech and clearly not designed for a human head, sat on display. There were dents and scrapes that she assumed had come from combat, but she had no idea what had worn it. The other items in the display gave her some hints—a chest plate, also battle-scarred, and various weapons that were unlike anything she'd ever seen.

"My God, this is…" She turned to Keyes. "Am I allowed to swear?"

Dr. Keyes raised his eyebrows. "Knock yourself out."

Casey stepped closer, studying the long battle staff. "Holy. Fucking. Shit. This is alien technology. *This* is what you brought me here to see."

Keyes showed her his grin, then pointed further along the corridor. More plexiglass awaited, and now Casey found her breath freezing in her lungs. Ice trickling along her spine, she stepped toward the glass and stared in at a medical facility that was like something out of a science fiction movie—or more specifically at the treatment table in the center of the room, around which med techs were fluttering like flies around a banquet.

She gaped and gaped, her mind trying to assimilate what she was seeing. Because strapped to the table was something she had waited her entire life to see.

Eventually she let out a gasp, suddenly aware both that she'd been holding her breath and that her heartbeat had become a drumroll. But why wouldn't she respond that way? Hell, in the space of a few seconds her whole life had changed.

She stared again at the creature on the table. It had to be at least seven feet in height, and massively powerful. *Bipedal humanoid*, she told herself, trying desperately to reassert an air of scientific professionalism. The skin of the creature seemed reptilian at first glance, but she realized almost immediately that that was a lazy comparison—mental shorthand for something not of this earth. What she'd first taken to be hair, considering the way it hung like dreadlocks from the alien's head, now appeared to be a cluster of thick appendages, but she had no idea what purpose they might serve. Its mouth hung slightly open, and what a mouth it was—arthropod-like mandibles, and sharp inner teeth. There were undersea creatures with uglier mouths, but not many. The thought made her wonder if the alien might be amphibious, but that was a question for later.

Later, she thought with excitement, mind already racing ahead to the moment when she'd be able to examine it in person.

"Agent Traeger," Church said.

A man inside the lab turned toward the window. Handsome, intelligent, arrogant, was Casey's snap judgment.

"Dr. Brackett?" Traeger asked. She gave a tentative nod and he smiled. "Would you like to meet a Predator?"

Predator, she thought. Fuck, yeah, she wanted to meet a Predator.

Dr. Keyes stepped aside with a chivalrous flourish to allow her to precede him into the decontamination chamber. Casey had never thought of herself as claustrophobic, but stepping into the blinding-white, antiseptic box room made her skin crawl. Her thoughts flashed back to an old Meryl Streep movie, *Silkwood*—a true story about a woman purposely exposed to radiation in order to shut her up. Casey had been twelve when her mother showed her that movie, to let her know that the truth always had enemies. Science had always been about truth for Casey, and the movie had been one of the foundations of that quest. She'd had nightmares, yes, but she hadn't let them stop her. Karen Silkwood had died for the truth. Mama Brackett hadn't raised a fool—Casey didn't want to die—but she'd risk anything for answers to the questions that haunted her.

The decontamination chamber had a partition down the middle, so two people could move through it at the same time. She and Keyes entered through the airlock hatch, which sealed shut behind them with a loud hiss. She'd have jumped at the sound, but Casey felt keenly aware of the attention turned toward her in that moment. She was the newcomer here, the wild card, and she didn't want to give them any reason to rescind their invitation. Not when she was this close to a truth denied to all but a handful of people on the planet.

She stared at the sign on the wall. *MANDATORY DECON—STERILE IN, STERILE OUT.*

"*Chamber secure,*" announced a recorded voice. "*Remove garments.*"

Casey scanned the chamber for the speaker broadcasting the voice. Sounding braver than she felt, she said, "You're not gonna buy me a drink first?"

On the other side of the partition, Keyes would be stripping too, but Casey was sure that anyone with a good view of this particular process would have their eyes on her. She did not hesitate, nor did she care. She'd grown used to people taking a second look at her with her clothes on, and she certainly understood why a gaze might linger on her without them. It wasn't arrogance, just acceptance of something she had no control over— namely, her genetic make-up—and she didn't have time to waste worrying about it.

"You do this sort of thing a lot?" Casey called across to Keyes.

"Pays the bills," he replied through the partition. "My, uh, father headed up one of the first contact teams."

Curious, Casey felt an urge to ask him about it, but

Keyes quickly changed the subject.

"So, how'd they rope you into this?"

Through the plexiglass, she could still see the Predator on the table. Suddenly, she didn't want to be talking anymore, didn't want to think about Karen Silkwood or her mother. She didn't want to answer Keyes' question. The Predator waited for her, an answer to so many questions, but one that would lead her to thousands more. Still, Dr. Keyes was her host, so she had to make nice.

"I wrote a letter when I was six. Said I loved animals and if NASA ever found a space animal, they should call me. A couple years ago, they put me on a short list because of a paper I wrote on hybrid strains. A computer had cross-referenced my letter."

"NASA still had the letter, huh?"

Casey shook her head. "The Oval Office. I wrote the letter to Clinton. He thought it was cute, so it's been in there ever since."

With a hiss, the room abruptly flared with white heat. Casey flinched as the top layer of her skin burned off. It lasted only seconds, after which she felt a prickling over her entire body. It stung a little, but just for a moment.

"*Protocol complete*," said the recorded voice.

Still inside the decontamination chamber, they stepped past the partition and quickly shrugged into hazmat suits. Casey had worn the gear plenty of times before. Keyes went to the interior hatch and placed his hand on a palm scanner while pressing his eye to the retina scan.

"Keyes, Shawn H."

The hatch shushed open. This time, Keyes forgot all

about chivalry. He led the way, and Casey didn't blame him. This was his territory now, and the spring in his step told her that the presence of the Predator excited him as much as it did her.

Inside the main lab, Traeger approached with his hand extended. "Thanks for coming. I'm sure you have questions."

"Two, actually." Casey nodded at the creature on the treatment table. "Why do you call it a Predator?"

Traeger gave a small shrug. "Just a nickname. The data suggests it tracks its prey, exploits weakness. Seems to… well, enjoy it. Like a game."

"That's a hunter."

"I'm sorry?" Traeger replied, brow crinkling. His dark features gleamed in the bright laboratory lights, and she couldn't help thinking he probably got plenty of second looks himself. Though he seemed like he knew it. The man clearly thought a lot of himself and didn't like being corrected.

"That's a hunter," she reiterated. "Not a predator. Predators kill for food, to survive. There's only one animal on Earth that hunts for sport."

Traeger rolled his eyes.

But Casey barely noticed his reaction. Once again, her thoughts had turned away from conversations with those around her. Traeger had intrigued her for ten seconds, but Traeger was only human. She moved closer to the table where the Predator lay, studying it with a sense of wonder she had always yearned for but rarely felt.

"You," she said to the unconscious creature, "are one beautiful motherfucker."

Traeger slid up beside her, so silently she wasn't aware of him until he spoke. "I'm going to assume your second question is: 'Why am I here?'"

She turned, shot him a grin. It didn't take a genius to figure that one out.

"Our test results yielded something a little... odd," Traeger went on. "We were wondering if maybe you could shed some light on it."

He nodded to Dr. Keyes, who produced a tablet and turned it to show Casey the readout on its screen. She studied it for a moment, deeply intrigued, and then she felt the blood draining from her face. No, no, no. This couldn't be.

"Is this a joke?" she asked, hoping sincerely that it was.

Keyes shook his head. "We ran the gene sequence ten times. This specimen has—"

"Human DNA," Casey said. She turned to stare at Keyes and Traeger, wondering how such a thing could be possible. It didn't make any sense at all. One look at the Predator and anyone could see it was extraterrestrial. This wasn't a lab-created monster. Humanity didn't have the scientific knowledge to breed a creature like this.

Close to the recumbent alien she noticed a blood centrifuge. And perched above it was a vial of clear, viscous liquid, which made her wonder...

But Traeger was speaking again. "We know about spontaneous speciation," he said. "Mostly plants and insects, but—"

"Some mammals," Keyes interrupted. "Sheep, goats. Red wolves are known to be a hybrid of coyotes and gray wolves."

"Exactly," Traeger replied. "Possibly some form of recombinant technology, or—"

Casey frowned. "Guys, I get it." Who did they think they were dealing with here? "You want to know if someone fucked a Predator."

8

McKenna slumped half-asleep in the strobing darkness in the back of the rumbling bus. Not merely a prison bus, as he'd first thought of it, but a bus full of head cases being treated by Veterans Affairs. Prisoners and patients, all in one. Had they all been railroaded the way he had, or were the loonies actually loony? He thought he knew the answer, but really, what was crazy? All he knew was that the men who had captured him and put him on this bus were not about to forget about him, which meant there was nothing simple about this bus, or where it might be headed.

Exhausted, lulled by the jostling of the bus and the growl of its engine, he slipped deeper into sleep and found himself lost in something that might have been a dream or a memory, or perhaps a little bit of both.

In the dream-memory, McKenna can still hear the crack of a baseball bat against the ball. He can still see the astonishment on his son's face as Rory realizes he's just gotten the first hit of his life. Awkwardly, in shock and disbelief, Rory begins to run toward first base, helmet bobbling on his head. It's way too big, that helmet. McKenna said something to the coach about it the previous week, but budgets for pee-wee league baseball being what they are, what can the heart-attack-in-waiting Coach Jeff do?

McKenna's in the stands, surrounded by other parents. People whose kids have all done this before, dads who've all had the remarkable pleasure of their sons having even rudimentary skills at baseball. Hit, catch, run. Now McKenna watches Rory stumbling around the bases and knows his own astonishment is even greater than his boy's. A cheer burbles up in his throat and he begins to shout, "Go! Go!"

Rory's headed for second base, a mixture of exultation and terror on his face. McKenna sees the ball arcing across the sky from the outfield, and he knows this dream is about to shatter.

"Slide!" he shouts. "Slide, buddy, slide!"

For a second, McKenna thinks Rory is going to make it. But that's when his stumbling gait causes the bobbling helmet to jostle right off his head. The helmet falls, hits the dirt, and McKenna is still thinking Slide, buddy, slide! *when Rory stops and turns around, crouches and reaches for the helmet.*

McKenna feels himself deflate. He can only watch, helpless, as the second baseman tags Rory out. Kids in the stands erupt in laughter... and not just kids. One beefy dad sitting just over McKenna's shoulder swears loudly.

"What are you doing, you moron?" Beefy bellows amidst his profanity.

McKenna reacts, no hesitation. Slams an elbow into the asshole's sternum. The guy crumples, gasping for air.

Out on the field, Rory glances around in confusion. He knows he's been tagged out, knows he screwed up, but he doesn't understand the laughter yet. Doesn't understand that it's directed at him. In a few seconds he will get it, the moment will sink in. Rory will see the cruelty for what it is, the mocking, and he will be angry… but he'll never be able to sort out just why the people are so mean. And if it happens again, if his helmet bobbles off his head, he'll still turn around and pick it up because he needs his life to be orderly, and the helmet is supposed to stay on.

In this moment, though, none of that has happened yet. Rory hasn't had that cruel epiphany. Half in dream and half in memory, McKenna wants desperately to wake up before he sees the sudden change that knowledge will have on his son's features. He's not a praying man, but this is a dream, and so maybe a little of his childhood churchgoing lingers. Maybe there's a tiny bit of praying going on in this dream.

For once… for fucking once… it's a prayer that is answered.

McKenna snapped awake, fully alert, just as he'd been trained. But he remembered the dream, and he was grateful as hell to have left it behind.

"Hey, Baxley," one of the guys was shouting from the back of the bus, his eyes alight with that manic quality.

Coyle, McKenna thought. *The guy's name is Coyle.* Nebraska Williams had pointed out all the other guys, and provided him with their names, before McKenna had drifted off to sleep.

"Here we go," the guy called Baxley muttered, up at the front of the bus's cage.

"Question for ya," Coyle went on. "How do you circumcise a homeless man?"

Baxley's eyes thinned to slits. It was clear to McKenna in that moment that these guys had a history.

Undeterred by Baxley's forbidding expression, Coyle grinned. "Kick your *mom* in the chin!"

One of the MPs at the front of the bus turned and banged on the cage. "Shut the fuck up back there!"

Coyle cackled mirthfully at his own joke.

McKenna picked up a protein bar, which they'd given him as a meal. He turned to Nebraska Williams.

"Dinner and a show. Great." He nodded at Baxley, who had turned away from Coyle, slumped back down in his seat. "He just sits there?"

"Oh," Nebraska replied, "he'll kill him one of these days."

"What's stopping him?"

"He likes the jokes." Nebraska nodded toward the bald lunatic. "Coyle's here 'cos of a friendly fire incident. He got turned around, fired on one of his own vehicles. There were fatalities." He shrugged. "Now he tells jokes. Go figure."

McKenna nodded in the direction of the magician, who was still shuffling his cards, one-handed. "What about him? Lynch?"

"Ordnance man. They gave him a medal for blowing up half a mountain in Mosul."

"Why's he here?" McKenna asked.

"Blew up the other half, too."

Lynch overheard. His cards stopped shuffling and he glanced up at McKenna. "Entropy, boyo. That's my game. The universe favors chaos. How long's it take to put together a skyscraper? Five years. To knock it down? Five seconds. Things like to fall apart."

"And you hasten the process," McKenna said.

"I make it happen." Lynch held up a card, flicked it, and it vanished. "Poof, just like that. I work for Entropy. I'm aligned with the universe."

"Yeah, well, ask the universe to get us some coffee." McKenna settled back against the bus bench, his gaze landing on the guy in the back with the neck tattoo and the long hair.

"Him?" he asked.

"Nettles," Nebraska reminded him. "Three tours piloting Hueys. Now he gets jumpy when he's not in the air." He glanced toward the back of the bus. "Hey, Nettles. Is it the end times yet?"

Nettles glared at him, shifting slightly. The crucifix dangling from his neck glinted in the strobing of the streetlights they rumbled past.

McKenna kept his expression neutral. These men were broken. Crazy or not, they were certainly dangerous. They had a sense of brotherhood, and the sarcasm flowed freely, but violence simmered among them as well. All of them were used to combat, having someone to fight. McKenna had a bad feeling that if they went too long without an enemy, they might cast aside brotherhood and decide fighting each other was better than no fight at all.

Nebraska turned to him. "Everyone's got a story. What's yours?"

McKenna almost smiled, but thought better of it.

What was he supposed to say? "You wouldn't believe me," he muttered.

"This is the batshit bus. Try me."

McKenna shrugged, scrutinized Nebraska's face as though trying to gauge what his reaction would be from his neutral, patient expression. Finally, he said, "I had a run-in with a space alien. They want to put a lid on it, so… here I am."

They'd assume he was crazy, of course. Why else would he be among them? But Nebraska just shook his head and glanced out the window, making a disgruntled tsking noise.

"Goddamn space aliens," he said.

McKenna stared at him. It hadn't occurred to him that the loonies might be crazy enough to believe him.

Casey stood over the Predator, studying its skin. Its pores. The slope of its massive forehead. With gloved fingers, she touched the thick protuberances that gave it the illusion of hair, wondering what the hell they were for. Could they be mere decoration? The scientist in her didn't think so. The alien still lived, but seemed to be dormant, and she wondered if they kept it deeply sedated or if it had entered a hibernative state. The scientists at Project: Stargazer were far from above drugging a creature they certainly considered hostile—they'd named it "the Predator" not "the good neighbor"—and she couldn't say that she blamed them. But her thoughts were awhirl with questions that would only be answered by interacting with the Predator.

As she moved around the table, she smirked at her own arrogance. Interacting with it? She had seen its weaponry and armor, she'd seen its mandibles and the sharp teeth behind them. The creature's race apparently used the Earth—if Traeger and Church were to be believed—as their own big game preserve, and Casey had an idea what the game was. Did she really want to be face-to-face with one of these things while it was awake and aware of her presence?

Yeah. Hell, yeah, she did.

Where did they come from? What were their starships like? How had they first discovered Earth? The Predators were a spacefaring race, interstellar travelers, which meant that despite their obviously violent, apparently savage culture, they were also a people with advanced science and technology far greater than humanity had managed to create. It felt like a dream to her, so surreal that in the too-warm environment of her hazmat suit and the sterile whiteness of the lab, she grew a bit faint and had to shake it off.

It's real, she reminded herself. *Wake up, Dr. Brackett. This is not a drill.*

Casey smiled as she crouched for a closer look at the Predator's hands and the powerful fingers tipped with sharp claws. Awake, it could rip her heart out of her chest, she had no doubt of that. But what might it tell her, if she could convince it not to kill her?

She turned to Traeger. "That file they showed me. Do you have it?"

From behind him, Agent Church produced the file and handed it over. Casey took it and began to flip through reports and photographs. She came across a telephoto shot of the Predator—or *a* Predator, anyway—in a familiar cityscape.

"This one," she said. "Los Angeles, 2005."

She frowned and went back to the previous photo, which showed a tall man with white-blond hair and a strangely familiar, toothy grin. Quickly, she glanced up at Dr. Keyes, who gave her a sheepish look.

"Your father," she said. "Sorry. Shoulda seen it. The, uh…"

Resemblance, she wanted to say. But this was more than a resemblance. The man in the photo had to be Keyes' father. His son was a dead ringer.

"Anyway, in this photo," she said, flipping back to the shot in LA. The helmet it wore seemed different from the war mask in the display case she'd seen earlier. "It's wearing some kind of… atmosphere mask. A bio-helmet." Casey pointed at the tech mounted on the alien's wrists, wondering if they were also weaponry. "And what are these, wrist gauntlets?"

She glanced back at the dormant Predator and then at a nearby steel table, where its equipment had been laid out like a buffet of extraterrestrial bizarreness. There were other weapons and bits of armor, but not…

"Where are they? The mask and the other gauntlet?"

Traeger shot Keyes an uneasy glance. "We looked, believe me."

Casey flipped back to another, more recent photograph—one that had been on top of the file. The man in the photo had a grown-out buzzcut, but everything about him said military.

"Is this the man who made first contact?"

Traeger shot Church a warning look, but Church either didn't notice or ignored it.

"That's right," he said.

"I'd like to talk to him."

Traeger shifted, stood a bit straighter. Those handsome features hardened. "He's... being evaluated."

Casey scowled. "I see. Well, if you're going to lobotomize him, can I ask him some questions first?"

A squawk from one of the radios up front drew McKenna's attention. He saw one of the MPs reach to his belt and grab his radio, answering the call.

"Go ahead," the MP said, and as he listened to whatever orders were being given to him, his gaze drifted to McKenna. His eyes narrowed slightly. "Read you five-by-five. Out."

Gears ground as the bus began to slow. McKenna stared at the MP, saw the way the man's gaze shifted away from him. Whatever command he'd just received, it didn't bode well. But then McKenna had never thought this was all going to end in a cheerful sing-along with his new friends. Maybe all six of them, there in the back of the bus, had been marked for "accidental" death, a way to clean up half a dozen messes the military didn't want to deal with.

Regrets started to rise in the back of his mind, things he wished he'd done if his end had been accelerated.

He pushed those thoughts out of his head. Regrets were for quitters, and McKenna was still breathing. For the moment, anyway.

One thing lingered, though. His son's birthday had come and gone a few months back and McKenna had never gotten him a gift. He'd kept meaning to. The trouble was, he never knew what to get Rory, didn't know what his son liked. McKenna recognized that last part was the problem, but didn't know what to do about it.

Next year, he thought, glancing again at the MP and wondering about the orders the man had just received. *Yeah, next year.*

9

Rory heard his mom's Subaru Outback pull into the driveway. Through the open window of his bedroom, he listened as the engine shut off, and then the cicadas filled the night with their usual hum. He liked the cicadas. Their music reminded him of static on the radio, a comfortable fuzz that kept things from getting too quiet.

Downstairs, the front door opened. Mom would no doubt have shopping bags. He ought to go and help her, but he'd been thinking and felt no sense of urgency. She didn't really need him down there.

"Rory!" she called from below. "I'm home! I got you something."

Blinking, he shook himself from his reverie and left his room.

"Rory?" she called into the quiet house, as he padded down the steps.

His mother smiled when he entered the kitchen. She gave him a kiss on the cheek as she started to unpack her shopping bags. Rory loved his mother. She could grow distracted, nearly as much as Rory himself, but his dad had always said that was an "artist thing." His mother painted beautifully, her work hung in galleries, but she hadn't become famous yet. People weren't exactly clamoring for Emily McKenna paintings, but Rory knew she had sold plenty of them, and that made her a professional artist. It seemed very clear to him that this was an important thing, and he often wondered why his mother didn't give herself more credit for her accomplishments.

He smiled at her, but his mom had already become distracted by the stack of language books he had left on the counter. French, German, Swedish, even Russian.

"You did one of these after school?" she asked.

"I did all of them after school."

Her smile was so familiar that even Rory, who struggled with non-verbal communication, could read the meaning behind it: *Why am I even surprised?* He watched as she reached inside a big plastic bag from Target.

"So, look, I got you two options," she began, as she drew out a pair of boxed Halloween costumes. "Pirate? Or Frankenstein?"

His mother held up both costumes, proffering them as if each was a remarkable treasure. Rory studied her face, mostly ignoring the costumes. It occurred to him that he ought to explain to her that Frankenstein had been the doctor rather than the monster, but he had been learning strategies of social interaction and knew that sometimes people did not like to be corrected. It was difficult for him to resist the urge, but that was why he fought hard to stay silent on the matter. The hard things were the ones most worth doing.

"Frankenstein," she prompted, mistaking his silence for incomprehension. "You know, green skin? Met the Wolfman?"

Rory took a breath. *The doctor, not the monster.* The words were on the tip of his tongue, but he kept his expression blank. Michael Rosenn, his therapist, would be proud when Rory told him later on. For now, though, his mother gave an exasperated sigh and held up the other box, acting as if it had been the prize she intended to give him all along.

"Let's go with pirate!"

Rory took the boxed pirate costume and reached inside, pulling out the mask. "This is dumb," he said, no punches pulled. "Dad's always telling me to grow up. Be a big boy."

Still, no matter what his father said, he knew the idea of trick-or-treating ought to appeal to him. His classmates seemed thrilled at the prospect. Reluctantly, he donned the mask. He breathed evenly, but it sounded very loud with the plastic covering his face, and he didn't like peering through the eyeholes. He turned his head to experiment, wondering how much it would restrict his vision, and he noticed the water spot on the wall—the one he had tried not to notice ever since he had heard his parents fighting in the kitchen, heard his mother remind his dad that he'd once driven his fist through that wall and the spot was not water at all, but the place where it had been plastered over and the paint didn't match.

His dad had a temper.

Rory took off the mask and set it on the counter. "It's too small. The guys'll… you know, still be able to tell."

Emily frowned. "Tell what?"

"That's it's me," he replied. He caught sight of the sad look on her face, the sudden wetness in her eyes, as he turned to leave the room, but he didn't understand the source of her sadness. He was only being practical, after all.

"I love you, peanut," she said, her voice breaking a little.

"*Jag alskar dig*," he said automatically as he left the kitchen. Swedish for *I love you*.

Rory didn't announce that he was going into the basement. He never did, but somehow his mom always knew when to look for him there. Now he descended into his lair and glanced around at the many recycled computers, screens glowing with online games awaiting his attention. A sign hung on the wall—*CONTROL AREA*.

He sat and launched back into several games at once, but something in the room kept drawing his attention. In his peripheral vision, he could see his worktable, and when he finally glanced over, he saw the parcel that had been delivered by the postal worker with all of his father's mail. Rory had compartmentalized its presence, intending to open it just as soon as he'd made his way through the language books upstairs, but he'd forgotten.

Now he sucked in a sharp breath, went to the table, and tore open the package. He reached in, pulling back the dirty newspapers that the contents had been packed with. He reached inside, felt a smooth metallic surface, and pulled out an enormous scarred helmet that reminded him immediately of something out of one of his video games.

For a moment he stood frozen, his mind stunned into immobility, and then abruptly it began to race as he tried to determine precisely what he held. This was not a Halloween mask or a replica. Whoever this helmet might belong to—this thing his father had shipped to himself from Mexico, and which had only been delivered here because he'd forgotten to pay for his post office box—it didn't belong to Quinn McKenna. The thing didn't look like US Army gear. It had various markings on its surface, but not in any language Rory had ever seen. It looked like it might have some in-board technology, and he started mentally comparing it to games he'd played and movies he'd seen.

One thing was for sure. Whoever this belonged to, the guy had a massive frickin' head.

Rory set the helmet aside and reached into the box again. What he pulled out this time made him grin. The wrist gauntlet clearly had the same origin, the same tech. He started fiddling with it, pressing nearly hidden buttons. With a *click*, a small door opened and a long, trapezoidal object popped out of a compartment in the gauntlet. It reminded him of a fat, old-fashioned remote control, but there was nothing old-fashioned about the sleek surface or the strange texture of the metal. It felt unusual and heavy and strangely warm, almost alien.

He studied the gleaming device—Rory was certain this thing had a purpose. It didn't appear to be a weapon, but there were switches and buttons. Warily, he punched a button. When nothing happened, he frowned and turned the sleek device over again, cocked his head to study it, then thumbed another button.

A display blinked on. Rory frowned deeper, locked in fascination as he watched glowing red symbols scroll across the device. His eyes widened as he studied their cryptic patterns, trying to make sense of it all...

Far from Rory... far from Earth... a stealth ship, smaller and sleeker than the one that had recently crash-landed in the Mexican jungle, glides swiftly toward the Earth. Within it, a Predator quite unlike the one in Project: Stargazer's custody taps a button and a display appears on its viewscreen. The same glowing symbols scroll, but to these eyes, its patterns are far from cryptic. Instead, they reveal very much indeed. The hunter makes several satisfied clicking noises, and flies onward.

In his basement, Rory worked studiously, scribbling a transcription of the symbols from the alien device onto the outside of one of his school folders. He knew his heart ought to be racing, but he felt calmer than he'd ever been. Excited, yes... enthusiastic... but intent upon his task. Here was a real puzzle, a real mystery that he could sink his teeth into. He couldn't ever seem to unravel the mysteries that other people presented, and school had never presented him with a challenge, but here was something different—a *true* challenge. Languages, after all, had always been his specialty.

With a blip, the readout on the device changed. He scrunched up his face and furiously scribbled this new sequence, translating in his head. His eyes narrowed, and he stared at the device. He had begun to understand it, and now he tapped several buttons, causing the display to revert to the first sequence he'd awoken.

Aboard the pursuit ship, the strange Predator grimaces and glares with great displeasure at his viewscreen. The readout has changed as if it has a mind of its own. A malfunction? He taps the controls, correcting the sequence...

Rory could have laughed when the sequence altered again. It seemed to him that the device had reacted to him. For a moment he wondered if it had been programmed this way, or if it contained some kind of alien artificial intelligence that he could not hope to understand.

On second thought, he decided the odds of there being a language or technology he could not understand were very slim. Dismissively, he overrode the device again.

On the pursuit ship, the strange Predator—enormous even by the standards of its race—punches in a new code. The interior of the ship spasms. The seat beneath him trembles, but it is the outside of the ship that truly trembles. It shimmers and enters stealth mode. To the naked eye, or even to any instruments, it is now invisible...

N N N

Rory grinned, awash with sudden understanding. He would have preferred the AI solution, but this was fun, too. *It's a game*, he thought. He had seen enough of these cryptic symbols, scribbled enough of them down and gotten a basic translation worked out, so that he now understood how to revise the sequence of the code to reverse a command, which was precisely what he did.

In space, the pursuit ship decloaks. What issues from the strange Predator's mouth then, in clicks and spittle, is what passes for profanity on its home world.

"You okay down there, kiddo?"

Rory froze. He stared at the device, at the helmet and the gauntlet, and then at the steps that led up from the basement. This would be a bad time for his mom to come down to check on him.

"Just playing games, Mom!" he yelled, trying to make everything sound normal.

For a few tense seconds he waited, wondering if she would reply—or even whether he'd hear the clump of her descending footsteps. But there was silence from up above. She must have gone away.

His hunched shoulders lowered slowly as he relaxed.

N N N

The only thing Anya Martin didn't like about her job was that she could never tell the truth about what she did. Not that she worked for the CIA or anything—she wasn't going to have some Russian spy shoot her in the back of the head on a street corner, or poison her food in a London restaurant. Although eating in London restaurants did seem wonderfully exotic to her. It depressed her when her train of thought chugged down these particular tracks, because then she got thinking about traveling the world, and though the job of Tracking Analyst sounded fancy, her salary was anything but.

Whine, whine, whine, she thought to herself, sitting in front of a whole bank of radar and tracking arrays. Truth was, Anya made more than a decent living. If she hadn't been a single mother, saving for her daughter's college, she probably would have done plenty of traveling by now. She fantasized about various European river cruises, got all the catalogs and emails, and didn't even care that she'd probably be the youngest person on board by thirty years or more.

Someday, she'd do all that traveling.

For now, though, at least she loved her job. Many of the programmers she had gone to college with would surely be making more money than she did by this point in their lives. Others would be managers by now. Maybe executives.

The good news was that the US Air Force had paid for Sergeant Anya Martin's education. She had no college loans.

Also, she spent her days watching the skies for signs of alien invasion, or any other unidentified flying objects—

anything that might indicate that alien enemies were approaching or traveling through Earth orbit. The military wanted forewarning of any possible threats. But here in her very comfortable chair in the 6th Space Warning Squadron's headquarters in Sandwich, Massachusetts, Anya just loved the idea of aliens. She pretended to be quite serious about the work—as serious as the title Tracking Analyst implied—but in the end, really, it was all about Dana Scully and Fox Mulder and late nights watching *The X-Files* when her parents had told her to go to bed.

It didn't hurt that she got to live half a mile from the ocean on the coast of Cape Cod.

Blip.

Anya's heart jumped. She stared at the radar screen and then glanced at the PAVE PAWS tracking monitor. The blip vanished, and then reappeared. It repeated the pattern again. Quickly, she went through her protocol, including identifying its location and trying to make radio contact with the object, to no avail.

"Sir?" she said, gesturing toward the Lieutenant General.

He came across, a man so wiry she wouldn't have been surprised to find that his gray hair was made of steel. "What you got, Sergeant?"

"Weird-ass bogey, sir."

They watched together as the blip vanished and reappeared sporadically.

"One second they're on the grid, the next they're ghosting," Anya said, trying to hide her excitement. She'd caught plenty of weird shit during her time in this job, but this was odd as hell.

"Radio contact?" the Lieutenant General asked.

"Negative, sir." She narrowed her eyes, skin prickling with ice as her thoughts filled with wonder. "But it seems to have an ion trail."

The Lieutenant General had a pen in his hand. He started to chew on the back of it while he stared at the monitor. Then he turned and scouted the room for Anya's supervisor, Lieutenant Crain.

"Where's the 325th?" he asked.

"Tyndall, sir," Crain replied.

The Lieutenant General's gray eyebrows crinkled in a deep frown. "Let's scramble some jets. I don't want to take any chances."

Sergeant Anya Martin couldn't hide her smile. This was getting good. It was even more exciting than being poisoned to death in a London restaurant.

10

Casey could smell Traeger's cologne, not overpowering or even unpleasant, but strange under the circumstances. She was bent over an electron microscope, doing her job, and Traeger stood a little too close behind her. His proximity wasn't so intimate that it had become unprofessional, nor so close that she could turn around and tell him to back off. But still, it made her uncomfortable. Despite— or perhaps because of—his handsome features and the grin he'd flashed earlier, she thought maybe he was the kind of man who took power from making people feel unsettled around him. Not just women—anyone.

It had grown quiet in the lab, and silent between them, and that added to her discomfort with his nearness. She was relieved when Traeger's aide, Sapir, appeared, rushing up to them with a look on his face like his grandmother's ghost had just whispered sweet nothings in his ear.

"Sir," Sapir said, "NORAD's reporting a two-oh-two anomaly."

The weighted look that passed between the two men pissed Casey off.

"Look," she said, bristling. "I know I'm new, but it'd be *swell* if somebody would kinda, sorta, I don't know… tell me *what the fuck* is going on here?"

A visible calm descended on Traeger. He'd decided how to handle her.

"This isn't the first Predator we've encountered."

Casey waited for more. From the file she'd seen, and the information they'd already given her, that much was obvious. She cocked an eyebrow, inviting him to continue.

"Apparently," he went on, "they use Earth as a kind of hunting ground. We've even got unconfirmed reports of them abducting people. For sport."

And? she thought. *Haven't we already established all this? Try telling me something I* don't *know.*

But it was Dr. Keyes who spoke next. He had been hovering on the periphery of the conversation, but now he stepped closer, as if worried that Traeger might not give a fulsome enough account of the situation.

"They've left things behind," Keyes said. "Evidence. Weapons. You saw some on the way in."

"Your point?" she said, unable to conceal her frustration. Now it was Keyes' turn to bristle.

"The point, doctor," he said in a clipped voice, "is that our satellite defense stations have just tracked a new UFO." He nodded grimly toward the dormant Predator. "Our friend here might have some company coming."

The words were barely out of his mouth when

klaxons began to blare throughout the complex. Casey's pulse quickened.

"What's happening?"

Traeger glanced over to where his aide had already picked up an internal phone receiver. The guy grew even paler as he covered the mouthpiece and turned to stare, wide-eyed, at his boss.

"Proximity alert, sir!" the aide called. "Bogey's inbound! Range two hundred miles!"

To her horror, Casey saw the supposedly dormant Predator's eyes suddenly snap open. Her mouth opened in an 'O' of astonishment, and she let out a cry of alarm, but didn't think anyone had heard her over the klaxons. The Predator's eyes were calm and alert, and she wondered if it understood English—if it had been listening to them the entire time—or if the alarm had been the signal it had been waiting for.

She leaped backward, heart thundering in her chest, but her mind orderly, calculating, assessing the variables. Earlier she'd seen a wall rack with several tranquilizer rifles and now she took one and raised it to her shoulder, backing away and taking aim.

"Everybody, get out!" she barked. "Now!"

All eyes had turned to her, and then to the Predator. Agent Church must have seen it faster than the others, for he was the first to move. He bolted across the room toward the nearest exit—the hatch for the decontamination chamber—and put his hand and eye to the scanners.

"Church, Thomas J.— " he began.

The Predator snapped its restraints as if they were made of paper and began to sit up. Guards went for their sidearms in what seemed like slow motion. Keyes backed away, taking cover behind Traeger.

The decontamination hatch whooshed open. She could hear Church thanking God over the blaring klaxons, even as the Predator snatched up a scalpel from an operating tray beside it and flicked its wrist. The scalpel flew unerringly across the room and embedded itself in the back of Church's neck, just at the base of his skull. *Sliced right through the brain stem*, Casey thought numbly, even as Church collapsed like a marionette with its strings cut.

She saw her moment, and she took it. With the Predator turning to focus on the guards, she lunged across the room and jumped over the fallen Church, careening into the decon chamber just as the hatch shushed closed again. Sweating, all the air inside her wanting to burst out in a scream—and yet with a tiny voice of awe muttering in the back of her head—she pounded on the outer hatch. She had to get out of not just the lab, but the entire complex. Project: Stargazer was just about as compromised as it could be.

"*Chamber secure*," said the pre-recorded voice. "*Remove garments.*"

"Fuck!" Casey snapped. She put down the tranquilizer rifle and fumbled at the catches of her hazmat suit with her heart thundering in her ears. She stared at the sign on the wall—*STERILE IN, STERILE OUT.*

Inside the main lab, security guards rushed the Predator. It ducked and parried. Snapped a guard's arm. Hurled a screaming man aside and then tossed another across the lab to crash against a wall full of shelved samples and instruments. Things clattered down, and the guards flew like rag dolls.

"Come on, come on!" she muttered as she kept glancing into the lab.

Terror rose within her, like her courage had sprung a leak and fear had come rushing in, flooding her insides. The Predator moved with mind-numbing speed and agility, dispensing violence and death with an efficiency and ruthlessness that was almost obscene, and suddenly all Casey wanted was to get the fuck out of there, *to be anywhere but here*, to forget she had ever met Agent Church—who lay dead just outside the decon chamber, glassy eyes wide and accusatory.

Breath coming in short gasps, pulse throbbing at her temples, she struggled to tear off the hazmat suit. A spray of blood arced across the examination room and splattered the glass window of the decontamination chamber, making Casey jump. She glanced past the dripping stain and saw the Predator's swift handiwork. Corpses littered the floor. It had to know she was there—had to be perfectly aware of her presence—but it ignored her and marched across the lab to the table where its gear had been laid out. Chest armor, gauntlet, a kind of chainmail.

The Predator dressed quickly, even as Casey tore off her own clothes. She saw the way it paused and tilted its head very slightly, hand freezing over the array of gear as if noticing that something was missing.

Then the decon chamber muttered something overhead and the spray came down. Casey stood and let it burn off yet another layer of her skin. It had barely finished when she kicked aside the hazmat suit and snatched up her street clothes, bundling them against her chest. With the other hand, she grabbed the tranquilizer gun.

In her peripheral vision she saw the Predator stalking across the examination room toward a man cowering behind an upturned bench, his knees drawn up to his chest, his back pressed against the wall as if he wished he could melt into it, pass right through. It was only when the man, sensing the Predator looming over him, glanced up and let out a yelp of terror that she realized it was Keyes. As the Predator leaned over, grabbed him by the hair and lifted him into the air as if he weighed nothing, Casey thought of how the son had continued the father's work, of how the family obsession had had such disastrous consequences for them both. Waiting helplessly for the outer door of the decon chamber to open, she could only watch with sick horror as the Predator scooped up another scalpel and used it, with one swift and devastating sweep of its massive arm, to cut off Keyes' screaming head. As the body fell like a sack of wet cement, the alien stooped and unhesitatingly sliced off the scientist's right hand. Now carrying its spoils, Keyes' head in one taloned hand, his severed hand in the other, the Predator crossed to the door of the decon unit and pressed Keyes' body parts to the retinal and fingerprint scanners.

Hideous though this was, even more grotesque in a way was when the Predator opened its mouth and spoke in a voice that was a perfect imitation of the dead scientist's.

"Keyes. Shawn H."

It's a fucking mockingjay, Casey thought, as a green light beeped. At the same moment, the outer door finally opened behind her. But now it was too late to run, because the door at the other side of the decon chamber was also opening, and the Predator, making a horrible Geiger-counter-like clicking sound, was ducking forward to step through it. All but naked, Casey spun to face it, clutching the tranq rifle.

Trying to control her trembling hands, Casey leveled the rifle at the alien hunter. She pulled the trigger and the weapon did nothing more than utter a dry *click*. Whether it was jammed, or empty, she had no idea, but either way she knew she was about to die. Desperate, she lifted her gaze to stare at the Predator.

It cocked its head, regarding her. Its mouth—the mandibles, the razor teeth inside—if the thing could smile, it seemed to smile at her, almost indulgently. Then it swept past her, sparing her, as if it had already forgotten she had been there at all.

Casey stared at the weird 'dreadlocks' on the back of its head as it strode away. Her breath thawed, and she inhaled ragged, short, terrified breaths. She set down the tranq gun and started to dress in a panic, even as she saw the Predator fitting its one wrist gauntlet onto its arm.

A guard came around the corner at a run. His eyes widened in terror as he raised his machine gun. Had he seen what Casey had seen, he wouldn't have bothered even trying to take aim. The Predator smashed the gun barrel aside and picked him up, then slammed his skull against the wall with a wet, horrifying crunch.

Two more of Stargazer's mercenary goons rounded the corner, their rifles up. Weaponless, the Predator seemed to shrug as it stomped on the stock of the machine gun that had spilled from the dead guy's hand. The weapon flipped upward like a yard rake and the Predator snatched it in its talons, lifted the gun, and opened fire. The guards fired as well, but too late, and inaccurately. Bullets raked their flesh, driving them backward to topple in a bloody pile in the hall.

Casey tugged her shirt on, darted her gaze around for her left shoe—the last piece of her wardrobe—and slipped into it. Only then did she hear the shushing *thunk* behind her. She glanced back and saw that the inner hatch door hadn't closed all the way. It opened slightly and then slid again, trying to shut—blocked by Dr. Keyes' severed head. The Predator must have simply dropped the head when it was no longer any use, and now the door was jerking open and closed, pummeling the severed head each time it did so. Casey felt bile burn up the back of her throat, but she forced her gorge back down. Her life depended on self-control now.

She nearly bolted then, but her gaze paused on the centrifuge inside the lab, and the vial of clear liquid that remained perhaps miraculously unbroken, dangling above it.

Now that the Predator had left her behind, her thoughts had begun to slow, to seek order, and, more particularly, answers. Staring at the vial, she found herself wondering how many answers the liquid inside it might contain.

N N N

The Predator strides along the corridor with purpose, disposing of irritations and intrusions as they present themselves. The guards are neither a concern nor a challenge. Only when he passes the display case near the front of the complex does his inexorable march toward freedom halt. With a click of satisfaction, he turns to look at the wide plexiglass window of the case and to admire what is displayed there.

He shatters the glass and reaches inside.

The bio-helmet does not belong to him. It was collected by these humans from some historic hunt years before. He can only assume the hunter who'd worn it had met an honorable death. The facemask is scarred and pitted from battle and the Predator tells himself it is an honor to acquire this mask, though he did not earn that damage himself.

He lifts the mask aloft and holds it over his face, taps the side. The eyeholes light up with their familiar internal readout and he taps again, making a connection. A personal connection. The bio-helmet adjusts to this Predator's bio-signature and abruptly the internal readout blurs and shifts to static, and then a viewpoint reveals itself. The Predator wants his own gear back, his own bio-helmet, and most importantly his missing wrist gauntlet, and the vital tech sealed within it.

Matching his bio-signature, this mask connects to his own—though it is many miles from here. The two masks sync, and now through this one, he can see through the eyes of the other. See what it sees.

Through the eyes of that mask, he sees a human child. A boy. Somehow his own bio-helmet has fallen into the child's possession and he needs to locate it immediately. Too much depends upon it, and the urgency overrides any other concerns he might have. There is no hunt, no battle, no hunger more important than this.

The boy works at some kind of table, and the Predator thinks of the lab from which he has just departed.

On the wall beyond the child is a crude drawing of an animal. A dog? A smaller paper is attached to the larger one, and on that smaller tag there are typewritten words. Rory Declan McKenna, Grade 6. Gordon Middle School, GA.

Pleased, the Predator taps another button on the mask and it seals to his face. This bio-helmet will serve him, for now. He scans the gear on display in that shattered glass case—items stolen or acquired from dead warriors over many years. He selects several throwing stars, slips them into a sheath on his armor, and then taps at his wrist gauntlet…

And vanishes.

McKenna had never imagined he could grow bored with being in federal custody—secret, black box, down-the-rabbit-hole federal custody at that. He'd certainly never have figured he would be bored being in the back of what was essentially a prison bus with a motley crew of military lunatics who were his new therapy group. But by the time they rolled through the gates of the mysterious compound, and he glanced out the window and saw the mercenaries guarding it—men and women much like the ones Traeger had brought to Mexico to put a noose around his neck—McKenna had reached the boredom stage.

He'd let his thoughts play out the future like a tangled

ball of string. How long did Traeger think he could be kept under wraps? What would the son of a bitch do if McKenna tried to escape, or get the truth out? Would anyone believe him, or would they think he belonged in some VA psych hospital with the other loonies on the bus?

As the gate rattled shut and the bus rolled across the compound, he smiled, half-asleep. People would believe him—at least some would—when they saw the evidence he'd shipped home to himself from Mexico.

Yeah, no way in hell would McKenna stay Traeger's pet nutjob. At least not for long.

With a shuddering squeal of brakes, the bus rattled to a halt. McKenna frowned and glanced around at the Loonies. Coyle and Lynch didn't even glance up. Nebraska and the others appeared more irritated than curious, but McKenna glanced out the window and frowned when he saw the other mercenaries in the compound. Wherever they were, it didn't look like any VA hospital. Maybe Traeger had other plans for him—and for the Loonies—after all.

The bus driver cranked the door open and a mercenary stepped on.

"Sit tight," the guard said, "there's been a breach."

Breach. McKenna didn't like the sound of that. Wherever they were, it was no hospital—and whatever secrecy it involved, someone who didn't belong there had entered the compound.

He started to wonder if this might be his chance to get the fuck out.

N N N

Casey had taken a moment to catch her breath. Almost unconsciously, she'd opened and closed her grip on the tranq rifle and then started forward. When she'd first glimpsed the fluorescent green liquid spattered on the floor, it had made her halt, but the moment she realized what it had to be—the Predator's blood, from its fight with the guards—she started moving forward again. She'd seen it kill the men and women in the lab, seen it murder the guards who'd tried to stop it, but now that her terror had abated, and now that she'd seen the Predator could be hurt, could be wounded, her old fascination and ambition had returned.

With a grunt, a bleeding med-tech came around the corner. The guy flinched when he spotted her, maybe thinking she would finish the job the Predator had begun. Then he exhaled, cringing with pain from his injuries. His eyes were alight with panic and despair.

"It… it can't get away," the med-tech said.

Casey gripped the tranq rifle even tighter. "It won't," she replied determinedly. "Not my space animal."

She followed the blood trail, knowing with every step that she had left the world of safety and good decisions behind, and not giving a single goddamn fuck.

11

Aaron Pinsky knew he belonged in the cockpit of his F-22. Some people never felt comfortable in their work. He had friends from high school who were high-priced lawyers or doctors who told him they felt like frauds, and more than one old friend working construction who admitted they thought they were meant for more in life. Over the past year he had found his thoughts straying more and more to Shayla Woods, who'd spent high school as a waitress and then gone to culinary school. Shayla dreamed of having her own restaurant, of being the kind of chef who won awards and became the buzz of the city. For now, she was just a sous chef, but she loved it. Lived and breathed, she said, for the rhythm and the smells and the constant crisis of the kitchen. She knew in her soul that she belonged there, and that was how Pinsky felt about flying, and about the Air Force.

He sliced the sky and scanned both instruments and visual, searching for the bogey that had everyone in an uproar. Pinsky was totally at ease. He could breathe up here. There were no distractions, no arguments, no pissing contests. As a pilot, his confidence felt pure. He had a job to do, and he performed his duties as surely as he drew in breath.

His comms crackled as he checked his instruments again.

"Catfish one," came Suarez's voice, "triangulate SAM radar."

Pinsky's hands moved confidently over the instruments as if he and his jet were simply different parts of the same organism, man and machine in a state of perfect symbiosis.

In his basement, Rory sat at the table with the device in his hand. He'd abandoned it for a while to play video games, and had just come back to it a moment before, tapping in the same code he'd tried earlier. Just for the hell of it.

He smiled curiously. What the hell was this thing? And that code… what did it do?

Rory figured he would never know.

There were three of them all together—Raptor jets— flying in formation. Pinsky heard hesitation over the comms, like Suarez was about to say something else. Then alarms sounded in the cockpit and something blinked onto his display. The instruments went crazy and he glanced up as a gleaming craft appeared directly ahead, right in their flight path.

"Holy shit!" Pinsky barked.

"Heads up! Bandit!" Suarez announced, as if they didn't know.

Pinsky veered to starboard. Suarez and Obie peeled off to port, missing the UFO by meters. The other two pilots were shouting profanities and generally losing their shit, but Pinsky snapped at them to lock it down. He didn't know about the others, but he knew for sure that he belonged up here, and whatever that bogey was—it sure as hell did not.

But when he glanced at his instruments, he couldn't quite believe what they were telling him. They had all seen the bogey, clear as day, but according to all the readouts there was suddenly no sign that it had ever been there at all.

McKenna rubbed his eyes and sat up a little straighter. *Breach*? What the hell was going on? And where exactly were they? He craned his neck and peered through the dirty windows, trying to get a better look at the compound. Something caught his eye, and he stared as something dropped from a rooftop. It took him a moment to realize that it was a human being, a guard, their arms flailing wildly. Then the body smashed into the ground, bounced, and went still.

Son of a bitch, he thought, putting a hand against the glass and staring up at the rooftop. There was something else up there. Something big, moving. It strode swiftly to the edge of the roof and peered over at the ground below. As light slid over it, McKenna felt a cold ripple run through his body. It was the creature he had seen in the jungle—or something like it! As he gaped at it, it flickered, and then vanished into the darkness as if it had never been there.

Only then did McKenna realize Nebraska Williams had been staring, too. The man looked shaken, but sensing McKenna's scrutiny he tried to hide it.

"Your little green friend?" Nebraska asked with mock casualness.

"Yup."

"Turns invisible?"

"Yup."

Nebraska grimaced. "Goddamn space aliens."

Out across the compound, half-lost in darkness, a guard swept his MX3 in a low arc. McKenna watched the mercenary searching the shadows between buildings, then one of those shadows took shape and the alien leaped out of nowhere—literally nowhere—and raked talons across the guard's throat before vanishing again.

The other guys were moving now, joining McKenna and Nebraska at the windows. The driver and the guards up at the front of the bus were whispering, all of them drawing weapons.

"That thing killed my men," McKenna said, starting to rise, watching the guards, ready to enter the fray.

"Yeah, they'll do that," Nebraska said. "Stay on the bus."

McKenna scowled at him. "What are you, nuts? We gotta move!"

"Brother?" Nebraska replied dubiously. "It's a bus." He glanced over at Coyle and gave him the nod, a signal to start some shit.

Coyle picked up on it immediately. "Hey, Baxley! If your mom's vagina was a video game, it'd be rated 'E for Everyone!'"

One of the MPs up front rattled the cage with his baton. "Knock it off!" he snapped, as nervous as the rest of them.

"Seriously," Coyle said, leering at Baxley with those mad eyes. "What's the difference between five big black guys and a joke?" He glanced around, as if hoping for an answer, then grinned. "Baxley's mom can't take a joke!"

That did it. Baxley lunged from his seat, a blur, and wrapped the chain connecting his manacles around Coyle's throat. Coyle gasped and sputtered, grin still on his face until he began to claw in strangled panic at the chain.

The MP who'd shouted at them swore again, key ring jangling as he grabbed hold of the gate. The other guard unclipped his sidearm and stepped to one side to get an angle on them.

"Everyone on the floor, face down!" shouted the one aiming his gun.

Everyone but Coyle and Baxley obeyed—Baxley because he was trying to murder Coyle, and Coyle because he was trying not to die. McKenna ground his teeth as he went to his knees with his head bowed and his hands behind his head. He glanced up to see the MP with the keys grabbing a Remington 870 pump action shotgun from its mount outside the cage. Then the two guards were rushing up the aisle, weapons drawn, sweeping the barrels as they went to Baxley and Coyle and started to drag the troublemakers apart.

Coyle and Baxley struggled, spitting, trying to get at each other.

The first MP reached for the baton at his belt. McKenna saw the surprise, and then the fear, in his eyes as his hand closed on nothing and he realized the baton had gone missing. Alarm bells were clearly going off in the guy's head as he started to glance around, but too late. Baxley had snatched the baton while they were grappling, and now he swung it swiftly and savagely at the back of the MP's legs. The guy went down hard on his knees.

The second MP raised the shotgun, but he barely had a second to register what was unfolding before Coyle brought his hand up, smashing his palm against the barrel of the shotgun. The weapon's stock slammed back into the MP's forehead with a loud *crack*, dropping the man to the aisle floor.

Coyle grabbed the shotgun and tossed it to Nebraska, who cocked it even as he spun and leveled the weapon at the driver.

"Whoopsie," Nebraska said.

The driver put up his hands. Baxley and Coyle, the best of friends now that their bit of theater no longer had a purpose, relieved the two MPs of their keys and swiftly began to unlock the other prisoners' shackles.

The moment Nebraska's manacles were removed, he hurried up to replace the driver. Baxley unlocked McKenna's cuffs as Nettles and Lynch bustled the two MPs back out through the open cage door and then shoved them off the bus, followed by the driver.

Unsure what the ultimate motives of his fellow prisoners were, McKenna said, "Hate to interrupt your little prison break, but I could use your help."

Nebraska fired up the engine, glancing over his shoulder at McKenna. "Does this green boy of yours have a bus pass?"

McKenna narrowed his eyes. He'd been half afraid the Loonies would want to try to run. Fortunately, they seemed either too brave or too crazy to do that. Maybe both.

"Just get me close," McKenna told him. "I'm a sniper."

Nebraska jerked the bus into gear. "Oh, you wanna *kill* him. Hell, why didn't you say so?"

With a look of grim purpose, he hit the accelerator, gunning the engine, and the bus lurched forward.

As Casey raced up another flight of stairs, following the trail of green blood, she felt grateful for all the spin classes she'd taken. She reached a metal door that hung open, its lock torn out, the hinges twisted. With a shove, she pushed through and burst into the night air.

Heart thundering, she glanced around. Her skin prickled with fear as she oriented herself. The Stargazer compound was on one side of a hydro dam, part of the base and the lab built into the dam itself. Now her pursuit had led her out onto the roof of one wing of the facility. To one side, she could see yet more of the base still under construction. Below her was the wide dam, the road that went across it, and the compound just in front of the base. She turned to look out at the dark water.

Casey was terrified, yes, but she felt far more determined than afraid.

At her feet, she saw a spattering of that gleaming green blood, and wondered just how wounded the Predator was, whether it had been weakened, incapacitated— she hoped so, though conversely she didn't want it to die; despite everything, she still harbored the hope of communicating with it. Before she could talk herself out of it, she ran, following the Predator's trail. Below her, vehicles roared along the road that ran atop the dam. Alarms wailed throughout the complex, both up top and down below, and echoed from within.

Casey followed the blood trail out along a catwalk. Breathless, she reached the end and saw the fresh green ichor dripping off the edge. A frown creased her brow. Had the Predator jumped, or…

Motion above drew her attention. She glanced up into the new construction to see the creature moving along a gantry overhead—moving easily, as if it hadn't been wounded at all. As if aware of her scrutiny, it paused and cocked its head, like it was listening to the sky. Casey held her breath, thinking it would turn and leap at her, but instead the Predator glanced up with a sudden quick movement, as if something had alarmed it.

Good, she thought. Whatever had gotten its attention, she was grateful for the diversion. She raised the tranquilizer rifle, thinking it was probably out of range. Even so, she was desperate enough to take a shot.

Maybe it was her heart pounding in her ears or the intensity of her focus or the rumble of military vehicles behind her, but she didn't hear the ship coming until it blasted across the sky—a silver pod that sheared through the atmosphere overhead with a *boom* that reverberated across Stargazer base. Casey froze, so caught up in the moment that when the sky opened again, her heart nearly stopped. A pair of F-22 fighter jets flashed overhead in the blink of an eye, their noise deafening, as if they'd just shattered heaven in two.

But heaven was somebody else's problem. Casey's was here on the ground.

The bus punched through a fence with a brittle *clang* and thundered forward, chain link whipping across the windshield and away. McKenna held onto the cage with one hand and knelt on a seat, scanning the compound. Nebraska drove like they were on a minefield, swerving back and forth, but he wasn't avoiding anything—he kept bending to peer out the windshield, trying to get a look at the jets and the damn spaceship even as he eyed the buildings around and below them.

"Eyes on the fucking—" McKenna began.

The next word would have been *road*, of course. But McKenna lost track of his thoughts the moment he spotted the woman off to the right of the bus, running along a catwalk twenty feet off the ground. As he spotted her, the woman swung up onto a metal bridge, taking the high ground. McKenna tracked her, wondering if she was running away from something, or toward it. He checked her trajectory, and then he saw it.

For all its bulk, the alien moved fast. It leaped, agile as an ape, from one steel beam to another, above her, the woman just about keeping pace. McKenna's eyes widened as he realized this one woman, who didn't even look like a soldier, was the only person in the entire complex who seemed to be in foot pursuit of the space creature that had murdered his men. She had some kind of rifle in her hand, but from this distance he couldn't identify the weapon.

What the hell does she think she's doing? he thought.

The bus jerked to the left, Nebraska cursing at an obstacle that McKenna hadn't seen. McKenna took a jolt, but held onto the gate, and when he glanced out the window again, he saw the woman raise the rifle—some sort of tranquilizer gun, like a zookeeper might use. She got off a shot, and then another, but whatever her ammo was, it smacked impotently into the steel beams. The creature leaped out, away from her, but McKenna didn't think it was out of fear. It wasn't fleeing its pursuer—it had a goal in mind.

As the bus roared forward, the alien suddenly dropped from overhead. It touched down dead ahead of them, but McKenna was only half paying attention as Nebraska swore and twisted the wheel to avoid it, the Loonies shouting from the back. The creature corkscrewed away from them, disappearing into the darkness. By this time, Coyle and Lynch had become aware of the woman as well. Together they watched her race to the end of the bridge she'd been on.

No way, McKenna thought. *No fucking way is she going to—*

But she did. He caught a glimpse of the determination on her face, and the terror that bloomed in her expression when she realized what she was doing, and then she was out of sight. The bus had passed right beneath her.

McKenna whipped his head back and stared at the ceiling of the bus, even as he heard the thump and roll of the woman landing on the roof above them. Coyle and Lynch grinned at each other.

"You gotta be kidding me!" Baxley shouted in excitement, pumping a fist.

Hold on, McKenna thought, but he'd already turned to look back out the windshield. He spotted the alien, heading for the perimeter fence like the White Rabbit, late for a very important date. McKenna flashed back to the jungle, to the sight of his men and the way they'd been torn apart.

"Open the door!" he barked.

Without hesitation, Nebraska jerked the lever, the door accordioned open, and McKenna gripped the sidearm he'd stolen from one of the MPs. He threw himself sideways onto the steps, poking his head out through the open door, and took aim. A flash of *Jaws* went through his mind. *Smile, you son of a*—he thought.

The air distorted around the alien as it ran. McKenna knew what that meant—he'd seen it in the jungle; hell, he'd used the tech himself. But before it turned invisible, the alien reached the perimeter fence and vaulted it easily. Still in midair, it threw back its arm in an almost casual gesture, and suddenly a spinning blade was flashing toward the bus.

McKenna felt the bus turn into a skid even before his brain registered the bang of the tire exploding. The bus slewed sideways, shuddering, whipped with such force that McKenna felt himself flung out the door. He tucked into a roll, tumbled across the ground, and came up on one knee just in time to look back and see the woman staggering on the roof. She was trying desperately to keep her footing, but looked like Bambi on the ice. McKenna saw the moment when she fired the tranq gun involuntarily, and as the bus shuddered to a ragged halt he saw her totter toward the edge of the roof and tip over, as if boneless as a rag doll . Only then did he realize she'd shot herself in the leg or the foot, and the tranquilizer had already taken effect.

By that time he was already up and racing toward the bus, wondering if he'd reach her in time, picturing her landing in his arms.

Then he spotted a cadre of security guards—those merc bastards who'd captured him in the first place—converging on the bus from the darkness, and he hesitated. Whereupon the woman landed with a *whomp* on the turf.

So much for Prince fucking Charming, he thought, as he ran to help her up.

Chagrined, he got her to her feet, but her legs were like silly putty and she hung around his neck, barely able to stand as the tranquilizer rushed through her bloodstream.

The Loonies scrambled out of the bus as the guards approached. Nebraska came out last, but he'd been scanning the compound the whole time he'd been driving, and it seemed he'd already figured out his plan. He pointed to a Quonset hut that looked to be the compound's motor pool. A row of Indian Scout motorcycles was lined up in front.

Turning to the others, he shouted almost gleefully, "Get to the choppers!"

12

Pinsky had tried yoga a few times. He understood the concept, the way it was supposed to relax you, let you breathe and connect with your body. He wasn't ever going to suggest that it didn't work, because it had worked for him, to a certain degree. But other than some useful stretching, yoga didn't provide anything to him that flying jets didn't offer a hundred times over… and never more so than when he had a bogey in his sights.

"Light up your winders on my mark," he said into his comms mic. "Go, zero-two! Go, zero-three!"

As the other members of his squadron banked off on either side to flank the once-again-visible ship that streaked across the sky below them, a blissful calm enveloped him. The world that existed for him now was only his ride, the voices on his comms, the steady in-out of his breathing, and the UFO he'd been tasked with blowing out of the fucking sky. He smiled to himself and thought of childhood visits to the dentist and the happy gas they'd given him when he'd needed a tooth pulled. Even the oxygen mask attached to his face reminded him of that day. There was no gas in the air he breathed—he wouldn't be seeing dragons on the wall or thinking his mom had floppy puppy ears—but he felt the same elation.

As soon as his colleagues were in position, he opened his mouth to bark the order that would send a triple whammy of missiles from the three F-22s converging on the bogey, to what should have been devastating effect. However, at that moment the alien ship shimmered and began to vanish, engaging its cloaking mode. A split-second later, before Pinsky even had time to realize that this was his last moment on earth, the three F-22s that had been about to fire on the alien vessel were instantly atomized by a deadly, all-engulfing wave of energy expelled by the ship, similar to the way that a squid will expel a cloud of ink to mask its escape from predators.

As Pinsky and his jet truly became one, their conjoined atoms dispersing to swirl and dance forever in the endless skies, the alien ship gave one final ripple, and then vanished.

Traeger stood with his aide, Sapir, and stared at the place where the vial ought to have been. A numbness spread over him. He tried a smile, but it didn't hold. He glanced around, looking at the table where the goddamned Predator had been playing possum.

"The floor," he said to Sapir, without looking at the man. "Check for fragments."

"Sir, I've been checking. There's debris everywhere—"

Traeger shot him a withering glance. "Don't you think I see that? You think I didn't notice how trashed this fucking lab is, Sapir? I need to confirm that vial is shattered on this floor, that the contents of that vial—which we could not afford to lose, right? You know we couldn't afford to lose it. But I need to confirm that the contents are in this fucking mess and not in the hands of someone who has no loyalty to us."

Sapir nodded, scanning the debris on the floor again.

Traeger swore, staring once more at the place where that vial ought to have been.

His headset crackled. A voice cut in. "Stargazer," said one of the mercs in his employ. "I have eyes on the woman. Instructions?"

Traeger lowered his head and took a deep breath. Sapir stopped trying to pretend the vial might have shattered in the melee and watched him, waiting to see what he would do—because, of course, the other significant thing missing from the lab wasn't a vial or a sample or even a secret, it was Dr. Casey Brackett.

"She was asking all the wrong questions," Traeger said.

Sapir gave a slight nod. Traeger sneered at him. He didn't need empathy from his aide and he certainly didn't need sympathy from anyone. Casey had crossed a line, and she had crossed Traeger.

"Cancel her," Traeger said. He gave a small sigh of regret—*only human, after all*, he thought. "Retrieve any contraband."

He could practically picture the hardcase mercenary with one hand on his weapon already.

"Wilco, Stargazer," said the merc.

Just as Traeger was about to sign off, he heard the roar of an engine over the radio. He turned to glare at Sapir. "What the hell was that?"

Sapir didn't have a clue.

Traeger wanted to shout. He wanted to break things, to add to the debris scattered across the lab. But he had a job to do, and it involved making sure that Casey Brackett didn't leave the base alive.

Casey didn't have a long history with drugs and alcohol. In high school and college, she'd partied with the best of them, but when she had too much to drink she tended to stumble off to the nearest bedroom, lock herself in, and sleep until someone pounded hard enough on the door to wake her. She'd been high, and she'd experimented with cocaine and Molly—twice each—but she had never liked the way any of that felt. She didn't like the sensation of not being in control, like her body had become a vehicle and she had turned the keys over to someone else.

The tranquilizer coursing through her bloodstream now didn't feel like any of that. It felt like floating, as if she had been sleeping and now danced on the very edge of wakefulness, and at any moment she might come fully awake, when all she really wanted to do was pull the covers over her head and huddle down beneath them, warm and dry and dreaming.

Or it should've felt like that. If she could only have surrendered to the tranquilizer, given herself over completely to the lullaby swaddling her brain right now. Instead, she had to fight it, because while the drug tried to tell her all was well, her ears were still echoing with the explosion that had rocked Project: Stargazer only moments ago. She'd chased a Predator—a frigging space alien! She'd jumped on a moving bus and then it had crashed and she'd shot herself in the foot like the biggest dork in the universe—if the Predators were getting all of this on video to study for next time like some NFL team, they'd be laughing their asses off at what a colossal dope she must be.

These thoughts were in her brain, but they weren't streamlined. They didn't progress neatly. Instead, they cascaded, they spilled in and out and sometimes left nothing behind, so that there were moments of utter blankness. She blinked, trying to remember where she was. It occurred to her that there'd been a bunch of guys on the bus. One of the guys had been shooting at the Predator. Casey had caught a glimpse of him, and maybe he'd picked her up—but if he'd picked her up, at some point he'd put her down.

The bus lay on its side about fifty yards away. Casey lay on her side, in the shadows below the walkways where she'd chased the Predator.

Unsteady but ambitious, she forced herself to stand, and she stumbled along again as best she could. People were shouting. Alarm klaxons were blaring. Military and pseudo-military vehicles rumbled all over the place. The jets had been there—she hadn't imagined them, or the spacecraft they'd been pursuing—but now they were gone.

She blinked.

Turned, only just now realizing that she wasn't alone. One of the guys from the bus, she figured, but of course it wasn't one of those guys. Thoughts cascaded in her mind again, images and blank spaces, and when she came back from one of those blank spaces, she saw the mercenary raise his weapon and take aim at her. He looked sad. She thought she remembered him from the laboratory, or somewhere inside the base. *Sad*, she thought again.

But it wouldn't stop him from killing her.

"Wilco, Stargazer," the merc said, tapping the comms unit at his ear.

He frowned in determination. In the wonderful fog of tranquilizers, she understood that he'd just received his orders, and that she was about to die.

Cradled in the lullaby, eyes heavy, feeling warm and happy and terrified all at the same time, she heard the air around her fill with buzz-saw whining. Blinking, she let her head loll to one side and caught sight of the roaring motorcycle as it launched off an embankment and landed with a crunch right on top of the merc who'd been about to put her to sleep for eternity. The motorcycle fishtailed but miraculously, considering the flesh and muscle and bone it had just crushed, the rider stayed upright.

Other motorcycles thundered behind the first one, landing and skidding, riders whooping like a war party. She glimpsed the first rider for another moment, saw him accelerate toward her. His tires squealed and Casey felt her eyes grow too heavy, finally, for her to open them again. Her legs went out from beneath her as the motorcycle leaped toward her and she felt herself falling into a dream at last.

In her dream, floating, she had the vague sensation of an arm around her, and of flying.

The roar of the motorcycle became her new lullaby.

A troop transport roars out of the Stargazer complex, driver up front and six black-clad mercenaries in the back. These are determined men and women. Not one of them has a clear idea of exactly what they've been assigned to kill, but they know it's alien and they know it's proven to be a nasty fucker. This doesn't bother them. After all, each of them considers him or herself to be a nasty fucker as well.

Quiet, grim, ready for a fight and ready to be heroes, they hold on as the troop transport whipsaws into a turn.

Only one among them, Harry Curtis, Jr., hears the muffled thump on top of the truck. Junior glances up, but only for a moment. It could be anything or nothing—could be his imagination.

The Predator swings down into the truck bed. Spinning blades reminiscent of Japanese throwing stars fly from its fingers and two mercenaries go down. Then its blades come out. Harry opens his mouth to shout, tries to reach for his weapon, but the Predator's gauntlet blades crunch through his ribcage and cleave his heart in a single motion. His brain continues to receive signals for half a second; long enough for him to see another merc die before his body realizes his life is over.

Corpses slump in their seats. Blood drips onto the truck bed. The Predator slides the last body to the floor with the quiet precision of a born hunter.

Still, somehow, the driver senses something. Perhaps he smells the blood, or the silence of death is an alarm bell all its own.

"Everything okay back there?" he asks uneasily, peeking in the rearview mirror. Into shadows.

In what little light makes it into the rear of the truck, he spots a thumbs-up from one of the mercenaries. It eases his mind, and he returns his attention to the road.

In the back, the Predator lowers Harry Curtis, Jr.'s severed arm. The alien sits back, removes his mask, and allows himself to relax and enjoy the ride, as the blood continues to pool at his feet.

In a forest clearing not far from the Stargazer base, the alien vessel squats among surrounding trees like a coiled snake awaiting passing prey. Steam rises from its sleek surface, but disperses among the trees before it can rise high enough to give away the craft's position.

The hatch of the craft opens and a massive figure emerges, before climbing down to the forest floor. The figure stands impossibly tall, the shifting light and shadow of the night playing across its formidable body. This creature is different to the one that earlier that night had caused untold havoc at Project: Stargazer. Like the Predator, but something more.

An upgrade. That is how it thinks of itself. Something better.

It raises its head and utters a high, oddly musical chitter. Two silhouettes, stocky, rangy and powerful, slink out of the brush, padding forward on all fours.

From its tunic, the Upgrade produces a piece of mesh-like material, perhaps a scrap of clothing, which moves in the creature's taloned hand with a slithering motion, catching the light. The Upgrade crouches down and holds out the scrap of mesh. Its two companions, shoulder muscles rippling with panther-like grace, move forward like tracker dogs to sniff it.

13

Rory sat in his basement in an old BarcaLounger that had once been his dad's favorite chair. One of his earliest memories was of his dad reaching down and scooping him up into the chair, plopping Rory on his lap, and the two of them watching the original *Star Wars* together. Rory figured he couldn't have been more than two years old at the time. His father hadn't been around much, but most of his earliest memories of his dad had imprinted on some part of his brain that made him happy and sad at the same time. He remembered his dad taking him along on a Sunday afternoon when he'd gone to play basketball with some of his friends. Rory had been four or five, old enough to sit and behave himself in the bleachers and watch his dad and the other men play. Just some guys in a smelly school gymnasium, pretending they were still in high school, but for those two hours, Rory loved them all. When the game was over, and the men took turns hoisting him onto their shoulders so he could try to throw the ball into the basket—that was the only time he could remember ever caring about sports.

Those memories—the times his father had acted like a dad—shouldn't have made up for all the absence and neglect. Most days, nothing could make up for that. Rory understood the way the fabric of things wove together, like numbers and language and mechanics, and he knew his father should have been a larger part of his life, that it made a difference. But he could never have put his disappointment into words his parents could have understood. It was as if his ability to evaluate his father's parental performance existed in a locked room, and he knew he'd never find the key. All he knew was that it didn't feel right; that far too often he was left feeling hollow, and yet a part of him understood this wasn't fair. Rory's brain had been wired differently from birth, and he thought—in his way—that Quinn McKenna had also been wired differently.

He was who he was.

Sometimes, especially on nights like this, when Rory sat in the BarcaLounger and remembered *Star Wars* and basketball—and when he had questions he needed answers to, but didn't want to ask his mom—his memories of his father were enough for him, and he was just a regular kid who missed his dad.

Rory wasn't sure of the time, but he knew it was late. He felt a little cold, down in the basement. In his right hand, he held a tiny keychain viewer with a little button that turned a light on inside it. Peering into the eyehole, he glanced again at the photo inside—a picture of himself and his dad. In the photo, they were both laughing. Rory didn't remember the picture being taken. He wished he could remember.

He lowered the keychain viewer and glanced over at the tattered ottoman nearby. The helmet sat there, its blank eyes seeming to watch him. Beside it was the black doohickey that he'd popped out of the alien wrist gauntlet. It looked like some kind of tiny coffin or a miniature Lost Ark or something, except for the buttons and lights all over it.

Rory had never wished for his father's presence more than he did right now. Where had his dad found these things? What were they? Obviously, they were a secret, because this sort of thing didn't just get mailed from Mexico to an Army Ranger's private PO box every day, but what was the story behind them? Rory felt like that information would have been very useful to him in his efforts to figure out how to use the doohickey.

He leaned out of the Barcalounger and grabbed it, then sat back and tapped buttons, trying to wake it up again. At first nothing happened. He frowned and toyed with it some more, felt pleased when the lights glowed red, but then he began to chew on his lip. What next? He felt like his understanding of this instrument and the language behind it was just out of reach, that he could learn to translate it all with just a little push, a little more insight.

The lights flickered. He thought he saw a pattern in their sequence and tapped again.

A series of 3D projections burst from the helmet, making Rory jump. They flashed by quickly, but Rory read them as instantly as they appeared, capturing every one of them in his mind, sorting them the way he sorted mechanics or the way he saw every move in a chess game—or five chess games—before the first few pieces had even been taken off the board.

The projections were three-dimensional graphics of a spacecraft and its controls. Buttons, switches, gauges, star maps, a virtual-reality owner's manual that whizzed by faster than any ordinary human brain could parse. The 3D image flickered to a view of the Earth, as seen from space, which Rory guessed was not something from the owner's manual, but was either the view from the spacecraft right now or a recent recording. Something blinked red on the planet as the image zoomed in. Landmasses grew closer. North America; the southern United States; Mexico. Then the image became a map, landmarks getting bigger and clearer, as the tracker, or remote camera, or whatever, rushed closer and closer to the ground.

The red blinking expanded into the outline of a specific image. He knew from the owner's manual what it had to be, what its silhouette indicated it must be.

Another spacecraft.

Taking care with the doohickey, Rory got up and moved to the worktable, studying the hologram even more closely. He nodded in quiet understanding.

There was something wrong with this ship. Its outline looked wrong—buckled.

Instinctively he knew the reason why. This ship had not landed.

It had crashed.

N N N

The Iron Horse Motel had laid out the red carpet. Motorcycles crammed the parking lot. Music played loudly. Dozens of bikers were milling about, swigging from bottles of beer and spirits, reacquainting themselves with old friends, bitching about old enemies. An air of festive camaraderie suffused the night, so much so that the handful of people staying at the Iron Horse who *hadn't* come to town for the bike festival managed to find themselves mostly charmed by the crowds of bearded, tattooed men and leather-clad, tattooed women, instead of terrified.

The motel's marquee had been arranged to read: *WELCOME RIDERS! CORPUS CHRISTI OR BUST!* The *M* in *WELCOME* tilted slightly, but not so much that anyone bothered to fix it.

Among the other motorcycles in the lot, the stolen Scouts did not go unnoticed, but those who did take note of their presence only admired them, perhaps envied their owners.

In room 112, the television glowed brightly, the volume just loud enough to be heard over the commotion out in the motel's parking lot. On the TV screen, a nervous-looking man was entering a suburban house, while a voiceover was saying, "...the forty-one-year-old came to this Texan home to meet our decoy, whom he believes to be an underage girl."

Cut back to the nervous-looking man, who is clearly surprised and alarmed to be encountered by *Dateline* journalist Chris Hansen.

"And what are you up to today?" Hansen asked pointedly.

The child predator tried desperately to look casual. "Nothin'. Just came by to hang out."

"I see you brought some condoms and some Mike's Hard Lemonade," Hansen said, his voice casual but his words damning as hell.

Coyle and Baxley were sitting on the edge of the room's only bed, their eyes fixed on the screen. However, the third occupant of the room, Dr. Casey Brackett, missed the pervert's response, and indeed the entire encounter. Despite her attempt to fight it, the tranquilizer had done its work very effectively, and even now she was still snoring lightly, a candle of drool at the edge of her lips.

Out in the lot, Nettles stood guard over the stolen Scouts, but his focus had drifted to the nearby Winnebago Super Chief and the bearded redneck who had set up a table in front of it to sell guns and ammo, like he was running a kid's lemonade stand. Some of the ordnance laid out on the table was state of the art, and it had Nettles thinking. Lynch might be good when it came to card tricks, but he himself was the true hustler of the group.

The gun seller's business had thinned out enough that the man wandered over toward Nettles and cast an appreciative glance at the motorcycles behind him. He actually licked his lips.

"Those *Custom Scouts*? How much you want for 'em?" he asked.

Nettles merely snickered, and the guy shrugged as if to say: *Ah, well. Worth a try.* Clearly, though, his curiosity wasn't yet sated. "Where you boys headed, anyway?"

"Bikefest," Nettles replied. "You?"

"Gainesville Gun Show." He nodded to his guns, then jerked a thumb at the RV. "Anything you need, I got in the Super Chief. I'm not kidding. *Anything.*"

Nettles' ears perked up.

McKenna didn't think he could have slept even if someone had hit him over the head with a sledgehammer. His whole body felt lit up, crackling with the electric need to move, to fight, to extricate himself from the most colossally fucked up scenario he'd ever encountered. If the woman hadn't been tranquilized, there would have been no way he would have stopped here. Yes, they needed a plan, but he wanted to be far away from the base and the alien and the fucking spaceship that had shot down those F-22s before vanishing. Instead, here they were.

The only upside of the Iron Horse Motel was the damn bikefest, which enabled them to hide in plain sight. Without all these motorcycles, they'd have had to ditch the Scouts—too recognizable—and steal a minivan or something. Still, he didn't like this environment, not with the Loonies who had suddenly become his new platoon—temporarily, at least. Any one of these guys might be volatile enough to start trouble in a church on Christmas, but surrounded by a couple hundred bikers, all of whom perceived themselves as alpha males… it was guaranteed not to end well.

McKenna exhaled and sidled over to where Nebraska sat on a brick wall, smoking a cigarette. "You, uh… think she's safe in there with them?"

Nebraska blew out a plume of smoke and gave him a disapproving look. "They're soldiers. They'd fuck a woodpile on the off chance there's a snake inside. But sleepy ladies? Nah."

Motion off to his left caught McKenna's attention and he glanced over to see Nettles emerging from behind the motel sign, zipping up his pants.

"Hey, Nettles," Nebraska called, "there's a toilet in the room, y'know."

Nettles widened his eyes in shock as if he'd just seen God. McKenna allowed himself a moment of amusement and then sat heavily on the brick wall beside Nebraska. A moment or two of quiet contemplation elapsed, but his anxiousness returned. He wanted to be elsewhere.

To allay the jitters, he tried to divert himself with conversation. "Where'd you serve?" he asked Nebraska.

Nebraska wasn't overly chatty, but he had a laid-back attitude, and seemed happy to talk, which made him the most relaxing of the Loonies to be around.

The big man took another pull on his cigarette, and said, "Operation Enduring Freedom, '03. Went for the Taliban, stayed for the opium." He blew smoke, smiling slightly. "Came back, tried for contract work. They wouldn't take me. Tried to drive a bus…"

"Lemme guess," said McKenna. "They wouldn't take you?"

Nebraska slid him a look, still smiling. *You got it*, his expression said.

For a moment they sat in companionable silence. Nebraska might have been laid-back, but he had a keen intelligence. There was a weariness about him too, as if he had been pushing at life too hard for too long.

Weighing up the question in his mind, wondering whether he should ask it, McKenna decided to take the plunge. "So... the officer. Did he live?"

"Excuse me?" Nebraska replied.

"The CO—the asshole you shot. Did he live?"

"Funny." A small nod. "He did."

"Where is he now?" McKenna asked.

Nebraska's expression turned into something halfway between sadness and amusement. He studied McKenna's face and cocked his head slightly, like a hopeful comedian waiting for a tiny audience to get his punchline. McKenna frowned, not understanding, and then he got it and his face went slack.

"You're shitting me."

Nebraska sighed and lifted up his hair to reveal a puckered pale scar on the dark skin beneath his hairline.

He shrugged. "I missed."

McKenna blinked at him. "Why... why did you do that?"

"Miss?"

"Shoot yourself."

"The doctors keep asking me that." Nebraska took another drag on his cigarette. "I walked to the hospital with a bullet in my head. It's why I'm... y'know..." He waffled his hand in the air. "Fuzzy sometimes."

McKenna felt a chill trickle down his spine. He cleared his throat. "Should I be worried?"

"Probably," Nebraska replied grimly. He stood up, tossing the butt of his cigarette to one side, then tapped at his scar with a smile and pointed to Heaven. "God wouldn't take me neither."

McKenna expected him to walk away, but Nebraska stood for a moment, contemplating his new friend, as if debating whether to reveal more devastating truths. Finally, he seemed to decide, but what he said surprised McKenna—surprised him and moved him.

"I got your back, Chief."

The constant noise in the lot had been getting to Nettles, and now the sound of a biker noisily revving his engine only a few feet away managed to fray his last few nerves.

Scowling, he said, "You mind keeping it down?"

The biker shot him an incredulous look. "You gonna make me, fairy boy?"

Nettles jumped to his feet and started toward him. "Am I gonna make you Fairy Boy? How would that work? Do I, like, give you powers? A wand? I'm confused."

The biker strode to meet him, full of rage and swagger and a history that doubtless included a hundred such encounters, all of them ending the same way. Nettles relished that moment, the instant when the guy's confidence suffused him the way all the best emotions did—love, fury... humiliation.

Nettles shot out a hand with such fluidity that anyone looking on would have seen the motion as almost casual.

The biker wouldn't have agreed—not when he staggered, gasping, and crumpled to the ground.

Standing in front of a vending machine, McKenna saw the exchange and shook his head. *Great. Just fucking great. What did these guys not understand about the need to keep a low profile?* He banged the machine with his fist. Bizarrely, and without warning, a paper cup dropped down and started filling with coffee. McKenna stared at the cup a moment—he hadn't put any money in yet—and decided to take this as a good omen.

Nettles could take care of himself, right?

He sure as hell hoped so.

Nebraska walked by, headed for the motel room, and with a last glance toward Nettles, McKenna followed. Nebraska knocked at the door, a prearranged signal of two short, three long knocks, and Coyle yanked it open almost immediately.

"Good timing," Coyle said, glancing from Nebraska to McKenna before he stepped back to let them in.

McKenna understood his urgency the moment they entered. On the bed, the woman had turned over and seemed to be stirring. Baxley and Lynch were gathered by the bed of their sleeping Snow White with the air of expectant fathers. She stirred again, moaned a bit, and Nebraska moved in as well. He held up his hands as if she were already awake, like she might try to bolt and he wanted to calm her before she hurt herself.

"Easy," Nebraska told the others. "She's gonna open

her eyes, buncha motherfuckers hovering, she might be coming in hot."

"Got it," Coyle said, nodding anxiously, eyes even crazier than usual. "Chill."

McKenna frowned as he noticed a dinner tray on a stand that had been set up next to the bed. A tiny cup of coffee, a troll doll, a postcard, a drawing of a shopping cart, a foil unicorn. Like offerings to the God of Idiots.

"What is this shit, exactly?" McKenna asked.

Baxley looked sheepish. "We wanted to make her feel comfortable. When she wakes up. The postcard's from me, the unicorn's from Nettles—"

McKenna raised a hand to cut him off, nodding as if Baxley's explanation actually made sense. In a way, he guessed, it did. The Loonies were like some Dr. Moreau combination of children and feral cats, wild but aware of the weird allure of domesticity.

Casey moaned softly as she clawed her way back to the surface of the deep black pool into which she'd fallen. The dead time between the tranquilizer taking effect and her return to consciousness seemed like both an instant and an eternity. She tried to open her eyes for what seemed like the hundredth time, and this time managed it, light suddenly flooding in between her lids.

"Mornin', sunshine," said a voice.

That's not my name, she thought groggily. But when she tried to communicate the fact, it came out as: "I wish people'd stop calling me that."

All at once, it occurred to her to wonder who had spoken. The last time she had heard a human voice it had come from a man who was about to kill her. The adrenaline that flooded through her at the memory enabled her to open her eyes wide, to half sit up. She saw faces. Men's faces. They didn't look like doctors. In fact, each of them looked crazy in one way or another.

Her gaze shifted instinctively to her left, looking for an escape route. She didn't spot one immediately, but what she did spot was almost as good. Bounding out of bed, she grabbed the Remington shotgun, which was propped against a chair beside the bed, on which sat a tray piled with various bits of junk—a troll doll, a foil unicorn, other stuff. Whirling round, she leveled the gun shakily at the group of men. Her eyes were wide and her breath came in ragged sips as she studied them, maybe trying to decide who to shoot first if anyone made a move.

The men didn't look scared. In fact, they looked impressed by her moves—and in her present befuddled state that confused her a little. One of the men—sandy hair, handsome, maybe the least crazy looking of the bunch—stepped forward, his hands raised to show he was unarmed.

"Relax," he said soothingly. "We're the good guys."

She sneered at him. Backing away, she fumbled in her pants pocket while still trying to keep the shotgun pointed in their vicinity, then started to look panicked. Frantically she patted her other pockets.

"Looking for this?" asked the handsome guy mildly.

She glanced up. He was holding the pulverized remains of her cell phone in his hand, an expression of apology on his face.

Before she could speak, he said, "They know who you are, lady. And they can *trace* phones."

Casey gaped at him. "Are you insane?"

The men—all except for the handsome guy—seemed to take her question literally. They shuffled embarrassedly and started casting glances at each other. Some shrugged, others raised their eyebrows.

One of them said, "Maybe."

"A little," amended a scruffy guy in a baseball cap, holding his thumb and forefinger an inch apart to demonstrate.

Yet another of the men, a tall, bald, bearded guy, stared into space and murmured, "I dunno… probably."

Casey narrowed her eyes, clearly uncertain whether they were making fun of her or not.

One thing she *was* certain of, though, was that fearsome as these men looked, they meant her no harm. If they had, she was sure she'd have known about it by now. Indeed, now that she really thought about it, the most likely scenario was that they'd rescued her from the Project: Stargazer compound and had been protecting her ever since.

Unless, of course, they were desperate prisoners and she was their hostage. But again, that didn't really ring true. Their body language was wrong for a start.

Deciding to test her theory, she leaned the Remington against the wall and made for the door. She was reaching for the handle when the handsome guy barked, "They were gonna put a bullet in your head back there."

Now Casey stopped and glanced back at him, torn by indecision. She'd already guessed the reason for her ex-employers' sudden change of attitude toward her: it was either because she'd seen too much, or because of the vial she'd taken. But, ever the scientist, she couldn't help wondering how these guys fit into the equation, and what they knew that she didn't. She cocked an eyebrow, and the handsome guy said, "You're expendable. Just like the rest of us."

She breathed out slowly, glancing around at the motley crew. She couldn't help thinking she knew the handsome guy from somewhere, but she couldn't think where. "Expendables?" she said wryly. "More like the Seven fucking Dwarfs."

The guy with the baseball cap grinned bashfully. Casey sighed in surrender to the insanity, grabbed her pack, which was leaning against the closet door, moved across to a plastic chair, and flopped down into it.

"Don't you guys have… someplace to be?" she asked.

One of the men—goatee beard, bare arms covered in tattoos—shrugged and said, "VA Psych Ward? Military prison?"

Casey almost laughed. For some reason, his response— or the way he had delivered it—relaxed rather than alarmed her.

"Can I *borrow* a phone at least? I need someone to feed my dogs." When all she got in response was shrugs and grimaces of apology, she fished a tiny bottle out of her pack and took a swig, then focused on the handsome man, as it suddenly came to her where she had seen his face before. "I read the file. Those men it killed… Yours?"

The guy nodded.

McKenna, Casey thought, remembering. *His name is McKenna.*

"They're gonna need a patsy for that," she said.

"You're looking at him."

"Yeah. I figured. Textbook fall guy. Psycho ex-sniper, PTSD, divorced… has even got a flaky kid who curls up in a ball. It's perfect—"

McKenna's eyes blazed with fury. He felt himself flush, felt the desire to lash out. Instead, he glared at her, silently warning her.

Casey shrugged apologetically. "I'm just telling you what's in the file."

The guy with the tattooed arms put a hand on McKenna's shoulder and fixed Casey with his own imposing glare. "How about you tell us what you were doing at a secret base full of private soldiers? Mercs," he said accusingly.

"It was a CIA cover," said Casey.

Speaking for the first time since she had revealed to him what was in his file, McKenna said in a strangled voice, "It said 'flaky'?"

Casey glanced at him, but continued with her explanation. "I'm an evolutionary biologist. I was on call in a case of… contact."

McKenna paced up and down to release the tension inside him while the guys all took turns staring at each other, weighing the meaning of her words. Finally, McKenna halted, exhaling raggedly. They were all dancing around the truth, her unsure what they knew, them treating her the same way. But out there was an alien psychopath who'd murdered McKenna's men and a whole shit-ton of Traeger's people as well. There were people who'd known this secret for what seemed to be a long time, and who were clearly prepared to kill all of them to make sure it *stayed* a secret.

If Casey was in this with them now, there was no more room for secrecy. She could see that McKenna felt the same way. He was studying her face, assessing her. She wondered whether she ought to say it out loud—that she was prepared to go out on a limb and trust them. That if they wanted to stay alive they had to trust one another.

Before she could, McKenna spoke the words that were in her mind. "Look. If we want to keep breathing, we've gotta find this thing. Expose it. We all agreed?"

A look went around the motel room, a bonding moment. They were all exiles, the perfect scapegoats for whatever the government and their black box UFO research group decided to pin on them. Everyone nodded. They were all in.

"Good," McKenna said, turning to Casey. "First things first. What *is* it?"

"The Predator? Well… it has human DNA, for one thing."

"What the fuck?" said a guy with a brooding expression, who so far hadn't spoken. "Human—"

"That's not all," Casey went on. "I was there when it escaped. I think it was looking for something."

She saw the blood drain from McKenna's face.

"Its equipment," he muttered.

Suddenly, all eyes were on him. "I took it so I'd have evidence. Oh, shit…" All at once he looked antsy, as though his skin was crawling with the need to move. "I think I know where it's going."

He glanced at the tattooed guy, who nodded and went to the door. By the time he had opened it, McKenna had fallen in behind him. Casey could see that right outside the room, a small, tough-looking guy had set up a poker game with a bunch of bikers.

"How good's your hand?" tattooed guy asked.

The small guy glanced around at his buddies. "It's poker. I don't think I'm supposed to say… but good, yeah."

"We *got* Indian Scout bikes," tattooed guy said, then pointed to the Winnebago. "We *want* that RV."

"And some guns," McKenna prompted.

"Hmm? Oh…" Tattooed guy raised his voice. "And some guns," he echoed.

14

Rory liked candy, of course—mostly things made of chocolate. People who gave candy corn or jawbreakers simply didn't understand the allure of trick or treat, but they weren't the worst offenders. Folks who took it upon themselves to issue a silent condemnation of everything good about Halloween—the Stillsons, for instance, who gave out toothbrushes last year and Halloween-themed pencils the year before—were the enemy of all that was good and joyful about childhood. Rory's neuro-diversity might make it hard for him to pick up social cues, but wandering around in spooky costumes and getting free candy had never been something he had to struggle to understand.

There were some real assholes in the neighborhood, shitheads like Tom Kelly and Dom Cortez, who would vandalize an old woman's electric scooter if she'd just sit still long enough. Why those pricks hadn't ever hit the Stillsons' house with a hundred dozen eggs some Halloween night was a mystery Rory didn't think anyone would ever solve.

Not that he supported vandalism. But still... toothbrushes? For trick or treat?

He'd gone upstairs to use the bathroom, had a bowl of spaghetti his mother had foisted on him, and then retreated to the basement again. Now he sat staring at the shoddy Frankenstein mask his mom had brought home and tried to decide what to do. He loved her so much and he knew that she loved him and just wanted what was best for him, but the truth was that she didn't always know what was best—and neither did Rory. They were both learning, and that always made the decisions and the conversations difficult.

Trick or treat meant chocolate, yes. But what he loved about it most was the anonymity. He could go from house to house and mostly manage to avoid being recognized. The social encounters of the evening were so deeply ritualized that nobody expected any further interaction beyond the ringing of the doorbell, the chorusing of "trick or treat," and the grateful acceptance of proffered candy. Rory understood this exchange. It didn't require him to parse words, to search for hidden meanings, to gauge someone's tone of voice—all strategies his therapist had taught him that took enormous effort and focus.

Halloween meant he could be anything or anyone, that people would see only the mask. As much as he struggled with the word *normal*, and knew that being on the spectrum was not at all unusual, every year he went out trick-or-treating and felt like he'd been suffocating all year and he'd finally learned how to breathe properly.

And yet... Halloween also made him sad. That was the awful part, the double-edged sword of it all. While he was out collecting candy, out among the people who had no diversity in their neuro and didn't embrace it in others, he felt good. Happy. But at some point, either when he'd arrive back home or shortly before, he would begin to think about the mask and be forced to acknowledge that people were treating him normally because they didn't know it was Rory McKenna behind that mask. They hadn't had a conversation with him, only engaged in the ritual. The mask made them more comfortable than Rory himself would have, because they didn't have to make an effort with the mask.

He pondered all of this as he picked up the Frankenstein's monster mask and poked his finger through the eyeholes. At the same time, he wondered how many people would be giving away Hershey chocolate. Hershey chocolate and Reese's Cups were his favorites. He liked the neighbors who allowed him to choose from their candy bowl instead of choosing for him. Usually he came home with about forty percent candy he would eat, and his mother would complain for a week about her lack of self-control as she ate the other sixty percent.

The thought made him smile. Mom liked Baby Ruths the best, which was funny, because from his observations in overhearing the conversations of his classmates and other kids in the neighborhood, nobody liked Baby Ruths the best aside from Emily McKenna.

Amid these thoughts, Rory paused, a frown creasing his forehead. He turned to glance at the small box window, high up on the basement wall. A scratching at the window made him cock his head. He heard a snuffling noise, like a big dog might be right outside, sniffing and scraping at the ground. He remembered the pit bull from earlier and wondered if it might be the same dog.

The sound moved off and after a few seconds, he couldn't hear it anymore.

Rory turned his attention back to the Frankenstein mask. Unimpressed, he tossed it onto the table. After all, it wasn't the only mask he'd gotten that day.

Emily stood at the sink with the water running. The bowl from Rory's pasta was in her hand, but her mind had wandered a moment, as it often did. He seemed happy tonight—the prospect of chocolate usually accomplished that—but she always felt nervous about him trick-or-treating without her. Emily knew there were kids at school and in the neighborhood who were less than kind to Rory. There had been instances of outright bullying. He tried to put on a brave face, or hide the hurt from her, but even with the difficulty that sometimes came with deciphering his feelings, a mother knew. But Rory had a lot of heart and no one could deny he was brilliant—he would have to make his way in the world without his mother around. He had to learn to negotiate the social landscape in a way he could manage for himself, for a lifetime.

She sighed and rinsed the red sauce out of his bowl.

A creak on the floor behind her nearly made her drop the bowl, and she swung round. Had she heard the back door click shut? Placing the clean bowl in the drainer by the sink, she grabbed a dish towel and started for the kitchen door, wondering if Rory had gone outside.

The doorbell rang. She frowned—it must be that time already, but it felt to her as if the kids showed up earlier and earlier every year. She tossed the dishtowel onto the counter. She grabbed the bowl of candy as she made her way through the foyer to open the front door.

The men on her front steps weren't there for candy.

In the center, there stood a handsome guy in a dark suit. He flashed a brilliant smile at the same time as he brandished an ID badge. Armed men flanked him on both sides and Emily wondered how many more there might be, out there in the dark on a street where hundreds of kids were about to go door-to-door.

"Mrs. McKenna?" the suit said. "Can we have a word?"

She squinted at his badge. Last name TRAEGER.

"Let me guess," she sighed. "He's done something crazy."

That smile again. "Why would you say that?"

Emily silently cursed her husband—ex-husband— whatever he was to her now. "Because the look on your face says he's not dead, and yet here you fucking are."

Agent Traeger's gaze shifted past her. Emily glanced over her shoulder and saw that he was eyeing Quinn's gun case.

"Those are his," she explained. "He's a hunter."

Traeger nodded sagely. "Shot a buck when I was six."

Good for you, Emily wanted to say. *Get off my stoop.*

Instead, she mirrored his sage nod. "Our son never took to it. He's more a 'rescue bugs' guy. He actually burns ants he thinks might hurt other ants. And sports...

forget it." She frowned as a memory touched her. "His dad did teach him to slide, though."

"Slide?"

"Baseball," Emily explained. "Didn't go well."

"Your son. Where is he?" Traeger asked.

"Around here somewhere." She narrowed her eyes. "Why?"

"Mind if we speak with him?"

Emily shifted her body slightly, almost unconsciously. Smiling secret agent man and a bunch of black-clad fuckers with guns wanted to talk to her boy? Instinct kicked in, and she couldn't help the way every muscle twitched, wanting to put herself between these guns and her son.

"Why the hell would you want to do that?"

Traeger arched a questioning eyebrow. "Just being thorough, ma'am."

Emily inhaled slowly, running scenarios through her head. These guys weren't here because Quinn McKenna had won a medal. They were here because he'd done something he shouldn't have done, and it wasn't the first time. What worried her was the biggest question of all—if they were here looking for him, that meant the army didn't know the whereabouts of one of its Rangers, so where the hell had Quinn gone? In some ways, that question worried her more than what he might have done.

"Fine," she said, then pointed at the armed men behind Traeger. "But *they* stay out here."

"Agreed," Traeger said, stepping over her threshold.

Emily let him pass, then paused to take in the expressionless, black-clad men on her stoop. "It's

Halloween, boys." She handed the candy bowl to the soldier nearest her. "If kids show up at my door and you scare the shit out of them, at least give them some candy while you're at it."

The soldier seemed about to argue. One of the others gave her a "Yes, ma'am," and gestured for the rest to spread out. The one with the candy seemed to sigh and resign himself to trick or treat duty. He slung his gun across his back.

Satisfied for the moment, thinking the kids would assume the soldier was in costume, Emily led Traeger through the kitchen and down into the basement.

"Rory, honey?" she said as she descended the steps.

Silence from the basement. She heard his absence, felt it, even before she reached the bottom step and glanced around. Behind her, Traeger scanned the basement and then looked back up the steps.

"That's weird," Emily said, but already her mind was going back to the moment while she was washing the dishes, right before Traeger had rung her doorbell. The floor had creaked. The back door had clicked. In the moment, she had thought she might be imagining it. Now… "If he's not in his room—and he's not—he's always here. He said he was going trick-or-treating, but…"

Her words trailed off as she caught sight of the Frankenstein mask. And then the pirate mask. Both costumes she'd bought him were here, scattered on his worktable and laid across a chair. Her frown deepened.

If Rory had gone trick-or-treating, why would he leave his costume behind?

N N N

McKenna felt like a fool hiding in the bushes outside his own damn house, but he knew Emily and Rory might be in danger and he wanted to make certain he didn't make it worse. He and the Loonies were gathered in the bushes across the street, with a parabolic microphone that had been with all the weapons in the gun dealer's RV. They'd set up surveillance only twenty minutes before Traeger had rolled in with his team, and now they sat and listened to every word Traeger and Emily said.

Beside him, Nebraska held the parabolic mic and glanced at him. "You think this guy's low enough to hurt your family?"

"Under the right circumstances," McKenna said, "I think so, yeah. I don't trust that smile of his. He thinks he's charming; I think he's a sociopath. But if the Predator shows up, I don't mind Traeger and his men providing some cover—"

"You mean cannon fodder," Lynch interrupted.

"If they buy me time to get Emily and Rory somewhere safe, I'll be glad they're here," McKenna said.

"You really think the Predator's showing up here?" Nebraska asked.

McKenna thought about the jungle, and about the gauntlet and helmet. He'd hoped they would be at the post office, but a small fear had niggled at the back of his mind—the fear that he hadn't paid for his post office box, and when he'd checked on it and learned the truth, confirmed that the package had been taken here...

"I do, yeah."

Nebraska grinned. "Good. Saves us the trouble of hunting it down."

Rory had never owned anything this cool in his entire life. He knew he shouldn't have taken it, knew that his father probably shouldn't have taken it from wherever he'd gotten it. He was smart enough to know an Army Ranger didn't pack something like this up in a tiny Mexican town and ship it to his private post office box without risking some serious trouble. Which meant that as soon as his father found out it was in Rory's possession... it would no longer be in Rory's possession. But while it was, the helmet was so damn cool.

The gauntlet remained on his wrist. The helmet was too big and bobbled as he walked, and he stumbled over a curb here and there and trampled Mrs. Markowitz's bushes, but he could not make himself care. He was surrounded by kids in costumes and their parents, but he felt as if he was isolated—not the way he usually felt alone, but in a good way. Crazy good.

The helmet had an interior display. The eyepieces showed human heat signatures in every direction. The tech left Rory almost breathless, giddy with excitement. He knew he might never get to wear it again, and certainly not with so many people around—it'd look weird on any other night of the year. But tonight, everyone looked weird. The DiMarinos had set up their usual haunted house in the garage. The Khans had the inflatable screen out front showing *It's the Great Pumpkin, Charlie Brown* on a loop. Steve Bronson always set up a scarecrow at the end of the driveway, tied to the lamppost, with a speaker inside so that he could talk to the trick-or-treaters in a spooky voice and make it seem like the scarecrow was alive. Autumn leaves skittered along the street. Kids screamed happily. At Cheryl Gorman's house, her drunken boyfriend had a toy chainsaw that made very real-sounding noises, and he chased teenagers down the street in a Leatherface mask. Cheryl and her boyfriend were alcoholics, but on Halloween, everyone pretended to ignore that sorry fact.

Rory loved it all.

It felt to him as if he was seeing his entire neighborhood for the very first time.

Like an alien, just setting foot on Earth.

Casey sat inside the RV with the guy they called Nettles— the one who had made her the foil unicorn, which she had now tucked into her pack, because she found it kind of cute. She wasn't sure if Nettles was his real name, or a nickname because he got under everyone's skin. She studied his tattoos while he blathered on, but after a minute or two she pulled her attention back to the task at hand—trying to figure out what the federal government had up their sneaky, stupid sleeve.

She peered into the portable microscope, which had been set up on the RV's dinette table. The vial she'd stolen from Stargazer sat on the counter beside her. She had some of the liquid from it on a slide. The microscope wasn't of the quality she would have preferred, but it was all she had to work with. Under the circumstances, she was glad to have it.

Adjusting the focus, she gazed at the smear of liquid, then pulled back from the microscope and blinked, incredulous. "Jesus. It's like a… supermatrix of trihydroxy and amino acids."

Nettles perked up expectantly. "Does that mean we smoke it or snort it?"

Casey glanced at the vial, talking to herself as much as to Nettles. "If I'm right… and I hope I'm not… it means they're trying to upgrade themselves."

Holy shit. She could barely believe she'd just uttered those words. It spooked her badly. Shaken, trying to tell herself she must be wrong but knowing she wasn't, she picked up the two-way and keyed it.

"McKenna?" she said, after a small burst of static. "I've found something."

The implications of Casey's discovery echoing in his head, McKenna burst through the front door of the house that hadn't felt like home for a long time. Heart thundering, he scanned the entryway and the short hall before he even let himself acknowledge Emily's presence. She'd frozen when he whipped the door open and now she glared at him, her expression worthy of Medusa.

"Hi, honey, you're home," she said.

A beat went by, a breath, and then she glanced pointedly at the shotgun in his hand. McKenna had barely remembered that he carried the weapon and he didn't have time to explain or apologize for it now.

"Where's Rory?"

"Oh, I get it," Emily said, falling into the old rhythm of their relationship, the familiar tone. "You think you can just waltz in here and—"

"I asked you a question."

She leaned toward the stairwell, put her hand on the banister. "Agent Traeger, he's in here!"

McKenna narrowed his eyes. "Nice try." He tapped his earbud. "I was listening. Oh, and, 'He's done something crazy?' Thanks for that."

"What was I supposed to say?"

"How about, 'Is my ex-husband all right?' Normal families ask that."

"There's your answer."

"Emily, now's not the time," McKenna said, thinking, *as if the shotgun shouldn't have told you all you needed to know.* "Where's Rory?"

Her mask slipped, and she revealed how worried Traeger's visit had made her. She had loved him once, McKenna knew that, and maybe she still cared about him, but nothing mattered to her—to either of them—more than Rory. That maternal terror filled her eyes now and she turned to look back toward the kitchen.

"He's not in his room. He was in the basement earlier," she said. "I bought him two different Halloween costumes, but he went out without either of them. I think he's trick-or-treating, but I have no idea what he's wearing. Maybe last year's outfit."

McKenna moved past her, headed for the kitchen. "He's spending a lot of time in the basement lately?"

"He always does," Emily said, following him.

"I mean the last couple of days. More than usual?"

"I guess. Maybe."

The basement door stood open. McKenna double-timed it down the steps and scanned the room, Rory's worktable, his posters, the computer screens still open, ready for him to re-engage with the video games he'd been playing. Then he spotted a parcel on the floor next to the table and he rushed over to it. He could almost smell the dust from the tiny Mexican village on the box, and when he picked it up, the return label confirmed its origin.

He shook the box, but the weight alone told him it was empty.

"Shit!" he said as he tossed it aside.

Emily had paused on the steps. Now she descended two more stairs. "What? So he ordered some video games."

"No, no, no, no," McKenna said as he rifled through Rory's things, checking under discarded sweatshirts and behind a stack of books and inside a chest that had once held toys. When he spoke again, it was a low rasp, mostly to himself. "The whole fucking reason I sent it to a PO box was so I wouldn't put you in danger! Goddamnit!"

He spun around and stared at Emily. "We need to find him. Now!"

McKenna bolted, passing her on the stairs.

Emily pressed herself against the railing, staring at him as he rushed upward. "Quinn, you're scaring me."

He strode across the kitchen, almost dragging Emily in his wake. "You let him order any video games he wants?" he tossed over his shoulder.

Despite the situation—or perhaps because of it—she bristled. "Excuse me?"

"I specifically said no first-person shooters. No combat games."

He heard her swear under her breath.

"Did you ever think maybe he plays them to connect with his father?" she retorted, almost hissing the words through her teeth. Then Emily seemed to catch herself, realizing how often they'd been in this argument before. "Oh my God. We're doing this."

McKenna had the impression she was going to say something more, but then they marched into the living room and Emily froze. He couldn't blame her, really, as in the moments they'd been downstairs, the house had quickly and silently filled with lunatics. They'd apparently left Dr. Brackett—Casey—in the RV, but the rest of them were there: Nebraska, Coyle, Lynch, Nettles, Baxley. Every one of the crazy fuckers who'd become his de facto new unit, at least until this horror came to an end. McKenna surveyed his team, saw Lynch shuffling his cards and Coyle rubbing the stubble atop his shaved head, eyes wide. Baxley and Nettles were rummaging around the living room, picking up framed photos to look at them and wiping a bit of dust off the fireplace mantel.

The room was full of Emily's paintings, the beautiful and heartbreaking works of her imagination, and the paintings were drawing the attention of the men too.

Nebraska was leaning forward to peer at one with the intensity of an art critic assessing technique.

"What are you doing? Give me those!" she snapped, striding forward and snatching a couple of her paintbrushes out of Nettles' hand. She wheeled on McKenna. "Who are these people?"

The corner of McKenna's mouth lifted in the closest he could come to a smile. "They're my unit. They're soldiers."

She gaped at him, incredulous. "They look like ushers at a porno theatre."

Nebraska had now straightened from the painting he'd been examining and was looking at her. He raised an eyebrow.

Aware she might have overstepped the mark, Emily said, "No offence."

Eyebrow still raised, Nebraska addressed McKenna. "The wife?"

"For better or worse," McKenna muttered, wondering if Emily might grab a kitchen knife and murder them all. Seeing them through her eyes made them seem that much crazier. He sighed and tiredly waved a hand around the room. "Emily? Loonies. Loonies? Emily."

As the Loonies murmured shy greetings, McKenna hurried around the room, snatching up pictures of Rory—school photos, holiday pictures—plucking them off the walls and side tables.

"Wait, back up," Emily said, shaking her head as it all sank in. "Your *unit*? What happened to Haines? Dupree?"

McKenna took a deep breath. "They're dead. And the thing that killed them is looking for Rory. So. You can think

I'm crazy all you want..." He closed his eyes briefly. He wished to God he wasn't here, wished he wasn't having to say these words. "But now? Our son is in a kill box."

Emily looked shell-shocked. The color drained from her face. "Looking for Rory..." she repeated, her voice low and croaky. Then suddenly the volume ramped up, became abruptly shrill, panicked. *"What thing?"*

"It's..." McKenna saw the terror and accusation in his ex-wife's eyes, and was suddenly at a loss for words. Turning desperately to the Loonies, he said, "Guys, what is it?"

Coyle was the first to respond. Fumblingly he said, "Um... it's not, like, a person. It's... a *creature*."

Eager to help, Nebraska said, "You know Whoopi Goldberg?"

Emily looked at him in bewilderment. "Yes."

"It's like an alien Whoopi Goldberg," he said helpfully.

Emily just stared at him. And when she finally murmured, "Oh my God," it was unclear whether she was horrified by the image Nebraska had conjured in her mind, or horrified simply by the fact that she was having to trust her son's welfare to a bunch of crazy—and possibly dangerous—people.

McKenna decided it was probably best not to muddy the waters still further by allowing time for the other Loonies to chip in. Instead, he started to hand out the pictures of Rory, his voice brisk, authoritative. "I want a grid search. Three teams..."

His voice tailed off. In his peripheral vision, he saw that Emily was shrugging into her coat, having snatched up, of all things, a fireplace poker. He marched across and grabbed it from her hand.

Furious, she squared up to him. "Our son's in *danger!*"

"That's right. And last time I looked?" He hefted his gun. "This is match grade." Now he lifted the poker. "This? Not so much. But points for originality."

Casey's head jerked up as the door of the RV opened, her hand going instinctively for the handgun on the table beside her. But it was only McKenna and the Loonies. McKenna was all business.

"Nebraska," he was saying, "find some wheels. Nothing flashy." Nodding across the room, he added, "Casey, you're with me."

He paused for a beat, fixing each of the guys with a look of purpose and determination.

Then he said, "Let's find my son."

15

Rory had been wandering the street without ringing any doorbells. He had no candy, which didn't seem like the best possible result of trick-or-treating. Without his mother or father with him, it seemed unexpectedly frightening to just walk up to a person's door, ring the bell, and ask for... well, anything. He still loved the anonymity, but somehow his earlier excitement had dissipated. His focus, instead, had been on the helmet and the cool thermal imaging he saw through the eyepieces. That alone had been enough to occupy him as he had walked around the neighborhood.

Now, though, the absence of candy had begun to seem like something he would regret later, so he had begun to study the other kids who were going door-to-door, intending to replicate the process. It was so simple. He'd done it before, just never on his own.

Go on, dummy, he thought.

Rory took a deep breath, watched a Moana and a

zombie accept candy from a smiling middle-aged woman in a witch's hat, and took a step forward. It was time.

"Hey, Ass-burger!"

Wincing, Rory glanced over to see E.J. from school. Even with the helmet covering Rory's head, the prick had somehow recognized him. Maybe his clothes, or just his build. It was possible, given how much of E.J.'s focus had been on him over the past couple of years.

Rory turned to head in the other direction and nearly ran into Derek, E.J.'s troll-like sidekick.

"What're you supposed to be?" Derek sneered.

"Leave me alone."

"Or what?" E.J. asked, boxing him in from behind. "You'll wash your hands five hundred times?"

He snickered at his own joke as Rory hurried away. The bullies fell in after him, dogging his heels. They weren't going to let him off that easy—of course they weren't—so Rory made a beeline for the nearest house. Only when he'd already committed to that direction did he notice that the porch light was off, which meant the owners were either not home or not participating in trick or treat. The house had a patchy lawn and needed a paint job, and one of the shutters hung askew. If someone had told Rory the place was haunted, he wouldn't have been surprised—and he didn't even believe in ghosts.

Crap. He ought to veer off, find a different safe haven, one where people were home and kids and parents were gathered on the steps or the front walk. But when he glanced back, he saw E.J. and Derek standing on the sidewalk, smirking in pleasure at his terror. This house might not be the escape route he had hoped for, but he had no choice other than to try it.

He went up the steps and rang the bell. A buzz echoed deep inside the house.

"Trick or treat?" he called hopefully.

To his surprise and consternation, a voice replied immediately, a slightly slurred voice, which came from right behind the door, as if its owner had been crouched or slumped against it. "Fuck off."

On the sidewalk, just close enough to hear the homeowner's response, E.J. and Derek laughed, holding onto each other as they bent over with mirth.

Rory turned stiffly away from the door, gaze shifting as he tried to figure out the best path of escape—searching to see if there *was* a path of escape. Behind him, the door creaked open. Before he could turn, he heard the raspy voice speak up again.

"Here's a treat, you little shit."

Then he felt the smack of something hard and wet against the back of his helmet. It rocked him forward slightly and, inside the helmet, Rory blinked in shock and frustration. He wiped the back of his helmet and looked at his hand, fearful that the guy in the house had thrown dog crap at him or something. Instead, his hand came away with a smear of what he thought must be rotten apple, and a glance at the ground proved the theory.

E.J. and Derek were howling with laughter.

Without warning the interior of the helmet lit up.

Red lights flashed. Rory's heart jumped in alarm and he panicked, twisting around for help, for some solution. Symbols scrolled across his internal viewscreen. Targeting information popped up and he stared at the guy on the front steps—the apple-throwing stoner who still stood there, sneering.

"What?" the stoner asked, throwing out his hands in a challenge.

A click came from the side of the helmet. Rory heard a whine. Then hellfire erupted from the helmet and disintegrated the stoner where he stood, blowing out the entire doorway of the house, leaving it a flaming, charred wreckage.

McKenna and Casey had taken Emily's Subaru and started cruising up and down the streets, moving carefully. With all the kids in the street and on the sidewalks, all the parents holding hands, munchkins with their Jack-o'-lantern buckets, and swaggering teenagers prowling for candy with the laziest costumes imaginable—if any—looking for Rory was like looking for the proverbial needle in a haystack.

"Busy night," Casey said. "What a great place to trick or treat. Rory's lucky to have grown up here."

"Yeah," McKenna agreed. He didn't bother to make excuses for how much of Rory's growing-up he had missed. He had a feeling Casey wouldn't be surprised, but he didn't know her well enough to share, even if he'd had the inclination.

"You really think he's wearing the Predator helmet?"

McKenna turned up Sycamore Street. "Yeah. He found it, that's for sure. That and the wrist gauntlet. Knowing my kid, and seeing that empty box, I figure there's almost a hundred percent chance he's got them both on."

"At least it's Halloween," she said. "So, he won't stand out."

"From our point of view, that's not a good thing."

McKenna's gaze continued to shift, tracking each kid, mentally dismissing each costume as he searched for the Predator helmet, and the boy wearing it. He tapped the accelerator again, cruising slowly along Sycamore, watching the shadows and the front steps and the sidewalks.

"I've seen every alien encounter movie," Casey went on. "Sure, I hoped for gently inquisitive or frighteningly ambitious, but I was totally ready for hostile. I mean, let's face it, if the nature of off-world races is anything like that of humans, they're bound to be assholes, right? Farming our minerals or harvesting our people— something unpleasant..."

She let the words trail off as she, too, searched the sea of trick-or-treaters.

"Ignore the small groups with parents," McKenna said. "He wouldn't fall in with them. He might join a large group of kids, stick to the back where he might not be noticed, but chances are he'll be on his own. Shouldn't be hard to spot him."

"Sounds like a sad kid."

McKenna frowned. "You'd be surprised. There are things that bum him out or make him frustrated, but he's got a much better attitude than you'd think, considering how much crap he has to deal with because he sees the world a little differently."

"You don't talk much about him."

"I've been doing nothing *but* talk about him."

"About keeping him safe, yeah," Casey said. "But not about what kind of kid he is."

McKenna went quiet as he braked to let a family cross the street, then turned left on Briarwood Road.

"He's a good kid, Casey. A really good kid." McKenna hesitated a moment, then went on. "A hell of a lot better than his old man."

Whatever she might have said in reply was interrupted by an explosion on the next block. Over the roofs of houses, a pillar of flame flashed toward the night sky and then vanished, but the smoke rising from it remained visible.

Casey and McKenna exchanged a stunned glance, and then he stomped on the gas pedal. He wasn't a man who prayed—wasn't a man who believed in things he couldn't hold in his two hands—but McKenna now found himself praying with all his heart that Rory hadn't been at the center of that explosion.

Rory froze, mouth gaping inside the helmet. He blinked, telling himself that couldn't have just happened.

A pile of ashes sat on the top step.

The front lawn, on either side of the steps, was smoking from the heat.

Oh shit. Oh God. Oh shit, Rory thought, even as the more analytical part of his mind examined the event and tried to make sense of what had happened. A weapon had whirred out from the side of the helmet. Its sensors had reacted to the attack, thinking the stoner was a threat because of the impact of the apple.

Now he turned, in utter shock, and stared at E.J. and Derek, who seemed just as stunned. As soon as the bullies realized the mask was now pointing in their direction, however, they screamed and fled, moving faster than he had ever seen them move before.

He raised the helmet and turned to glance again at the ruin of the front door and the ashes on the steps, too shaken to appreciate the terror of his tormentors. At some point, he had dropped his trick or treat bag. Now he lowered the helmet and bent to retrieve it, numbly picking up items of candy that had spilled from it as he attempted to restore a semblance of order to his mind.

Once he had done, he looked again at the smoking ruin of the house, and suddenly the shell of shock that had formed around him cracked and fell away. Tearing off the Predator mask, he tossed it into the bushes surrounding the house.

Then he ran.

The two-way radio squawked. Nettles was back in the RV, monitoring local police chatter. Now his voice burst in from the static.

"McKenna, you hearing this?" he barked.

He must've put his two-way up to the police scanner, because McKenna and Casey heard the crackling voice come through, but it sounded like it was coming from deep inside a well.

"...got a male juvenile, ten to twelve years old," the officer was saying. "Ran right in front of my car, now moving east on Woodruff."

McKenna swore, spun the wheel, and turned the car into a squealing, smoking one-eighty. Emily wouldn't thank him later for the rubber he'd left back on the road, but the officer had spotted what could well have been Rory, and she wasn't going to give a shit about her tires if he could get their boy back in one piece.

"Repeat," the voice on the police scanner said. "Moving east on Woodruff."

Stay alive, kid, McKenna thought. *Whatever just blew up, stay the hell alive.*

"Nebraska," he barked into his radio. "You got wheels?"

Janice Pelham had joined the Neighborhood Watch out of civic duty. She wasn't a cop, not quite, but as a security officer she had been deputized to perform certain functions in conjunction with the police. She also had a sweet ride and a uniform that her boyfriend Elwin loved her to wear at home, and she didn't mind at all.

In the three years since she'd started this job, she'd mostly dealt with burglary, vandalism, and illegal parking, plus some domestic disturbances that had required the police to step in. Now she stared at the front of the house whose front door had been vaporized and realized that this job might be dangerous, that even though she wasn't a real cop, she could still be killed doing it, even in a neighborhood like this one.

The kid had bolted, but she'd radioed it in. The real police could track him down. She wanted to get home to Elwin and take the uniform off—and not in the fun way they both preferred. Janice was thinking about taking it off and never putting it on again.

She turned and started back toward her patrol car—and froze.

"Where's my fucking car?"

Nebraska Williams held onto the wheel as he blasted the stolen Neighborhood Watch patrol car around a corner. The tires shrieked. He had the flashers turning, strobing red light and pale shadows all over the lawns and houses. Parents and kids had scrambled out of the street when the explosion had erupted, and now they mostly stared from front lawns or had gone indoors, where they peered out of windows. Trick or treat had ended abruptly this year, but the kiddies in McKenna's neighborhood would never forget it.

When McKenna's question came through, he snatched up the two-way from the seat and thumbed the button.

"I got wheels," he said, and grinned. "Something flashy." Then he dropped the humor, was suddenly all business again. "Kid's spooked, he's rabbiting. Talk to me. Where's he gonna feel safe? Where's someplace he *knows*?"

N N N

Huffing, heart thundering in his chest, Rory raced across the middle school baseball field. His thoughts were beginning to return to their orderly nature as he went back through the events of the previous minutes. He had killed a man, but he told himself that he couldn't be held responsible… that he *didn't* hold himself responsible.

Dad, he thought.

But no. He couldn't be blamed either. Even though his father had sent the helmet and gauntlet, he hadn't expected the package to fall into his son's hands. Not even the manufacturer of the technology—whom Rory assumed must be some nation's military, some corporation that specialized in finding inventive ways to murder people on battlefields—could really be said to be responsible. They had all had a part to play in the death of the stoner and the destruction of his front door—Rory, his dad, the military, the postal worker, E.J., Derek, and the stoner prick who'd thrown a rotten apple at a kid.

But when it came right down to it, when you reached the end of the long rope of cause and effect, only one sure and solid fact remained: a man was dead. And despite everything, Rory still felt like it was his fault, and although he didn't process emotions the way other people did, he thought he might cry.

He reached the scoreboard and found the niche he had used several times to hide from the bullies. In the darkness there, he cowered and tried to catch his breath. He knew he ought to run home, but the police would be looking for him. They hadn't seen his face, but if anyone talked to E.J. or Derek, they would figure out pretty quickly that they were looking for Rory McKenna and then the cops would be at his house and his mother would know what he had done... and that was the worst part. The idea that his mother would learn that he had killed someone, even if it really wasn't his fault, even if it was just the stupid fucking helmet... Rory loved his mother more than anything. She understood him like nobody else ever would and he knew that. If his mom cried or screamed or felt horror or disgust because of him...

In the niche beneath the scoreboard, he kept trying to catch his breath, wondering how all this had happened.

Am I going to jail?

"Dad," he whispered in the darkness. "Where are you?"

A low growl replied from the shadows. Rory froze, turning slowly to see a flash of canine eyes in the dark. A dog—a big damn dog—ready to bite his face off. Still winded, he knew he should run, but knew he wouldn't get far before it caught him.

The dog shifted and some of the starlight bled in, letting him see the silhouette of its head. He recognized it immediately—Bugsy, the damn pit bull that menaced him every fucking day on his way home from school. It growled again, low, quieter this time... and moved closer.

Then the pit bull dropped its head and let its tongue loll out. It moved even nearer to him and nudged him with its huge, heavy head. Rory furrowed his brow in confusion. Tentatively, he reached out... and petted the pit bull's head. To his surprise, the dog didn't flinch. Instead, it lifted its eyes and looked at him, and a sound came from its chest that was different from a growl. A friendly, contented sound. Rory petted the dog again, smiling in amazement at the sudden sweetness of the dog that had so terrified him.

"Good boy," he said quietly.

All at once the dog froze. Its lips peeled back in a snarl that grew into a new growl and it backed away from Rory. For a moment, he didn't notice that the dog wasn't growling at him, and then he saw its eyes and realized something else had spooked it. Something behind him.

Slowly, Rory turned… to see a very different sort of dog.

Ice filled his gut. For the first time, he understood how someone could piss their pants from fear. He didn't—but it was a very near thing.

This dog was no pit bull. It wasn't any kind of dog Rory had ever seen before. In fact, one glance at its massive haunches and the insectoid mandibles that clicked and stretched open across its face, and he knew it wasn't a dog at all. Rory had been brilliant since birth. He knew more about biology than ninety-nine percent of the adults he'd met, including every science teacher who'd ever tried to teach him. Whatever this monster-dog was, it hadn't been born on Earth.

Alien, he thought breathlessly. *Or genetically engineered. Or both.*

The monster-dog snarled, its intent viciously clear. Its mandibles snapped open and shut and it advanced a single step. The pit bull whimpered and backed further away. For a moment Rory hoped, perhaps unkindly, that the monster would chase the ordinary dog. Unfortunately, it seemed only to have eyes for Rory.

He backed away, up the dugout steps and onto the

field, keeping the monster-dog in his sights… and then he heard a voice behind him.

"Kid. Walk to me. Slowly."

Rory turned to see a security guard standing about ten meters away, armed only with a flashlight and a nightstick. The guy, stuffed into his uniform, was overweight and over fifty, but at least he was brave. Nine out of ten guys in his position would most likely have locked themselves in their nice warm office and called the cops.

"Shhh," the guy said, as if Rory was causing a commotion instead of just standing there. "Come on, now…"

Rory was about to obey—though he wasn't sure what good it would do—when he noticed something that the security guard hadn't. Movement in the shadows under the bleachers. The stealthy movement of something big and predatory inching forward, readying itself to spring.

Before Rory could shout a warning—before he could even open his mouth—there was a blur of movement, and suddenly the security guard was on his back, arms outflung, nightstick and flashlight spinning away into the grass on either side of him. And there was something on his chest—a *second* alien animal, just as big, and just as mean-looking, as the first. Lowering its hideous face, all stretched-out mandibles and rows and rows of shark-like teeth, the creature bit into the security guard's shoulder and throat. It ripped a chunk away, as easily as Rory would take a bite out of a cupcake.

Until that moment, the guard had been screaming, howling in a voice that was hideously high-pitched for a man of his size and age, but as soon as the monster snapped back its head with a sizeable piece of him between its jaws, he stopped. Now there was blood, a shockingly vast amount of blood, that gushed from the hole in the man's body, and kept gushing, spreading out through the grass like an oil spill through the sea, a dark, gleaming purple in the meager light.

Rory was frozen by the sight of all that blood. He'd once seen a bird, standing on a wall as a cat stalked toward it, and he'd wondered why that bird didn't just fly away. Now he knew.

I'm going to die, he thought with utter crystal clarity. *I'm going to die just like that man on the ground.*

At first, when he heard the screech, he thought it was the attack cry of the other monster rushing in for the kill. But then he realized it was coming from the opposite direction, and turned his head to see his mother's Subaru barreling across the grass. Its engine roaring, the car smashed right through the scoreboard. Shrapnel sprayed across the ball field as the car accelerated straight for one of the monster-dogs, smashing into it and sending it flying through the air.

Even before it had landed, the Subaru had slewed to a halt on the grass. The doors burst open and two people leapt out. In the light of the moon and stars, and the glow from the Subaru's headlights, Rory recognized the car's driver immediately.

Dad?

McKenna and Casey jumped out of the Subaru, weapons leveled at the Predator dogs. He pulled the trigger, blazing shot after shot across the baseball field. The alien hound darted to the left, staying ahead of his aim. McKenna swore loudly, heard Casey doing the same, but then he heard another engine roar and had to throw up a hand to shield his eyes from the brightness of blazing headlights.

The RV hurtled across the field from one direction. McKenna spun to see another vehicle—the patrol car Nebraska had hijacked—sailing over the grass from the other edge of the baseball diamond. Behind the wheel of the patrol car, Nebraska aimed the vehicle directly for the chain link fence lining the diamond and slammed through it with a *clang*. The fence furled up in either direction, springing back as if it had been waiting years for someone to crash through it.

The patrol car fishtailed onto the field. Nebraska flung open the door and dove out, rolling on the grass and leaping to his feet, gun in hand, without even slowing the car down. The vehicle kept rolling.

The RV slewed to a ragged halt, tearing up the turf, and the rest of the Loonies piled out, laden with all the weapons they'd acquired from the RV's owner in the parking lot of the Iron Horse Motel.

"Three o'clock!" McKenna shouted, gesturing toward one of the Predator dogs, which had started across the field along the same path Rory had taken. "Ten o'clock!"

It was all the Loonies needed. McKenna clocked everyone's locations, kept Rory in mind, made sure his back was to Casey but also checked to be certain she could handle herself. A hailstorm of artillery tore up the field as they opened fire on the Predator dogs. McKenna saw bullets strike home, saw chunks of flesh and blood spray, though just as often the bullets seemed to do little more than nudge the monsters. The Predator dogs kept moving, but at least now they were distracted by their attackers—the focus off Rory.

McKenna ran toward his son, and Casey backed him up.

Still pale with shock, Rory called out to him, more out of curiosity than fear. That was Rory. McKenna packed away any regret or shame he had about his past with the boy, or about putting him in danger. Rory stood frozen on the grass and McKenna raced toward him.

Then he saw one of the beasts make a beeline for Nebraska, snarling, those hideous pincers around its mouth snapping. Its intent was clear.

"Casey!" he snapped, gesturing for her to grab Rory.

"I've got him!" she called.

McKenna barely knew the women, but he trusted the confidence with which she carried herself. Out of the corner of his eye, he saw Casey scoop Rory up into her arms. For half a second, it looked as if Rory might fight her. There was a real dog on the field, a terrified-looking pit bull, and Rory seemed to want to save the mutt.

Then there was no more time for distraction. McKenna had run almost into the path of the Predator dog as it raced toward Nebraska. Now he faced the beast, swung his M4 and pulled the trigger, unloading. Bullets tore the ground, pounded the monstrosity, smashed the air and his eardrums. The alien creature staggered and McKenna thought maybe, just maybe, he'd kill the damn thing. Then he clicked on an empty chamber.

Oh shit.

Out of ammo, with the creature ten feet away.

McKenna turned and bolted for the bleachers. Off to his right, he saw Nebraska struggling to load a 40mm recoilless grenade launcher and his eyes lit up.

"Umm… Gaylord?" he called.

The man jacked the round into the barrel and snapped it shut. "I thought I told you," he said, as he tossed the grenade launcher fifteen feet into McKenna's waiting hands. "Call me Nebraska."

McKenna caught the weapon on the run. The Predator dog slavered and snarled as it chased him— both man and alien hound knowing he had no chance of outrunning death. McKenna reached the bleachers and hurled himself between two crossbars. He hit the ground, rolled, and turned as he rose. The bleachers slowed the beast just half a step—it was enough. McKenna jammed the massive gun between the monster's mandibles, shoved it down the dog's throat, and pulled the trigger.

A muted *fwumpp* came from within the Predator dog. Its eyes went wide and then it buckled, toppling to the ground in a wet *slap* of flesh on cold earth. Dead.

A snarl made McKenna whip around. He'd been so focused on this fucker trying to kill him that he'd forgotten the other one. The background noise of gunfire and the shouts of his men had receded in the intensity of the moment, the urgency of trying not to die. Now he heard the chuffing of the other hound's breath and felt the ground thump under its tread. It leaped over the corpse of its dead companion and lunged toward the opening beneath the bleachers.

Nebraska Williams appeared as if by magic, a bolt gun in his hand. With a single motion, he brought the bolt gun up and shot the second monster point blank in the skull. The bolt impaled its forehead. For a moment, McKenna thought it hadn't made a difference, that the Predator dog would still rip his throat out. Then it wavered, listed, and started walking in a lazy circle as if it sought a comfortable place to lie down.

"You've gotta be kidding," McKenna muttered.

The thing had taken a bolt through the skull and it wasn't dead. No longer a threat, for sure, but still alive.

He glanced at Nebraska in astonishment.

Nebraska shrugged. "Goddamn space aliens."

16

The RV revved onto the street between the baseball field and the school. McKenna had lost track of who was behind the wheel now. All he could think to do was get to the vehicle. The Loonies ran in formation, boots pounding dirt, weapons clanking. They were following his orders now, but he didn't have to order them to withdraw. There was no telling how many of those Predator dogs might be prowling around the neighborhood in search of Rory—or rather, in search of the helmet and gauntlet that, as far as McKenna knew, were still in his possession.

"Dad?" Rory said.

He glanced down, satisfied himself that Rory was running alongside him. Casey had put the kid down. She'd shot at the creatures herself, had carried Rory, helped to save his life. She might be a scientist, but she had proven to be just as formidable as he'd suspected from the moment he'd seen her chasing the Predator.

"You're okay, kid," Casey said now, speaking up when McKenna failed to.

"I've got you, Rory," he added belatedly.

"What are they?" Rory asked, as they all crowded through the broken fence and raced toward the RV.

McKenna began to answer, but then he heard Lynch start in on a string of terrified profanities. The Loonies all pulled up short, bringing their weapons to bear. McKenna looked up to see the Predator itself, standing on top of the RV, waiting for them.

Casey said McKenna's name, very quietly.

Rory took a step backward.

McKenna took aim. But the Predator was all business. It fired a single shot that obliterated a lamppost at the edge of the ball field, purely to show them all what it could do to them if it chose to. The lamppost melted and exploded, all at the same time. Whatever the weapon was, nobody wanted it aimed at them.

The Predator signaled to them, gesturing for them all to lower their weapons. Several of the men glanced at McKenna, ready to follow his lead. If he started shooting, or gave the order, they would open fire. They had seen what the Predator's weaponry could do, but they had all had their chance to opt out of this fight and instead they had committed themselves to combat. None of these men were backing out now.

McKenna opened his mouth to issue an order—

Rory bolted for the school, the only shelter nearby.

"Kid, go!" Casey called, urging him on.

McKenna followed on his son's heels. He felt the target

on his back. If the Predator wanted him dead it would take only one shot, right now, and he'd be just as much wreckage as that lamppost. He wanted to scream to Rory to run a serpentine pattern, but the school was just ahead, and he knew that as long as he could keep himself between the Predator and his son, Rory would have a head start. The Loonies would buy them even more time. The only thing that mattered in that moment was his boy.

He glanced back and saw the Predator leap down from atop the RV. The Loonies moved in. McKenna spared a moment to hope they weren't all about to die—then he faced front again.

The lobby doors were locked. McKenna kicked them open and he and Rory barreled into the empty building, footfalls echoing across the vacant lobby. Both of them were breathless, wordless. No words were necessary. McKenna knew he wasn't as smart as his son, but he also knew they were both working overtime trying to figure out how to survive this.

Rory kept running. McKenna needed to slow him down, to keep the boy with him—protected. He reached for Rory but the kid squirted further ahead, running for the stairs. Going up seemed like a terrible idea—once they were upstairs, they'd have to find a way down that didn't involve jumping—but Rory had nearly reached the steps and McKenna had no way to stop him.

"Wait," McKenna gasped. "Rory—"

The lobby doors exploded inward. The blast nearly lifted McKenna off his feet. A cloud of shattered wood blew across the floor. Glancing back through the massive hole in the entryway, McKenna could see the Loonies rolling on the pavement, clutching at their ears, deafened by the blast.

In through the swirling cloud of debris stalked the Predator, its silhouette flashing McKenna back to the jungle. Yet again he cursed himself for not killing the alien when he'd had the chance.

Rory had headed up the stairs. McKenna followed at top speed, using the settling cloud of debris to buy him precious seconds, even whilst knowing that those seconds wouldn't be nearly enough.

McKenna chased Rory out of the stairwell and into a long hallway. Rory's sneakers slapped the linoleum. McKenna just needed him to slow down a moment, but damn, the kid was fast.

"Son, come on!" McKenna snapped.

Rory glanced over his shoulder and, at last, pulled up short. McKenna had more to say, but Rory's dreamlike expression startled him to silence. The kid wasn't even looking at him, just staring... past him.

A throaty clicking sound came from behind him. McKenna turned to look down the corridor, marveling that the Predator could be that fast, that it had already caught up to them. But no, it wasn't the Predator. This sound was different. It came from outside the line of high windows set into the outer wall. Turning, McKenna spotted a massive silhouette out there in the dark and he stiffened, his mind trying to make sense of what he was seeing.

Ice flowed along his spine and he reached out a hand, instinctively trying to put Rory behind him. He had no words left for this new thing. It was a Predator, yes, but the monster framed in the window had to be some kind of next-gen bullshit, because this creature stood at least eleven feet tall.

McKenna didn't have to say a word. As one, he and Rory began to back away from the windows. Together, they twisted around to flee for the next turn in the corridor, and found the Predator waiting for them. The one from downstairs. The original, the bastard from the jungle, who now wore a borrowed helmet and wanted his original gear back.

Rory practically plowed into the Predator. It swatted him aside and the kid went sliding along the smooth floor. Something skittered out of Rory's hand, a long black gizmo that McKenna thought looked like a video game controller or a big TV remote. He only got a glimpse of the thing before the Predator shot out a hand and grabbed the chest of his jacket. McKenna threw a punch at its body, and realized his mistake when his fist smashed against armor.

The Predator slammed him against the wall, so damn strong it could have killed him with very little effort. Instead, it cocked its head and seemed to scan him—and McKenna realized that was precisely what the alien was doing. The tech in the helmet must have been searching him for something that it didn't find. Still holding him against the wall, the Predator turned and fixed its gaze on Rory.

No, McKenna thought.

The Predator's head twitched, its focus no longer on Rory but on the black gizmo on the floor. It was clear that whatever that thing was, the alien wanted it.

Just take it, McKenna tried to mumble. *Just take it and go.*

Maybe, if he'd been able to get the words out clearly, the Predator would simply have done as he asked. But then McKenna heard the clicking noise outside the window again. He started to glance that way, and was aware that the Predator was also whipping its head round, alarmed by the sound—but too late. Abruptly the wall erupted, plaster debris flying everywhere, and an impossibly large arm smashed through the hole and reached for the Predator.

Stunned, McKenna dropped to the floor as the Predator let him go and raised its weapon. But before it could fire, the massive arm shot forward and the huge hand on the end of it tore the cannon-like gun from the Predator's hand and crushed it as if it were cheap tin. Dropping the weapon, the massive arm of the Upgrade Predator swung and swatted the original Predator effortlessly aside. As the Upgrade Predator hauled itself through the hole it had made, and the original Predator scrambled to its feet and rushed forward to confront it, McKenna took his chance and jumped up. Turning away from the Predators, he ran back along the corridor, toward the stairs, scooping up a still-dazed Rory as the howl and clash of the fighting aliens resounded behind him. His only hope was that the creatures would keep one another occupied long enough for him to get his son to safety.

He and Rory clattered down the stairs, McKenna all but carrying his son, taking the steps two at a time. Through the still-drifting murk of debris he saw dark shapes moving *up* the stairs toward them, and for a moment he faltered, before realizing it was the Loonies, Nebraska at their head.

"Go! Go!" he yelled, waving them back. There followed a Keystone Kops moment, everyone trying to turn at once and head back the way they had come, which would have been comical if it hadn't been for the dire circumstances. After a few seconds, however, they were all heading in the same direction, Lynch and Coyle leading the way, with McKenna and Rory bringing up the rear, just behind Nebraska and Casey.

They made it into the lobby, and were a few feet from the splintered gap that had once housed a pair of double doors when McKenna became aware of something at his back—a sixth sense kind of feeling, maybe a displacement of air—and turned to see the original Predator (it felt like too much of a sick joke to think of him as the small one) leaping straight down the center of the stairwell.

The creature landed with barely a jolt—indeed, without even bending its knees to absorb the impact of its fall. The Loonies froze, and for what felt like a long moment McKenna and his team stared at the Predator, and the Predator stared back at them.

What is this? McKenna thought. *An impasse? Or is it just waiting for us to run, so it can enjoy the thrill of the chase?*

So focused was he on the creature that he didn't notice Rory sidle away from his side. Now, though, he heard him gasp, and turned. His son was a couple of meters away, almost against the right-hand wall, looking at the Predator side-on. Curious, McKenna took a tentative step to his right, and suddenly he saw what Rory was seeing—the whip-like cord, which was wound around the smaller Predator's neck, stretching up into the dusty shadows.

The Predator hadn't jumped down the center of the stairwell. He had been pushed or thrown. And he wasn't standing there staring at them. He was dead.

The Upgrade had hanged him.

Now that McKenna looked more closely, he saw that the Predator's feet weren't quite touching the floor. As if the Upgrade was somehow aware that the humans in the lobby below had finally realized the truth, it gave several sharp tugs on the cord around its fellow alien's neck, making the Predator's limbs jerk and twitch in a ghoulish dance.

Then it gave a sudden sharp yank rather than a tug, and the cord, which was made of some type of metal, sliced straight through the meat and bone of the smaller Predator's neck. The creature's head flew off and hit the floor with a thud, right in front of the Loonies, the neck stump spattering them with green blood as the body dropped to the ground.

That was precisely what was needed to break the spell. As one, the Loonies, McKenna, Rory, and Casey turned and bolted out of the wrecked entranceway.

McKenna yelled, signaling toward the RV, and they all ran in that direction.

All except Rory, that is, who paused to regard the pit bull, which, despite everything, was still hunched down beneath the bleachers, too terrified to move. A thoughtful look crossed Rory's face, and for a moment it seemed he might even veer off to rescue the frightened dog.

Then McKenna grabbed him roughly enough to make Rory yelp out in pain. "Goddammit," he said, unable to rein in his exasperation at his son's lack of urgency, "we have to go!"

He leaped into the RV, all but dragging Rory after him, as Nettles threw himself into the driver's seat and fired up the engine. McKenna hated to retreat without finishing a job—which, now that he had found Rory, he saw as both ridding the Earth of the alien threat, and gathering enough evidence to expose Traeger and his goons, and clear all their names. Thing was, the Upgrade was more than he had bargained for. If they were going to fight it, they needed a plan, and standing here dying wasn't anyone's idea of good strategy.

He didn't let go of Rory's arm until the RV's door was shut behind them and they were heading away from the kill zone, but as soon as he did, the boy crawled under the table of the dinette and curled into a fetal ball. McKenna felt a twinge of guilt and shame at how roughly he had handled his son, but he told himself it was necessary— in this case, rough love might have proved the difference between life and death.

Around him the Loonies were whooping and hollering—more a release of tension than anything else— but they quieted down fast when the Upgrade suddenly appeared behind them, stooping through the shattered doorway and rising to its full height, its massive form spattered in the glowing green blood of its enemy. The Upgrade was clutching the weird remote control doohickey in its taloned paw, and as it watched them go it had a look on its face that McKenna couldn't help interpreting as a kind of calm contemplation. Perhaps it was something in the creature's eyes. From this distance, they looked almost human.

He glanced again at Rory, cowering under the table, and couldn't help but feel a pang of dismay as the boy winced—almost as if he was more terrified of the violence inflicted by his own father than he was of an eleven-foot-tall alien killer with the face of an angry crab.

Then he became aware of Casey beside him, holding on but still staggering against him as the RV swung around a corner and the school fell out of sight.

She caught his eye, and he could see that she had been shaken to the core by what she had witnessed tonight.

"Holy shit," she muttered. "They're hunting each other now?"

On the baseball field, the Upgrade stands in the moonlight and examines his prize. The black box gleams in the dark. The Kujhad, it is called, in the language of his people. He feels a certain satisfaction at the death of his prey, but there is more to be done. The massive Predator raises his wrist gauntlet and a hologram display blossoms into light and life.

It depicts the young human, the one previously in possession of the Kujhad. The boy appears to be staring at the Upgrade, examining him, assessing him, though the Upgrade knows that what the young human is really assessing is the Kujhad itself, and that this footage was recorded by the device earlier that day.

The Upgrade is intrigued by the boy. There is intelligence in his eyes. More than intelligence. For a human—and, more particularly, one as unformed as this—to work out the intricacies of the Kujhad so quickly takes something very special indeed.

In some ways, he could consider this boy his nemesis. He had the intelligence to adversely affect the workings of the Upgrade's ship, after all, and that alone makes him far more dangerous than all those bigger humans with their primitive weapons.

The Upgrade tweaks a control and suddenly there is sound to accompany the holographic image. The voice is scratchy, high-pitched, and to the Upgrade his words are meaningless.

"Just playing games, Mom!" the boy says.

17

The grounds of the school had been cordoned off, and the basement hurriedly converted into an autopsy room/pathology lab. It wasn't an ideal room for such purposes, as the school boiler, old and in need of an overhaul (if not outright condemnation) chugged and burbled away in an alcove on the far wall, filling the damp space with a stuffy warmth that encouraged mold and fungi to sprout in shadowy corners.

Dominating the center of the room was a large table—in truth, four tables requisitioned from the school dining hall and clamped together—on which lay the now deboned, headless corpse of the Predator that had broken free from the Project: Stargazer complex. The white sheet laid over the corpse was stained with patches of alien blood, which glowed a luminescent green whenever the flashing lights of cop cars, strobing through the bank of high windows on the outside wall, passed over it.

Traeger strode into the room, wrinkling his nose at the

heat and the raw, fetid stench of dismembered alien, and marched up to the table. His aide, Sapir, scuttled behind him like an obedient pet rat.

"So this time they're hunting their own," Traeger said, and huffed out a sound that translated as: *Go figure.* He favored Sapir with a glance. "Now tell me again."

"Eleven feet," Sapir said.

Traeger whistled. "That's really fuckin' tall." He whipped the white sheet back from the corpse. Sapir recoiled at the sight of the Predator's head perched on its neck stump at the end of the table, above the body, its piercing, fish-like eyes glazed now in death. Traeger, though, leaned in closer, baring his teeth in a spiteful grin. "Shoulda stuck with us, buddy." He turned to Sapir again. "You said they had a kid with them?"

The aide nodded. "Yes, sir. Captain McKenna's son. Wife confirms—he has the operating system to the missing ship. Thinks it's a video game."

Traeger rubbed his chin. He paced around the sheeted corpse, looking thoughtful, while Sapir waited patiently.

At last he said, "I'm thinking this guy was a rogue. A runner. The big one was damage control. Sent to take him out."

"Retrieve the ship?"

"Or destroy it." Traeger came to a halt. His eyes narrowed. "We need to find that ship. Before he does."

Sapir licked his lips. Tentatively, he said, "Sir… we've been looking for forty-eight hours solid—"

Traeger raised a finger, cutting him off. So pompously that you could almost see the speech marks around his quote, he said, "'The difficult is done at once. The impossible takes a bit more time.'" He gave Sapir a smile that didn't reach his eyes. "The kid. He has the device."

Sapir spoke the words eagerly, to show that he was in tune with his boss's wishes. "Find the kid."

It was late enough that all good girls and boys should have been asleep. The RV sat, cooling and dark, beneath a bridge at the far edge of a patch of rural farmland so vast it was impossible to tell where it ended and the next property began. Despite technological advances, there were still places in America where a squad of military deserters/mental patients and a startlingly fearless and physically capable scientist could vanish for a few hours.

Despite the late hour, Rory was still awake. He had a stick in his hand and was drawing in the dirt. The stick made an imperfect artistic implement, but he thought he had the basic design and measurements of the alien ship correct. He drew it from memory, recalling the holographic image he'd summoned up from the gizmo that had popped out of the Predator's wrist gauntlet. The gizmo was gone now, so he wanted to solidify the memory in his head, just in case it was important. At the same time, he kept running through the symbols that had appeared on the readout, trying to understand what it all meant.

Nebraska Williams kept looking over his shoulder. He seemed like a nice man, but Rory grew antsy. He didn't like being the focus of anyone's attention.

"I heard you got a hole in your head," he said.

Nebraska smiled. "People been tellin' me that since I was five."

Rory frowned, but stayed on topic. "What happened?"

"Well… you get to be my age, your brain's like an attic," Nebraska replied. "All musty and cobwebby. Sometimes you need to air it out."

The soldier resumed the task of placing grenades gingerly into a box. Rory frowned. He wondered if Nebraska realized he was recommending a middle-school kid solve his problems with a bullet to the head and decided that, no, the man had no idea. Apparently, that was one of the side effects of shooting oneself in the head.

Casey had lost track of time. Ever since childhood that had been her MO. She'd find a thread that intrigued her, some bit of information or a word she didn't understand or a scientific idea, and she'd follow it down the rabbit hole, learning as much as she could until she fell asleep or her mother forced her to go to bed or come to dinner or go to school. It was warm inside the RV, the air heavy and close now that the engine had been turned off for a while, but she had her microscope—and more importantly, she had the Predator's gauntlet that had been in Rory's possession.

When McKenna entered, Casey had the gauntlet on her arm, studying it. She knew it was important to learn as much as possible about the Predator and its tech, but she also relished this time. The rest of the world, and the danger she was in—both from the gigantic Predator 2.0 they'd encountered and from her own government—all fell away while she focused on unraveling the mysteries before her.

McKenna grabbed a beer from the cooler, then paused

to glance at her, as if uncertain whether to interrupt her or not. But Casey was ready to talk, ready to demonstrate what she'd found. McKenna wasn't a scientist, but he was smart, and besides, it was sometimes good to share information, get your findings out into the open, rather than just letting them stew in your head.

Producing the vial of fluid she'd stolen from Project: Stargazer, she said without preamble, "They found this in the Predator's blood. In layman's terms, it's like distilled 'lizard brain,' the part that kicks in under extreme survival conditions."

McKenna took a gulp of beer. "So?" he said, sensing she was eager to tell him more.

"Remember I told you they rip out people's spines?"

"Trophies, you said."

"Right. But if a Predator's first and foremost a survivor, wouldn't it make sense to collect DNA 'souvenirs?'"

McKenna raised his eyebrows. "From people's spines?"

"Brain stem. Close enough." Casey knew she wasn't painting a clear picture. It was a bad habit. Her thoughts seemed to coalesce cleanly in her head, but getting the words out in the proper order was another thing entirely. "Look, suppose—just suppose—that these space creatures are… siphoning off our lizard brain juice."

Now McKenna laughed, although she could tell he was a little insulted. "You don't have to overdo the layman's terms."

She held up a hand in apology. "I think they're attempting hybridization," she said. "It would explain the human DNA, now, wouldn't it?"

McKenna's brow furrowed. Casey could see his mind working and knew she'd been right in her assessment of his smartness. McKenna might be a rough-tough soldier boy, but there was a brightness about him, an ability to take information on board, adapt, calculate the odds, make quick decisions. If she was being honest with herself, she guessed she should never really have doubted his intelligence. You didn't get to be an officer in the Army Rangers without being mentally agile.

"Collecting survival traits from high-end specimens," he said, nodding.

"From the strongest, smartest, most dangerous species on every planet they visit, to make upgrades to their own race. Hybrids."

McKenna studied her. "Are you just pulling this theory out of your ass?"

"This new Predator, the bigger one," she said, ignoring the question, "did you see its eyes?"

His nod was almost imperceptible, but it was there. McKenna knew exactly what she was talking about.

"They're evolving, Captain," she said. "Changing."

"Being upgraded," he murmured.

"And here's the clincher," she said. She leaned toward him, as if so eager to impart her information that she wanted to close the gap between the words leaving her mouth and reaching his ears. "Project: Stargazer? The shitshow that recruited me? A stargazer's a type of flower—an orchid. And not just any orchid…"

McKenna fixed his gaze on hers. "A hybrid," he said softly.

N N N

After speaking to Casey, McKenna did what he maybe should have done as soon as they arrived here. Using one of the burner phones they'd acquired, he keyed in the most familiar phone number of his lifetime.

It only rang once. When Emily answered, her voice was frantic.

"It's me," McKenna said.

"Tell me he's okay."

McKenna turned to look at his son, sitting apparently contentedly with Nebraska, who was smoking a cigarette, and taking care to blow the smoke in the opposite direction. "He's fine. He's with me. I'll bring him home when it's—"

"It's okay," she interrupted. "Don't say anything. Be safe."

She hung up. No explanation.

McKenna frowned. Emily's message had been loud and clear. She wasn't alone.

Emily ended the call, trying to hide the vengeful sneer on her face. Her boy was okay—that was all she had needed to know. She turned her back on the cadre of black ops agents who'd filled her kitchen, and dropped the phone into the sink's garbage disposal. One of them shouted and another reached for her, but they were too late to stop her from flicking on both the water and the disposal. The sound of the sharp blades chopping up the phone while the water ruined anything they might salvage gave her a thrill of pleasure, deep in her chest.

She turned toward them, letting them see her fury.

"You guys fucked with the wrong family."

Still blazing, she pushed through the agents filling her kitchen, crossed to the open door leading to Rory's basement sanctuary, and clumped down the wooden steps. Just before the call from Quinn, a couple of guys, surveillance techs, had gone down there without her permission, and she wanted to know what they were up to.

Entering the basement, she was incensed to see one of them pick up a remote-control T-rex that was standing atop one of Rory's notebooks in what he called his 'Control Area' and toss it disdainfully over his shoulder. The T-rex hit the floor with a clatter. Emily hurtled across the room like a tornado, snatching up the dinosaur as she went, and shoved her way between the two men. Waving the T-rex in the startled tech's face, she barked, "Hey! Don't throw the toys!"

The tech looked at her with an expression that was half-sneer, half-apology, as if he was uncertain how to respond. Before he could decide, there was an almighty crash from the kitchen above, and it wasn't merely the sound of something being dropped or falling over, but the sound of major damage—the kind of sound you might hear if the kitchen ceiling collapsed, and the entire contents of the room above smashed through onto the floor below.

Emily and the two techs froze, looking up at the basement ceiling, as if they expected that to collapse in on them too. Then the two guys reacted, drawing guns almost in unison, one of them dashing past a bewildered Emily and up the stairs, while the other—the one that had thrown the T-rex—looked at her and held up a hand, suddenly solicitous: *For your own safety, stay here.*

They waited. Heard running footsteps. And then— suddenly, shockingly—the sound of gunfire. Three, four, five shots.

Emily went rigid, raising herself up on her toes, her fingers spasming out like the defensive spines on a puffer fish.

Holy shit, what was happening up there? She couldn't believe she was hearing this. Gunshots! In *her* house?

She was terrified, yes, but she was also angry. How dare they? Whoever this was, how *fucking* dare they? Almost unconsciously, she began to walk toward the basement stairs, her steps slow, cautious, her eyes fixed on the now closed door at the top.

Maybe she should hide? Arm herself? Who would be next through that door? Friend or foe?

And then, a hard, bright, furious thought: *What the fuck have you got us into here, Quinn?*

After the crash and the running footsteps and the gunshots came silence. Three seconds of silence… four… She took another tentative step forward.

And then the world fell in on her.

Or rather, it fell in behind her. Another crash at her back, like a small bomb had gone off, and suddenly she was throwing herself forward as her head and shoulders were showered with splinters of wood and flecks of plaster.

Rubbing her streaming eyes, choking on dust, she

clambered to her feet and turned—and in an instant, it was as though everything she had believed, everything she had relied on her entire life, was ripped unceremoniously away. Because standing in her basement, beneath a hole which even now was raining swirls of white dust down onto its shoulders, was what appeared to be a demon from Hell. Ten feet tall, maybe more, it had a face like all her worst nightmares rolled into one, and in its fearsomely taloned right fist it was clutching the still twitching body of a dead mercenary.

No, scratch that. It was holding *the top half* of a body. Because its poor victim, whoever he had been, had been severed, or pulled apart, or twisted off, at the waist. Blood and other weightier things were now sliding and pouring out of the massive rent and splatting on the basement floor. But if the sight of this alone wasn't bad enough, Emily now saw the demon take hold of the corpse's dangling, exposed spine in its left hand, and with one practiced tug, rip it from the body as casually as a child might rip a Band-Aid from a wound.

She almost passed out. She almost threw up. It was only a fierce sense of self-preservation that prevented her from doing either. Her entire focus since turning around had been on the demon and its victim, but now she realized that the second tech, the one who had thrown aside the T-rex she was still clutching in her hand, was still standing over by Rory's now dust-shrouded Control Area, much closer to the demon than she was.

His face was ghost-white—though whether through fear or simply plaster dust it was impossible to tell—and he was whimpering, cowering, like a beaten dog that didn't want to be beaten anymore. Not that the demon was prepared to show even a shred of pity. With a lightning-quick spin, it flicked out its wrist, and the spinal column lashed toward the man, like a striking cobra made of bones, and wound tightly around his neck, garroting him.

Emily had seen enough—*more* than enough. This latest atrocity galvanized her to spin round and race toward the basement stairs. With every step she took, she expected to hear the clattering *crack* of the demon's bone-whip, expected to feel herself lifted off her feet. As she scrambled up the stairs, she had only one thought in her mind: *If I'm going to die, please God, let it be quick.*

The Upgrade watches the human creature scuttling to safety with dispassion, even disgust, and considers crushing the life from it—it is a worthless thing, after all. But in the end, it is the sheer insignificance of the creature's life that saves it; the Upgrade has more important concerns.

Looking around, it focuses on a bank of screens and other devices. Lights are blinking and flickering, and images swirl on the screens themselves. To the Upgrade this technology seems primitive, basic, and yet there is such a wide range of equipment here, all of it operative, and all of it contained within a small, domestic space, that it is suggestive of an acute intelligence, of a mind that is both enquiring and forever striving to better itself—and that the Upgrade can admire.

Turning in a slow circle, the alien scans a series of framed photographic images on the walls. Here is one of a young male human and a mature male human, both wearing identical garments, the older human with his arm around the younger one's shoulders. Here is another image of the older human, and this time he is wearing garments and carrying a weapon, which the Upgrade knows identifies him as a warrior, a soldier.

Tramping through human offal, the Upgrade moves across to a seating area and picks up a receptacle made of a pliable synthetic material. The contents of the receptacle do not interest the Upgrade, but the label attached to it does. Scanning the human markings, it translates them as 'R. McKenna'. A label of identification, which may at some point prove useful.

Moving from surface to surface, the Upgrade now spies something infinitely more interesting. It knows the young human has had access to some of its species' equipment, and even that it may have deciphered some of the readings on that equipment—certainly enough, whether intentionally or unintentionally, to affect the systems on the Upgrade's own ship. But this document here—primitive, fashioned by hand— suggests an even greater understanding and intelligence than the Upgrade had previously given the young human credit for. Picking up the flimsy sheet of what its sensors inform it is mostly plant-based pulp and chemicals, its analyzing and translation systems identify the strange markings as a map, on which interstates and landmarks, all of which have been meticulously labeled, surround a tiny shape—a shape that the Upgrade recognizes instantly.

It is the ship. The ship that it has been searching for.

N N N

Nettles wandered down to the privacy of a small clump of trees to relieve himself. It wasn't that he was shy, it was just that with Casey and the boy around he wanted to display a little decorum.

After zipping himself up, he stood for a moment, enjoying the coolness of the night air on his face, the gurgling of a brook close by and the soft chirrup of insects.

Then he frowned. Along with the chirruping, he could hear a weird clicking sound, as if something were purring, or growling, deep in its throat. He peered into the darkness of the trees... only to realize, when the sound came again, that it was behind him.

He whipped around, raising his weapon.

But by the time he saw the Predator dog's gleaming eyes and the flash of its clacking mandibles, the opportunity to pull the trigger had passed.

The tread of a boot caught his attention, and Rory turned to see his father appear. Stashing his phone in a pocket, he crouched down.

"Talked to your Mom. She's fine."

Rory let an awkward silence grow even more awkward before he replied.

"Mom says you're a killer."

His father's brow furrowed. "I'm a soldier."

"What's the difference?"

Nebraska seemed not to be listening. He shifted away from them. Over in the RV, Casey stood by the window. Rory could see her, and they were close enough that she could probably hear as well, but like Nebraska she acted as if she couldn't hear a thing.

"When you like it," his dad said. "That's when you're a killer."

He looked suddenly at a loss, as if he didn't know quite where to go from here, as if he didn't know how to talk to his own son. He glanced up at the stars, and then pointed. "Which one do you suppose they're from?"

"The one on the left," Rory replied confidently. A joke. His father never really got his jokes.

This time, though, Quinn McKenna nodded. "That's the one I was gonna say."

Silence between them again, but now it was almost companionable. Rory shifted a little, tapping his stick on the ground. Then abruptly he said, "Sorry I never grew up. Y'know, the way you wanted."

His father sighed and ran his hands over his face as if scrubbing it clean. "Yeah, well. Truth is… I never grew up the way I wanted either."

Rory liked that. He watched as his father stood up and stretched his back.

"Are we gonna get killed?" he asked.

His father seemed to really think about it for a moment. Then he shook his head.

"Nope."

"Okay."

McKenna shifted uncomfortably. He'd never been good at communicating with Rory, but he was trying. The kid went back to drawing in the dirt, and McKenna took stock of his unit again. He spotted Nebraska standing guard. Casey remained in the RV—it occurred to him that she'd become just as much a part of the unit as any of them, for as long as she wanted to be. Of course, given that some black box spookshow division of the federal government was after them, she might not have another choice.

He was just wondering whether he could risk getting a couple of hours sleep when he saw Nebraska tense up and spin round, taking aim at the brush at the edge of the field.

"Company's coming!" Nebraska snapped.

McKenna heard it, then—they all did. Something crashing through the brush, moving fast in the dark. Gun barrels came up, everyone taking aim... and a second later Nettles burst from the brush into the moonlight, and he wasn't alone. On his tail, bounding and crashing, mandibles clicking, was a Predator dog.

"Son of a bitch!" Baxley shouted, taking aim.

"Whoa, whoa!" Nettles said, throwing up his hands as if to ward them off.

What the hell? McKenna thought.

But it only took another moment for him to realize the Predator dog was not chasing Nettles, but merely bounding after him like an excited puppy. A glint of metal in the dark, and they all recognized the monster—it was the one from the school. The one Nebraska had shot through the skull with a bolt gun. It seemed the big, ugly bastard had tracked them like some faithful mutt!

Clumping to a halt, laughing a little, Nettles said, "Jesus, Nebraska, you lobotomized the poor sumbitch."

They all watched curiously as the thing wandered around like an obedient, if addled, puppy. It gazed at Nettles as if he was its master, then looked around and suddenly started trotting toward Rory. Remembering that the boy had been its original target, and wondering whether it might have some residue of its former duty still rattling around in its damaged brain, McKenna jumped up to intercept the beeline it was making toward his son, but even as he started to run he knew he'd never reach Rory before the alien did.

Fearful, Rory rose and grabbed a length of wood. He hurled it at the Predator dog, but the monster ducked, and the wood sailed over its head. Instead of continuing toward Rory, however, it turned… then padded away to retrieve the wood! The clicking, grunting monster rushed over to Nettles and dropped the small log at his feet.

"Well, I'll be all go-to-hell," Nettles said. He grinned around at them like a proud but bashful father.

While the Loonies played with their new pet, throwing sticks for it and laughing as it retrieved them, Casey went back inside the RV. After a while, satisfied that the Predator dog wasn't about to eat his son after all, McKenna joined her, grabbing himself another beer to steady his nerves.

Blowing a lock of hair away from her face, Casey gestured toward his bottle. "Gimme a sip of that."

She took the beer from him and gestured out the window, nodding toward Rory, who was back to drawing in the dirt, ignoring the antics of the men. "You know, a lot of experts think being on the spectrum's not a disorder. Some think it might even be the next evolutionary step."

"Yeah?" McKenna replied, displaying no emotion. He looked at her a moment, then said, "Goin' down the street once? He sees this homeless guy, runs right over. 'Hey man, what's your name?' Meanwhile, I'm thinkin': *Where's the nearest edged weapon?* I see a target; he sees a friend." He gave a crooked grin, half-affectionate, half-regretful, and took a swig of his beer. "All I can do is ruin him. So, I stay away."

His words almost felt like a confession, and for a few seconds he studied the beer label on the bottle, embarrassed and ashamed. When he finally glanced up, he was surprised to see Casey was looking at him with an almost tender expression.

"Can I be honest with you?" she asked.

He nodded.

Gently, she said, "That's the dumbest fucking thing I've ever heard."

He started to chuckle, but didn't reply. In the conversational lull, Casey cocked her head at a distant, growing burr. It took her a moment to realize the sound was the approach of a helicopter, chopping at the air.

McKenna, however, recognized the sound instantly. By the time Casey had figured it out, he had already jerked upright and then slammed out the door of the RV, into the darkness. Casey took a deep breath and followed him out. Whatever came next, they were all in it together, for better or for worse.

She had a terrible feeling it was going to be worse.

18

Bursting from the RV, McKenna nearly ran headlong into Nettles, who stood frozen in the field, listening to the sound of the incoming chopper. All the amusement that had been on the man's face just minutes earlier had vanished, leaving just the soldier behind. The warrior.

"Sounds like a Pave Hawk," Nettles said, glancing at McKenna. "Sikorsky. Not civilian."

This was all McKenna needed to hear. He whirled around, scanning the team. Baxley, Coyle, Lynch, Nebraska, Nettles himself, Casey... and Rory. Jesus, he wished he could have taken the kid home, but nowhere was safe for Rory right now. Nowhere. He consoled himself with the thought that as long as he was with his son, he could at least try his best to keep the kid alive.

How the hell had it come to this?

"Lights out! Move!" he barked, even as he darted back to the RV, reached inside, and killed the lights.

When he turned, he saw that the Loonies were all

looking to him, waiting on orders. He'd become their ersatz CO, which meant it was on him to formulate a plan. Right now, his only plan was to keep as many of them alive—and out of the clutches of their various enemies—as possible. Whatever happened in the next few minutes, if some of them kept to the shadows, there was always hope for the others. If they were all captured, the government could tell any story they wanted about the violence and fear unfolding tonight.

Yet, in their faces, he could see that they thought of themselves as a team—that they wouldn't like the idea of splitting apart. They needed something to cling to. The Loonies needed a mission.

"We're gonna need air transport," McKenna said. He glanced at Nettles. "And maybe some incendiaries. Nebraska, you're with me. The rest of you, go. Get moving!"

They all stood a little straighter. Even Rory. One by one, the Loonies saluted McKenna, sealing the deal—making it official. He was their commanding officer. He snapped a salute in return, trying to hide how absurdly moved he suddenly felt, and the Loonies took that as their cue. They bolted, grabbing weapons on the way, and disappeared into the woods at the edge of the field.

McKenna grabbed Rory's hand, nodded to Casey and Nebraska, and the four of them ran across the field. Tall grass waved around them, but he knew it wouldn't be enough to hide them. They'd only run five yards when they nearly tripped over the Predator dog, a thick stick clenched in its mandibles.

Casey rushed at it, making silent shooing motions

with her hands. "Go," she urged, but the bolt through its head hadn't just tamed the monstrosity. Dumb as a stump, it capered back and forth with every shooing motion, thinking Casey was playing with it.

While they'd been in the area, the men had spread out to clean their weapons and take inventory. Casey spotted something on the ground and bent to retrieve it. Only when she stood up did McKenna see that it was an errant grenade, sloppily left behind by one of the Loonies. He'd have ripped them a new asshole if they were still standing there. Instead, he felt relief as Casey tossed the grenade—pin still safely in—toward an irrigation ditch. The Predator dog raced after it, snatched it up, and then tumbled into the ditch.

"Dad, we're never gonna make it," Rory said.

McKenna gave him a tug and they started running again. Casey and Nebraska fell in behind them, racing toward an old barn a hundred yards across the field.

The helicopter roared in from over the tree line. The chop of its rotors went from loud to deafening as it swept overhead, circled back, and then hovered above them, its spotlight stabbing down onto McKenna and the others like God had decided it was time for them to have a conversation. They were caught dead to rights, nowhere to run.

McKenna let go of his son's hand and spread his arms, to make sure the shooters up in the chopper knew he didn't have a gun. Nebraska and Casey did the same.

Moments later the Sikorsky was on the ground, tall grass bent by the blowback of the rotors. The door slid open, and a figure jumped down into the field. McKenna recognized Agent Traeger immediately, and reluctantly had to admire the man's courage. Though his men followed him out of the chopper, all of them armed and with their weapons trained on McKenna, Nebraska, Casey, and Rory, Traeger had exited first and unarmed. Whatever he wanted from them, it wasn't a firefight.

Even so, McKenna shifted to put himself between the mercenaries' guns and his son.

Traeger stopped a dozen feet away and regarded them impassively. "Where is it?"

"Where's what?" McKenna replied.

"The device," Traeger said. He mimed placing something on his arm, as if he was wearing the same type of wrist gauntlet the Predators wore. "It goes right in here."

McKenna knew instantly what he meant, remembered the thing in Rory's hand—what the original Predator had come for, and what the Upgrade had killed him for.

"That... *thing* has it."

One of Traeger's men—not a soldier, but an aide of some kind—gave them a look of disdain.

"I see," the aide said. "Well, if that's your position, I think it's time for some *robust* discussion."

As the helicopter's rotors finally stopped spinning, throwing an eerie silence over the farmland, armed mercenaries hustled forward and grabbed McKenna and Nebraska. Rory started to argue, but McKenna quieted him with a look. The mercs started marching McKenna and Nebraska toward the barn across the field. In the dark, Casey and Rory were accompanied by Traeger and his aide. No guns were aimed at the scientist and the boy, but they were no less prisoners, and in no less danger.

McKenna had his face in the dirt. He didn't like the taste. His thoughts were all static fuzz, like a TV screen when the cable connection went out. His face throbbed where boots had kicked him, and his ribs ached. He tried to get his knees under him and another boot kicked him. He grunted and went down on his face again. Thoughts of Rory filled his head. He pictured the kid drawing in the dirt... then sliding in the dirt to get to first base... and somehow that led his mind to an image of the Loonies saluting him.

An image flickered in his head—the men he'd lost in the jungle, the smell of their blood, the Predator uncloaking, soaked in gore. He should have killed the bastard at the time, but it was dead now, wasn't it? Muddy as his thoughts were, he knew that. The giant one, the Upgrade, had hung that son of a bitch like a side of meat. He wondered how many more there were, how many on their home planet. How many on *his* home planet?

"You hid it once," a voice said.

McKenna glanced up at the two mercs who loomed over him. They had him in some kind of holding pen beside the barn. One of them kicked him again.

"In the mail," the mercenary reminded him. "Where'd you hide it this time?"

With the next kick, McKenna coughed up blood.

Fuzzy as his mind might be, he knew that was a bad sign.

N N N

The mercs had taken Casey up into the barn's loft, and secured her to one of a stack of rickety wooden chairs that had no doubt been left over from a hoedown or something. The barn's interior was not nearly as romantically antique as she'd expected, given the general condition of the structure from the outside. The place was big and sprawling, with wooden crates stacked next to the rows of chairs at one end and a string of lights along the beams overhead. Not the sort of place teenagers would come for a roll in the hay in the torrid novels she'd read in secret in middle school.

She tugged against the handcuffs, but it was a futile gesture. Traeger, who had been leaning against the wall, observing her as if she was an interesting specimen in an aquarium, now wandered casually across and stood in front of her—loomed over her, in fact.

"You're pretty handy with a gun," he said. "Where'd you learn?"

She wasn't about to discuss her family history with a creep like Traeger. He wasn't worth it. "America," she said.

Traeger snorted. "Funny. Know what my job description is?"

Casey thought back to the moment when the Predator had first burst to life in the examination room back at the Project: Stargazer complex, and how Traeger had suddenly been conspicuously absent.

"Guy-who-flees-when-monster-appears?" she snapped, and winked at him. "You're good."

Ignoring the jibe, he said, "Close. I'm in acquisitions."

Casey glared at him. In truth, she wanted to know more, but the handcuffs and the armed guards in the barn and whatever Traeger's men were doing to McKenna didn't make her feel like developing any sort of rapport with him right now, however false and temporary, so she remained silent.

Undeterred, he went on, "I look up, I wait—and catch what falls out of the sky."

"Alien tech?" she said, interested despite herself.

"Yup. Seems Predators, they don't just polish pelvic bones twenty-four seven. They conquered space. I wager there's a whole faction… like you."

"Acerbic?" She weighed her options, mind racing. "Listen, I can help you. I've been studying the biolog—"

"*Shut the fuck up!*" he screamed at her suddenly, shocking her, causing her to dig her heels into the dirt floor, rock back in her chair. For a moment, the wooden walls boomed with the echo of his fury, and then abruptly he was calm again, smiling at her. Only this time his smile didn't seem as charming as it once had. This time, it seemed cruel and bottomless. "You stole our secrets, Dr. Brackett. That's not one 'no,' that's two 'nos.' That's a no-no. Now, I need to locate that ship so… one more time. *Where is the device?*"

Casey felt her throat go dry. She licked her lips. "What's on that ship?" she asked.

Traeger's smile slipped again, but this time he didn't scream at her. He simply let out an exasperated sigh and rubbed a hand over his closely cropped hair. He was clearly frazzled, stressed out. Which may not have been good news for Casey and McKenna, but she felt a certain satisfaction at seeing it nonetheless.

"You wanna know what's on that ship?" he snapped. "Okay, for starters—*a ship*. A fucking interstellar spacecraft. We don't got one of those."

"That's a really good point," she conceded.

"So." He leaned closer to her. "*You* tell *me*—what's on that ship?"

She looked into his eyes. Brown as roasted chestnuts, but cold all the same. "Gravy," she said.

He nodded, straightened up. "Exactly. Gravy."

Rory sat in the RV, drawing in a notebook one of the soldiers had given him. He preferred it to drawing in the dirt. The helicopter sat dark and silent about twenty meters away—the pilot had moved it closer to the barn. One bored-looking guard had been posted to keep an eye on Rory, and he didn't mind so much. He was just waiting to find out what the soldiers were going to do with him and his dad and Casey and Nebraska. He liked Casey and Nebraska, he had decided.

His dad and Nebraska were soldiers too, so he thought it wouldn't be so bad. The alien monster, the huge one, was clearly the bad guy. Rory had seen enough monster movies to know what happened when the military went up against a giant monster, so he figured they would work all of this out together, eventually.

For now, he just wanted to draw.

Agent Traeger's aide, whose name—Rory had learned—was Sapir, sat inside the helicopter with his laptop open. Rory wasn't sure if Sapir thought he was deaf or that his Asperger's made him stupid, but the man wasn't making any attempt to keep him from overhearing the conversation he was having over Skype on his laptop.

The man on the other end of the Skype call was a cryptographer. Sapir had said as much, but Rory would have figured it out anyway. He wasn't stupid, no matter what Sapir thought. The cryptographer sounded tense, but Rory wouldn't have been able to identify what sort of tension the man's voice betrayed if Sapir hadn't kept telling him not to get so irritated.

That's what irritation sounds like, he told himself. His mom had told him he needed to focus on strategies of socialization, and trying to identify emotion by tone of voice was one of those. Rory had been trying, but didn't feel like he was getting any better at it.

"You haven't found the spacecraft," the apparently irritated cryptographer snapped at Sapir. "Why are we trying to crack the entry code?"

"Because when we do find it, it would be great if we could get into the fucking thing!" Sapir barked.

Now *that* sounded like irritation. Rory felt pleased with himself for recognizing it, but he supposed shouting and swearing were big clues, so maybe he shouldn't pat himself on the back too much.

The guard had taken an interest in Rory's drawing. The guy came a bit closer, peering over his shoulder.

"What's that?" the guard asked.

"Map," Rory said.

"Map to what?"

Rory shrugged without looking up. "The alien's ship."

The guard went quiet for a few seconds before bending over and reaching toward the drawing pad. His hand paused a few inches from it. The smile on the man's face did not reach his eyes. Even Rory could see that.

"Do you mind if I…?"

Rory shrugged. The guard took the pad and Rory started tapping his pencil on the toe of his sneaker. He didn't want to give up the pad—drawing was the only thing he could do to occupy himself here, and it helped keep him calm. His mother was an artist, and though he didn't aspire to follow her in that vocation, he understood the way she lost herself in her art. He found himself able to do the same thing and he always enjoyed the places that drawing took him, even just doodling. Sometimes he drew things to help himself envision them, or to make sure he wouldn't forget.

The guard walked the pad over to the helicopter, trying to get Sapir's attention, but Sapir waved him away.

"I'm busy."

On the Skype connection, the cryptographer continued to plead his case. "Sir, we're trying. I'm telling you, the access sequence… it could be a hundred digits, for all we know."

"Fifteen," Rory said aloud.

Sapir and the guard both froze. Even the cryptographer on the laptop had gone silent.

Rory glanced across at Sapir through the open door of the RV. "I'm pretty sure it's fifteen."

Less than ninety seconds passed while Sapir rushed inside and emerged with Agent Traeger in tow. Rory knew he was the guy responsible for people pointing guns at them tonight, and for all the trouble his dad was in. Traeger had the drawing pad in his hand as he walked over to him and smiled like they were best friends.

"Hi, Rory," Agent Traeger said. "I'm Will. I understand you know where the spaceship is."

Rory bit his lip, shoulders tense.

Suddenly, Traeger was no longer friendly. He tapped the drawing Rory had made. "You want to play grown-up? Man to man? We're not going to let your dad go. Not until you give us what we want."

"What if I won't tell you?" Rory said.

Traeger shook his head and looked just like Mr. Cushing, his math teacher, sometimes did when one of Rory's classmates disappointed him. "Oh, now, Rory... I thought we were playing grown-up."

For the first time, Rory felt a little afraid.

19

The world tilted beneath McKenna. He still had a mouthful of dirt and he was certain there was cowshit mixed in there, too. Groggy, he had just enough of his wits about him to hope this wasn't a concussion. The two mercs still loomed above him, but they'd held off on the kicking for a minute.

He spat a wad of blood and soil onto the ground. His face was swollen, his jaw stiff. He breathed through his nose with a reedy whistle and the copper stink of his own blood. They'd worked him over good. Internal darkness kept washing over his thoughts, as if unconsciousness was an ocean trying to drown him.

Taking a breath, he glanced up, eyes narrowed as he peered through the slats in the fence around the holding pen. The helicopter sat there, and its rotors had started to turn. The familiar whine of the chopper gearing up forced him to pay attention. He saw several figures climbing aboard and wondered where they were off to. Had they found the Upgrade Predator? Had they found the gizmo Rory had gotten his hands on?

The mercs were talking among themselves. As far as they were concerned, he was done. As good as dead. The only thing remaining would be the bullet that punctuated the end of his personal sentence.

McKenna squeezed his eyes shut. One of the people getting on board the chopper seemed so much smaller than the others. If he hadn't been kicked in the head, it might have gained him a second, but then he blinked his vision clear and realized the little guy was Rory and that he was being dragged on board. These fuckers working for Traeger weren't content to question them—these assholes were about to take his son on a chopper ride, take him away from his old man, use him somehow.

The chopper started to lift off. It whorled skyward.

That moment or two had cost McKenna a chance to reach Rory. Rage boiled behind his eyes.

"Golf tomorrow?" one of the mercs asked the other, ever so casual, as he drew his gun to finish Quinn McKenna. Whatever they had needed him for, they clearly didn't need him anymore.

"Why not?" the other merc replied, so reasonable, so personable. They had a golf date, these two assholes.

McKenna coughed up ropey strands of blood. "You know what burns me up..." he managed. "You never even... read my file. Did you?"

The mercs traded amused glances.

"What makes you think that?" the gunman asked, voice thick with condescension.

"'Cause you're making plans for tomorrow," McKenna said.

The mercs laughed, thinking about their tee time.

"Worst part," McKenna went on, "is you making me lie to my son. I really don't like to do that."

The second merc snickered. "What lie did you tell him?"

"That I wouldn't enjoy this," McKenna grunted.

His hand darted out, snatched the first guy's forearm. Using his other hand for leverage, he twisted, put his weight behind it, and snapped the asshole's forearm with a satisfyingly audible *crack* that echoed like a gunshot across the holding pen. He liberated the gun from the merc's flopping hand and pressed it to his eye, then pulled the trigger. Muffled by eyeball and brain and skull and hair as it exited the back of the guy's head, it didn't sound much like a gunshot at all.

The dead merc dropped with a thud as McKenna stood and leveled the gun at the second merc, who froze, staring at him, trying to figure out how the hell a guy who'd looked halfway dead could move so fast.

On the other side of the holding pen, Nebraska, his hands tied behind his back, snorted up a mouthful of blood and phlegm and spat it into the straw. His body was throbbing from the beating he'd taken, but it was all just bumps and bruises. He was pretty sure nothing was broken.

He'd heard the helicopter taking off, and not much since. He'd been left unguarded—surely it was too much to hope that Traeger and his goons had lost interest in them and headed off to pastures new? If Nebraska were in Traeger's position, he certainly wouldn't be leaving any loose ends behind. The thought had barely formed in his mind when the door of the holding pen opened, framing a black-clad merc.

Me and my big mouth.

Then the man stumbled forward, going down on one knee. Nebraska was about to hit him with a quip—*What's this? A proposal or an execution?*—when he saw that behind the merc was McKenna, looking a little worse for wear, but pointing a gun at the guy's head.

"Untie him," McKenna said, nudging his prisoner with the gun.

The merc scrambled to his feet and obeyed, making quick work of it despite his trembling hands.

"They have Rory," McKenna explained, then frowned as Nebraska rose to his feet with a groan. "Shit, they rough you up?"

Nebraska rubbed his wrists, which were chafed and bleeding. "Whatever. Done worse to myself back in the day. I was the kinda drunk who thought the fastest way down a long flight of stairs was to just relax." He nodded at the remaining merc. "What about him?"

Three seconds later, the merc's face had left a permanent impression in the barn's outer wall. Streaking the wall with blood, the merc slid down to thump to the ground like a discarded laundry bag.

Nebraska winced. "That's what I get for asking dumb questions."

N N N

When the gun barrel prodded the back of Casey's skull, she closed her eyes tight and waited to die. Her heart beat loud in her ears and she found herself remembering the first time she'd ever looked through a decent telescope. Her pulse had quickened then, too, and her imagination had been set afire. All her hopes and ambitions had been born in that moment, and now she was going to die because of them.

Not only that, she was going to die on her ass, wrists handcuffed to a chair. Somehow that bothered her more than the concept of death itself. If she had to die, she wanted to do it standing up.

She felt the gun barrel twitch against her head. No bullet followed. Her guard had paused at the sound of heavy footfalls in the corridor, clumping noises approaching. They had an intruder.

"Who goes there?" her guard demanded, his voice tight. Maybe he was wondering who to shoot first, or whether he needed her alive, so he could use her for a shield.

The intruder poked his head around the corner, and Casey heard the thin intake of air as the guard started shitting his pants, albeit metaphorically.

Standing there, in the shadows, massive shoulders hunched and mandibles clicking, was the Predator dog with the bolt through its skull. It was a big, dumb, snuffling, drooling brute—it was even wagging its tail, for Christ's sake! But the guard didn't know that the creature had been tamed by the cranial trauma that the bolt gun had inflicted.

In fact, the guard was making little squeaking,

mewling noises now, clearly unsure whether to shoot at the thing and provoke it or just stay still in the hope it would go away.

Casey saw what the Predator dog was carrying in its mouth before the guard did—the grenade from the clearing, which the dumb monster had leaped into the ditch to fetch and had now finally brought back to continue its game. Still lashing its tail from side to side, the beast trotted happily toward her and dropped the grenade into her lap.

She heard the guard mutter something about Jesus as she snatched up the grenade, lurched from the chair, pulled the pin with her teeth and spun toward him. The guard's eyes went wide and he tried to take aim with his gun, but she was too close and he was too distracted, both by the grenade and the Predator dog, and he could only fumble with the barrel as she jerked her handcuffed wrist, whipping the thin wooden chair up at him. The impact caused the gun to go off, the report echoing off the walls and making the Predator dog whine. Before he could fire off another shot, Casey put the grenade down the front of the guard's shirt and turned toward the railing of the loft, dragging the chair behind her. She knew the guard wouldn't have time to shoot at her if he wanted to live.

As she leaped, the chair smashed against the railing and she had a flicker of a moment to fear she'd be snagged on it. Then she plummeted to the floor of the barn, hit the ground and rolled as the chair shattered on impact beside her.

Overhead, the loft exploded. Her ears buzzed, felt like they were stuffed with cotton. From the corner of her eye she saw another merc rushing at her and she pistoned to her feet, swinging the remains of the broken chair around on the handcuff chain in a single, swift motion. The shattered wood smashed the merc in the skull, nearly taking his face off. Blood sprayed out in an arc and spattered the ground as he fell.

More blood showered down from above, in a cloud of dust and dry wall and straw from the explosion in the loft. Casey staggered away, her ears still ringing. As the smoke cleared, she saw the Predator dog clumping down the steps from the loft, totally unscathed. He had something else in his mandibles this time and he dropped his new toy at her feet, still interested in fetch.

Casey had no desire to pick this new toy up, though. It was the scorched head of the guard who'd just been blown to pieces.

Hot bile burned up the back of Casey's throat, but she managed not to puke. As she fought the urge, her ringing ears caught the sound of muffled boot steps approaching on the double. She lifted her cuffed wrist, ready to use the remains of the chair on its chain as an improvised weapon a second time. But then she saw McKenna and Nebraska hustle around the corner, both looking like they'd just survived a gang war. They were both armed, both breathing heavily.

"Hey," McKenna said, almost casually. "Can I interest you in getting the fuck out of here?"

Casey grinned, breathless. "'Getting the fuck out of here' is my middle name."

McKenna shot a sidelong glance at Nebraska. "And I thought 'Gaylord' was bad."

They started to head out, then abruptly McKenna halted, grimaced, clutched his abdomen.

"Oh boy," he muttered.

Casey looked at him in concern. "What?"

"Must be the coffee," McKenna said apologetically. "Uh… excuse me."

He bolted, disappearing around the corner, heading toward the barn's exit door.

Casey turned to Nebraska, bewildered. "Where's he going?"

Nebraska smiled and raised an eyebrow. "I think he's about to give us a tactical advantage."

20

Five minutes later McKenna was back, looking washed-out, sweaty, but no longer in gastric distress. Clearly embarrassed by what had just happened, he looked at Casey and said without preamble, "Doc, if what you're saying is true, my son's headed for a spaceship, and so is a ten-foot monster."

"Eleven," Nebraska corrected, and shrugged. "I used to be a contractor. Got an eye for measurements."

McKenna scowled at the irrelevancy. Sensing his agitation, Casey laid a reassuring hand on his arm. "Hey," she murmured. "We'll get him back."

McKenna looked anguished. "He's just a kid, he can't—"

"He's not just a kid," she interrupted firmly. "He's a chess prodigy with an eidetic memory who decrypted Predator language. He'll be fine."

McKenna nodded, though not entirely convincingly, and they went outside. Looking at the RV, McKenna knew it wasn't going to get them anywhere—not without being picked up fast. As soon as someone bothered to check on the dead bastards back at the barn, they'd put a BOLO out on the vehicle. McKenna knew they needed new transport, and hopefully the rest of the Loonies were on to that. His main priority right now, though, was to make sure they had enough firepower to survive the mission before them.

Together, he and Nebraska went through the RV, stuffing backpacks with as much ordnance as they could carry. A dozen ways to kill people—anyone who tried to get between McKenna and his son—went into those backpacks. Thanks to the lunatic gun seller who'd stocked up the RV in the first place, they also had earwig comms units, and McKenna grabbed them so they could all be linked up, whatever happened from here on in.

They had just finished loading up when a new sound made them all freeze, a whirring from over the trees. Another damn helicopter. McKenna drew a gun and glanced at Nebraska.

"Traeger coming back?" Nebraska asked.

If it is, McKenna thought, *then* this *time there will be a firefight*. All three of them hurried out of the RV and into the soft light of daybreak. They stared into the dawn sky and McKenna's jaw dropped.

"Is that… pink?" Nebraska asked in a strained voice.

It was. And what was more, it had the Victoria's Secret logo emblazoned proudly on the side.

"Jesus tap-dancing Christ," McKenna said slowly.

"That what you asked for?" Nebraska asked, as Casey laughed.

McKenna shrugged. "It'll do."

By now the chopper had descended enough that McKenna could make out Nettles in the pilot's seat, and Coyle waving merrily at them from the side hatch. Despite himself, a grin spread across his face as he hurried toward the helicopter. He heard Nebraska whooping behind him as the rotors slowed. The tall grass in the field bent and waved, and the door popped open and now McKenna could see Baxley and Lynch in there with Nettles and Coyle. If he'd thought these bastards were crazy before they'd somehow managed to steal a Victoria's Secret helicopter, he thought they were twice as crazy now, but he loved the hell out of them for it.

Yes, they needed transport. But they also needed to be inconspicuous. Flying around in this thing in broad daylight was a terrible idea, but it was still better than sitting on their asses in the middle of a grassy field without any way of going after Rory.

Carrying backpacks full of weaponry, McKenna, Casey, and Nebraska climbed into the helicopter, enduring the welcoming cheers and the cocky grins of the Loonies, and moments later they were lifting off. McKenna looked down at the RV and the field and the barn that had been the last place he'd seen Rory. He promised himself it would not be his final memory of his son.

"Very inconspicuous," he yelled, over the roar of the chopper.

"We had to kill seven Victoria's Secret models," Coyle said proudly.

Casey's face went white. "Tell me you're joking."

"I'm joking," Coyle replied, horrified that she'd taken him seriously. "I'd sooner piss on the *Mona Lisa*."

Nettles throttled up and the chopper took on speed, careening across the sky. The landscape rushed past below as McKenna turned to Nettles.

"Anything on board we can use?"

Nettles shrugged. "We got some low-grade pyro and about three dozen promotional tote bags."

Nebraska held up a tube of exfoliating gel. "Yeah, Predators hate this shit."

Baxley edged over to McKenna. Almost matter-of-factly, as if he was asking where they were going to stop for lunch, he said, "Cap, we gonna die, you think? Just curious."

Hearing him, Nettles chipped in from the pilot's seat. "Yeah, we're dealing with a hybrid…"

"That thing," Coyle called. "It's a fucking survival machine."

Despite their casual bravado, McKenna could tell that the men were jittery, nervous, that they needed a pep talk. Looking at Baxley, but addressing them all, he said, "You. Yesterday you were on a prison bus, barking to yourself. Now you got a gun in your hand. Who's the fucking survivor? Huh?"

Baxley nodded enthusiastically: *Hell, yeah.*

Glancing at Nebraska, McKenna continued, "We put bullets in our head and walk to the fucking hospital. That's who *we* are."

Nebraska grinned.

"So, when it comes to standing on the right side of the dirt?" Now McKenna looked at each of them in turn.

"That motherfucker ain't got shit on us."

The Loonies whooped, punched the air. When the sound had died down, McKenna turned back to Baxley.

"And yes," he said decisively. "We may die."

The men laughed and cheered all over again. Baxley grinned. "Thanks. Just checking."

"Nettles," McKenna said. "We got a twenty?"

"I can follow their chopper," Nettles replied. "I just need to lock in on its frequency."

Casey's brow furrowed. McKenna followed her gaze as she leaned over to look out the window.

"Or," she said, "we can just follow that thing."

Far below the chopper, they could all see the Predator dog hauling ass across country roads and farmland.

The forest pressed in on all sides. The only light came from the headlamps of the military jeep, which seemed to give the looming vegetation a jolting, shadowy life as the vehicle lurched in and out of ruts in the makeshift road.

Rory had been dozing, but now he was awake. Sitting in the back of the jeep, he alternated his gaze between the back of Traeger's head, poking above the seat in front, and the chiaroscuro of white, pitted tree trunks and flat, pale, spade-shaped leaves embedded within a blackness so profound it was like a vacuum.

Beside Rory sat Sapir, Traeger's aide, who hadn't acknowledged him once throughout the entire day-long journey. Rory wondered where they were, and where they were going, but he didn't ask—he wasn't that sort of kid. He shifted his position slightly when the jeep slowed, so he could peer between the two front seats.

He saw temporary floodlights on metal tripods illuminating a row of sawhorses, beyond which a couple of lowboy tractor trailers were parked nose to tail at the side of the road. The temporary barricade was guarded by soldiers in black, like the ones at the barn. Rory counted four of them, their weapons leveled. A fifth approached them. Traeger wound down his window and brandished his ID.

"You mind telling the Wild Bunch to chill out?" he barked.

Rory's mom had once referred to his dad as an alpha male, and so Rory had read up about them. He had learned enough to know that Traeger was one too—or at least, that he tried to be. Rory wasn't sure, though, whether it was the CIA man himself or just his job that made the soldier cower a little, and nod, and scurry away to obey his superior's orders.

After a moment, the sawhorses were pulled aside and the jeep drove through, and at a command from Traeger pulled into the side of the dirt road, just in front of the tractor trailers.

Traeger got out and motioned that Rory should do so too. The vegetation was pressing so close to the door on Rory's side, though, that he had to wait until Sapir had vacated the jeep before he could scramble across the seat and exit on the same side.

The air smelled green and hot and damp. Rory saw Sapir wipe sweat from his brow with a handkerchief that he produced from his pocket. Traeger, on the other hand, looked as cool as ever. He marched off, indicating that they should follow him.

Rory was surprised when they left the road and plunged into the jungle. A route had been marked with arc lamps, but it was still a little tricky picking their way down the side of a ravine thick with undergrowth and dotted with dark rocks that pushed up out of the carpet of verdant green like the humped backs of whales.

Soon they came to an area where the ground was a sea of black mud, which formed a track as wide as a highway through the surrounding vegetation. There was a strange smell, like the ghost of an oil drum fire, and although it was hard to tell in the dark, Rory thought the vegetation on either side of them looked scorched, blackened. He imagined men coming through here armed with flamethrowers, using fire to blast a route through the jungle. But when, after another five minutes of walking, they came to a clearing, surrounded by temporary stadium lights, he saw that what had burned its way through the jungle was nothing so mundane as a few flamethrowers.

Immediately he thought of the map he had drawn in the warmth and safety of his basement den at home, and knew exactly where he was. He was at the crash site of the ship that the Predator—the one that had been killed by the Upgrade—had used to reach Earth.

Even though the ship was broken and spattered with charred, pulped jungle debris, it was still a thing of beauty. Rory gazed up at it in awe, admiring its sleek lines, its economical, streamlined shape.

They had arrived here just in time. A squad of soldiers was unrolling a huge tarpaulin, and even as Rory watched they began to haul it over the ship, presumably to conceal it from potential rubberneckers who might be peering down from passing aircraft.

Rory couldn't understand why the crash site hadn't been discovered before now—he could only suppose that the blackened ground was less visible from the air, and that the original Predator had cloaked the ship, then led Traeger's men well away from it, before allowing itself to be captured—but now that it had, it was a hive of activity. Over on the far side of the clearing, a group of techs were rolling in a giant screen, while others followed behind like an honor guard, holding armfuls of cable attachments to stop them trailing in the mud.

And on the periphery, more soldiers were variously hammering in posts, unrolling lengths of wire fencing, or engaged in the setting up of a generator, so that— Rory assumed—the site could be enclosed within an electrified barrier.

So engrossed was he in all this activity, and in the ship itself, that he had almost forgotten about Traeger. It was only when the man crouched beside him that he recalled who had brought him here.

"So, what do you say?" Trager said. "Think you can get us in there? Because I'm not sure that you can."

Rory was not so out of touch with human emotions that he couldn't recognize Traeger's intentions. "Good reverse psychology, fuckface," he said, deliberately using a word he thought his dad might have used.

Traeger chuckled, but his next words were anything but kind. "Put it this way, then. You love your dad, don't you? You want to see him alive again, right? Then do me a favor…"

He put one hand on his sidearm and gestured with the other toward the hatch of the newly revealed ship. Then he leaned toward the kid and whispered, "Let your love open the door."

Rory might have been on the autism spectrum, but he got the message loud and clear.

If Rory had known where his dad was at that precise moment, he wouldn't have been all that surprised. Despite their differences, he had absolute faith in his dad's prowess as a soldier, and was sure, even though his dad hadn't been around all that much in the last couple years, that if he, Rory, was ever in danger—as he possibly was now—his dad would move Heaven and Hell to help him.

It would almost certainly have given Rory some comfort to know that his dad was looking at him right now. Quinn McKenna, who knew this terrain far better than Traeger and his bozos did, was currently perched on the highest spit of land overlooking the crash site. He was shrouded in foliage, completely camouflaged, his rifle leveled and his eye glued to the sniper scope, which allowed him to see what was happening with crystal clarity.

The pink helicopter was parked in a clearing just over a mile away, and the Loonies and Casey were out and about, doing their stuff. The Loonies might be a maverick bunch, but McKenna had faith not only in their loyalty, but also in their abilities. He didn't know where any of this was ultimately leading, but right now he felt like the leader of *The A-Team*. Just him and his rag-tag bunch of oddballs against the world.

Through his sniper scope he saw Rory approach the crashed Predator ship, flanked by Traeger on his left and his smarmy sidekick, Sapir, on his right. Last time McKenna had been here, the hatch of the pod had been open, sticking straight up in the air like the damaged wing of a crumpled dragonfly. Now, though, it was closed—presumably by the Predator, which had sealed up its ship before allowing itself to be "captured" by Traeger's men and transported to the Stargazer facility. McKenna watched as Rory halted in front of the hatch and examined a panel beside it, Traeger and Sapir looking on. Then his son reached out and began to tap a code sequence into the keypad.

Even though Rory was proud of his dad—and more so than ever after today—he had never wanted to be a soldier like him. He had little desire to shoot anyone, or to be shot at, no matter how noble the cause. But as he stood in front of the Predator's ship, he wished he still had the helmet and gauntlet that had helped him accidentally vaporize the stoner while he was out trick-or-treating. He felt bad about that guy—figured he always would—but if he could have vaporized Agent Traeger, he wouldn't have hesitated for a second.

For most of his life, Rory had never had to consider whether he had courage. He would never have said he was brave in the way his father was brave, but he stood up for himself. Now that he had to think about it, he supposed he had some courage in him. Cornered by bullies, he'd speak up, even fight back if he had to. But he wasn't stupid. Agent Traeger struck him as the sort of person who had no sense of honor or nobility. If this guy needed to murder his father, maybe even his mother, to get Rory to do what he wanted, he did not doubt for a second that Traeger would do it.

So, he unlocked the ship.

Once he'd punched in the code, the hatch opened with a whisper. A cavernous darkness yawned within as the hatch rose. Tentatively, Traeger went first. Rory stood with Sapir, hanging back a moment. If he hadn't stepped inside on his own, he figured Sapir would have nudged him. Traeger had recognized that Rory's brain was an asset, and he had announced his decision to his aide the way a king might. The soldiers around them might think it was crazy for him to bring only Sapir and Rory into the ship, but they took their orders from Traeger and no one would dare challenge him.

Rory didn't have to wonder about the decision, either. Traeger kept the others out because whatever might be inside the alien craft, it was top secret. Which meant that whatever happened after this, Rory would be forced to keep that secret. He imagined that meant Traeger intended him to be dead, but he was alive so far, and he planned to keep it that way.

So, he opened the door and he followed Traeger into the ship, and he didn't even protest when Sapir gripped his arm to keep him from wandering. And he sure as hell didn't try to run. Because where would he go, aboard an alien ship that might have homicidal monsters hiding away somewhere?

Once inside, the three of them gazed around in wonderment. There were symbols everywhere, but it looked precisely as Rory had imagined it. Once they had gotten past the entryway, they spotted several storage units set into the walls. Rory had seen enough movies to know this didn't bode well, that these things might be hibernation chambers, and he shouldn't want to know what they contained.

Except he *did* want to know. He couldn't help himself, and he knew Traeger and Sapir and their whole gang of assholes at Project: Stargazer would also not be able to help themselves, given enough time.

Sure enough, Traeger grinned and rubbed his hands together, like a fat and greedy king who has just had a banquet laid out for him.

"Hook the translator into the mainframe, download everything," he said. Turning to Rory—though only, Rory suspected, because there was no one else there for him to boast to—he added, "Been trying to figure out what these bird-chirping motherfuckers are saying since '87. Gave the Harvard School of Linguistics a billion-dollar grant. Voilà!"

Gazing uneasily around at the tubes, Sapir said, "What's inside these things?"

THE PREDATOR

"It's the property of Project: Stargazer, that's what the fuck it is," Traeger replied.

As he spoke, Rory noticed a control panel, like a podium that jutted from the floor between two of the cylinders. The panel was covered in symbols, the components of the Predator language, or at least some form of iconography that their species understood. Rory could see that each of the stasis cylinders was highlighted in red on the display, with a time-code beside them. The numbers were blinking, as if something had stopped them from continuing to count forward.

Or count down, he thought.

A countdown. It had stopped mid-sequence, the blinking an impatient signal, suggesting that all it would take was someone with the right code to get it moving again.

Rory shook himself from his reverie, abruptly aware that Sapir and Traeger were reacting to a commotion outside the ship. He turned to listen, and heard running footsteps, shouting. Then Traeger's radio squawked. He snatched it angrily from his belt and held it to his ear. Rory heard the urgent voice of one of Traeger's mercenaries.

"Code Three, Code Three, we have motion at the south fence line."

"Send a fire team to take a look," Traeger barked. "Extreme prejudice."

"Local wildlife?" Sapir ventured, but Rory was smiling. "It's my dad. He's gonna save me now."

Traeger knelt beside him. His voice was silky, but he had a look on his face like the bullies at school—mean and spiteful. "Well, if it *is* your daddy—and I truly hope it is—he has to be just about the dumbest motherfucker I've ever met. I mean, a Ranger sniper tripping motion sensors? He'd have to be…"

Then his voice tailed off and his face went slack, his eyes opening in horrified realization. Once again grabbing his radio, he looked wildly at Sapir and said, "He's creating a diversion! It's a fucking divers—"

Before he could bring the radio up to his mouth, it flew from his hand. As though attacked by an invisible force, he was knocked off his feet, his body smashing against a control panel.

Sapir whirled this way and that, eyes and mouth stretched wide with fear, looking for his boss's assailant.

"Howdy," said a voice.

Rory saw the air behind Sapir shimmer and coalesce, and next moment his dad was standing there, face blackened with dirt, a tranquilizer gun locked and loaded, and pointing at Sapir's face.

Sapir looked nervous, but he did his best to sneer. "What, you're gonna kill us with a tranq gun?"

McKenna's voice was low, his hand steady. "You took my boy, so yeah."

He pulled the trigger. The tranq dart passed through Sapir's eye and into his brain.

For an instant, Sapir looked outraged. His remaining eye glared at McKenna. Then the life went out of him and his body dropped in an ungainly sprawl of limbs, so much dead meat.

Even before Traeger's aide hit the floor, McKenna was moving. In one smooth motion he dropped the tranq gun and drew a pistol, which he pressed to Traeger's temple as he hauled the CIA man to his feet by the collar of his jacket.

Rory smiled at Traeger. "Told you," he said brightly.

Traeger looked as if he would have cheerfully strangled the life out of the boy there and then. Instead, he gawked at McKenna, as if unable to believe the sheer insolence of the man.

"You out of your mind?" he exclaimed, spittle flying from his lips. "We literally have you surrounded."

"That's why you're coming with me," said McKenna mildly. "I just want the kid, nobody has to die."

"Umm, Dad?" said Rory, ever the pragmatist, and pointed at Sapir's corpse.

McKenna shrugged. "I mean… y'know… from here forward. Now let's go out there and tell your men to put their guns down."

He shifted his grip from the front of Traeger's collar to the back, and shoved the agent toward the hatch. They exited the ship and started down the ramp. The area directly in front of them was populated by armed mercs, all on high alert. Traeger cleared his throat and the majority of the mercs turned. It took a moment, but suddenly guns were coming up, all pointing in their direction.

Pressing close in against Traeger's back, McKenna hissed in his ear, "Tell 'em."

Traeger raised his voice. "If Captain McKenna doesn't lower his weapon in the next ten seconds, shoot the kid's knees out." He twisted his head back to regard McKenna, curling his lip. "That work for you?"

McKenna jerked his head at Rory, who moved to stand behind his father, pressing himself against McKenna's back as tightly as McKenna was pressed against Traeger. To McKenna's dismay, however, he saw the mercs fanning out around them, and he knew that if he wanted to absolutely guarantee his boy's safety, their only option was to withdraw to the dubious sanctuary of the Predator's ship.

In truth, he'd misjudged Traeger's reaction, and that irked him. He'd potentially bet his life—and worse, Rory's—on the fact that Traeger, with a gun at his head, would turn out to be a coward. But the CIA agent had displayed a reckless bravery that had surprised McKenna.

"Fuck you!" he snarled into Traeger's ear, trying to reestablish the upper hand. "My guys have this place covered from every angle."

But even now, Traeger refused to be cowed.

"Funny story," he said dismissively, "I don't care. Ten… nine… eight…"

McKenna took another look at the mercs surrounding them, and thought: *Shit.*

21

Armed with a long rifle, Lynch was crouching close to where McKenna had crouched before him, looking down on the crash site below. His vantage point, though, wasn't quite as good as McKenna's had been. He had only a partial view of the site from here. He couldn't see what was going on over by the alien ship, mostly obscured as it was by an overhang of rock and a drooping sprawl of decimated trees. Propped against a bush in front of his face, his radio hissed and crackled, but remained annoyingly silent for now.

Never a patient man, Lynch twitched and fidgeted, glaring at the radio as though it was a toddler that stubbornly refused to eat its greens.

Come the fuck on, he thought. *Just give the fuckin' word.*

From the corner of his eye he caught a flicker of light. Fireflies?

He glanced to his right—and saw a trio of red dots dancing on his trigger arm. *Red fireflies?*

Then realization crashed in on him. *Shit!* He was being targeted! The sniper was being sniped! He scrambled upright, spun round, raising his gun.

Before he could take offensive or defensive action of any kind, a lightning bolt shot down from the heavens and hit him dead center. He was lifted into the air, as if by a giant hand made of sizzling light and excruciating pain, and smashed back down again. His ears hissing, his thoughts screaming, his body full of fire, he looked wildly around, and noticed something very odd indeed— his own arm, lying on the ground, fingers still twitching at one end, smoke rising from the other. Wondering if he was dreaming, or hallucinating, he turned to look at the place where his arm should be, and saw nothing but a charred stump, drooling blood.

I'm dead, he thought, and felt a kind of wonder. *I'm actually dead. Aww, shit. Now I'll never get to find out how this ends.*

Above him, in front of him, he heard the crashing of undergrowth, the sound of something big heading his way.

Scrabbling in his pack, he pulled out a flare gun and fired it blindly into the air… illuminating a huge, dreadlocked shape, which pushed its way out of the trees and loomed over him like the Angel of Death.

Still calm, still counting down, Traeger said, "Three… two…"

McKenna wondered whether to shoot him in the head before he reached one, just for the hell of it.

Then a flare lit the sky above the jungle somewhere to the east, and was followed almost instantly by the hideous, drawn-out scream of someone or something dying a horrible death.

McKenna thought instantly of the Loonies, and Casey. They were out there. He hoped to God—

The momentary distraction was all that Traeger needed.

Spinning round, he made his hand flat and rigid as a blade, and stabbed it toward McKenna's throat, intending to jab him right in the Adam's apple. McKenna flinched away just in time, and Traeger's hand scraped painfully against the side of his neck. It was still enough, though, to enable the CIA agent to break free of McKenna's grip when the Army Ranger stumbled backward. As Traeger leaped from the ramp of the ship, hit the ground and rolled, the world suddenly erupted with gunfire.

We're dead, McKenna thought, assuming that without Traeger there as a shield, the mercs had opened up on them. He threw himself backward, his only instinct being to protect Rory—with his own dead and twitching body, if need be.

It took him maybe a second to realize that the bullets weren't coming their way. No, they were coming from the jungle, from the Loonies, God bless 'em, raining in on all sides, with the mercs as their target. And the mercs—those that weren't cut down in the first volley—were scattering, running for cover, returning fire when they could. McKenna had been in firefights before, and knew he had to think and act fast, that he'd have only a few seconds before someone once again identified him and Rory as targets.

Rory was lying on the ramp, curled into a ball, his hands pressed over his ears. Crouching beside him, veiled by smoke, McKenna scooped him up, carried him to the edge of the ramp—Rory's body rigid, as if made of wood—and dropped to the ground. Blanketed by the haze, the two of them then rolled beneath the ramp and lay there a moment, recovering. McKenna could hear his son's heart hammering in his chest, and he held him close, murmuring words of comfort and encouragement. Eventually, he felt Rory's body relax, saw him crack open an eyelid. The ground was littered with the corpses of Traeger's mercenaries, and McKenna told his son not to look.

"Are you okay?" he said quietly.

Rory was clearly petrified, but he nodded. From his pocket, McKenna produced the invisibility ball, polished it briefly on his thigh, and offered it to Rory.

"Take this. You need to vanish, you *really* vanish. Understand?"

Rory nodded again.

Diego Galarza did not consider himself a bad guy. Yes, he'd been prepared to shoot the crazy soldier, and maybe even his kid, but what he did, he did purely so he could send money home to his ailing mama and two sisters in East Harlem. Without his monthly contributions, he feared they'd slip below the poverty line, especially once his mama's medical bills began to mount up. It was imperative, therefore, that he stay alive. And although it wasn't looking too good for him right now, he felt sure things would turn out okay in the end. After all, he was a lucky guy, always had been. He'd even been known as Lucky Galarza in the neighborhood where he'd grown up. He'd had scrapes in the past—many scrapes, and some bad ones, ones where other people had got killed—but somehow or other, he had always come out on top.

Right now, he was crouched behind the generator, close to the perimeter fence, cut off from the rest of his unit. Bullets had spattered the ground and spanged off metal all around him for what seemed like minutes. They had stopped now, but Diego knew it was a temporary lull, and that if he moved, if he showed himself, he would be shot down like a dog.

He was torn between staying here to finish the job he'd been hired to do, or opting out, crawling off into the jungle and making his way to safety. If he took the second option, he knew he wouldn't get paid, and there might well be other consequences if it was discovered he'd cut and run, but at least he'd still be alive. The perimeter fence was maybe three meters away, and the first clumps of blackened foliage at the edge of the jungle maybe another three meters beyond that. Six meters in all. It was nothing. If he crawled on his belly, if he kept to the shadows, he could make it.

He was still plucking up the courage, still wondering what to do, when he heard a sound coming from the jungle. It started off as a rustling, but quickly escalated into a crunching, and then a crashing, as something headed toward him. The something sounded big, maybe an animal, or even a vehicle of some kind. Maybe the guys who had fired on them had a tank, and were attempting to drive it through the jungle, right onto the crash site. He peeked around the edge of the generator, and saw trees and bushes whipping back and forth, as if a twister was working its way through them. He thought he could see something moving back there in the shadows too, something that walked upright like a man. But how could it be a man? Whatever that thing was, it had to be ten, twelve feet tall.

Slowly, he raised his gun as the figure moved closer.

Then the thing stepped out of the darkness of the jungle, into the light.

He had heard some of the other guys talk about the space alien they kept at Project: Stargazer, had heard them say the thing had escaped, but he hadn't known whether they were bullshitting him. Then he had seen the spaceship and he had thought that maybe there *was* something to their story, after all. Even so, he had never really expected to *see* a space alien, and certainly not this close. And even if he *did* see one, he'd half-expected it to look like the ones on TV: small and gray, with big black eyes. But this bastard was bigger and more terrifying than anything he could ever have imagined—hell, it was almost twice as tall as he was. And it was built like a Roman gladiator on steroids, its muscles huge and powerful, its massive hands tipped with claws that looked as though they could tear a man's head off with one swipe. But worse than any of that was its face. Oh man, its face…

As the creature turned in his direction, its mean little eyes fixing on him, and its mandibles stretching open,

Diego felt his bladder let go. Hot liquid squirted down his leg as a judder of fear started up like a motor in his guts and turned his limbs to trembling Jell-O. Whimpering, but not even aware he was doing it, he raised his gun and took aim at that hideous face. But the creature reacted with lightning speed, and even before his finger could twitch on the trigger, it had ripped aside the perimeter fence as though it was a lace curtain, and was reaching out for him. Within a split second, it had knocked his gun aside, and ripped him open as though he was a wet paper bag. Diego heard a tearing sound and a crack of bone, and realized it was coming from himself. Then, as his steaming innards slid out of the gash in his belly, he felt himself lifted off his feet like a doll. His last sensation, as his life and all he had been swirled away into a black drain, was of the creature using him like a puppet, squeezing his hand so that his finger pulled the trigger on his weapon, spraying the crash site with bullets.

Perched in a tree on the opposite side of the crater, Casey saw the Upgrade stride into the clearing, tear a man apart, and strafe the area with bullets to discourage retaliation. What she didn't see were several of the mercs making it across to a parked jeep, but she knew they must have done so when the vehicle's headlights suddenly blazed, and its engine roared, like a wild animal issuing an attack cry.

She saw the Upgrade straighten up, tossing aside the merc's eviscerated body like discarded packaging, as the jeep tore across the clearing toward it. At first, she thought the jeep was going to ram the Upgrade, and wondered who'd come off worse. But then the vehicle screeched to a halt and a trio of black-clad mercs spilled from it, each of them loaded with heavy artillery.

Casey had to admire their bravery. They must have concluded either that the previous attack had originated from the Upgrade itself, or that their attackers would see the Upgrade as a common enemy, and would either join forces with them or hold fire. On that last assumption— if that *was* their assumption—they were kind of correct. The Loonies *were* holding fire for now—but not out of any sense of commonality or fair play. If things were going as discussed, they'd be moving into position, their single aim being to retrieve McKenna and Rory, and get them out of the kill zone. As for Casey, for now she had a grandstand seat. Up in her tree, she watched events unfold with a horrified fascination.

Even as the mercs were spilling out of the jeep, the Upgrade was on the move. It was frighteningly fast, its movements almost a blur even without its cloaking technology. Although Casey had little sympathy for Traeger's black-clad soldiers, their massacre was still painful to watch. It was like seeing a tiger pitted against tortoises in a gladiatorial arena. Armed as they were, they appeared cripplingly slow next to the swiftness of their enemy. The Upgrade was on them before they could get their guns up and aimed, though not without the alien first reducing the odds by throwing some sort of whirling blade, which took one of the mercs' arms clean off at the elbows. As he lay in the grass, screaming, the Upgrade ploughed through the remaining two men, slashing one open with its claws, before picking the other up with both hands and simply ripping him in two.

Now, as the Upgrade strode purposefully toward the original Predator's craft, more mercs started to emerge from hiding—though whether to avenge their fallen comrades or simply because their orders were to protect the ship at all costs, Casey wasn't sure.

Even in greater numbers, though, they were no match for the eleven-foot-tall Predator. It simply cut through them like a barracuda through a pool of minnows, dodging their clumsy attempts to take it down, and dispatching them in a variety of ways—ripping some apart with its bare hands, beheading others with its throwing blades. It shot one man who tried to sneak up behind it with his own weapon, and it snapped a wrist cuff onto one merc's arm as it passed him by, then pressed a detonator on its gauntlet and reduced him to an explosion of chunky red confetti.

Leaving a battleground of dead and dying men behind it, it continued its remorseless progress toward the alien craft.

And toward McKenna and Rory, who were still crouched beneath the ship's ramp.

22

The armored personnel carrier was the pit bull terrier of the motoring world. Ugly, squat, compact and powerful, it was effectively a dark-gray metal box, which perched on eight wheels—four on each side—and had two narrow, widely spaced headlights at the front, which resembled mean little eyes.

Also known as a GPV, this was the vehicle that had been parked closest to the alien ship when Traeger had made his escape from McKenna. It was the one he had sought refuge behind, and it was the one he was still crouched behind now, hunkered down beside one of the massive muddy wheels with two of his remaining men, out of sight of the battleground, the perimeter fence and the jungle at his back.

Because he had been hiding behind what was, to all intents and purposes, a three-meter-thick metal wall, he had seen little of the massacre of his troops. He had heard the screams, though, and the explosions, and the grisly tearing sounds. And now he could smell the blood, and hear the groans of the injured and dying.

He had shown defiance, and even bravery, in his dealings with McKenna, but he didn't feel brave now. Cowering in the dirt, his clothes spattered with mud, he trembled, and sweated, and prayed to a God he had never really believed in, as the footsteps of the Upgrade thumped relentlessly closer to his hiding place.

Please don't let it know I'm here, he thought, squeezing his eyes closed. *Please don't let it know I'm here.*

Was the ground really shaking as the creature approached, or was that merely his imagination? As the footsteps seemed to boom right on top of him, he couldn't resist it: he opened one eye.

Backlit by arc lamps, he saw the Upgrade looming over the GPV, its shadow spilling across the top of the vehicle and shrouding him and his men like a black blanket. He half-expected the creature to pick up the vehicle in one vast hand and toss it aside, then lean down toward them in a macabre game of peekaboo.

But it didn't. It simply passed them by, either ignorant of their presence or uninterested in it. Traeger breathed a sigh of relief as its footsteps receded, and risked creeping to the edge of the vehicle and peering around it to see what the Upgrade would do next.

He saw it march up the ramp and enter the Predator ship, the hatch closing after it with a pneumatic *whump!*

Then there was silence. It was almost an anticlimax. Traeger's men who had been hiding with him looked at one another in fearful bewilderment, unable to believe they were still alive.

What the fuck now? he thought.

He made a quick decision. He had to get hold of this situation as quickly as possible, had to regain the upper hand.

He made a quick inventory of his men. There were six still standing, albeit scattered around the battleground, hiding behind trees and other vehicles.

"McKenna?" he yelled.

No response. Nothing but drifting smoke and silence.

He tried again. "C'mon, be reasonable. There's... what? Five of you? Seven of us."

That was a total guess. He was trying to recall from the intel he'd received how many crazies there'd been in the prison van with McKenna—this was assuming they'd all stuck together. He guessed one was now dead, if that scream from the jungle was anything to go by, and he wasn't counting Casey Brackett. She was a woman, and a scientist, so if anything, she'd be more of a hindrance than a help to guys like this.

In answer to his question, someone (Traeger thought it might have been Williams, but the movement was too quick for him to really tell for sure) popped up from behind a tree surrounding the area and let off a shot. The head of one of the mercs who'd been cowering behind the GPV with Traeger snapped back, and next moment he was lying in the dirt, his brains leaking out of his skull.

From the tone of his voice as he replied, Traeger sensed McKenna was grinning. "Who taught you math?"

Traeger seethed. The death of the merc was a clear signal that McKenna's rabble had them surrounded and could pick them off at will. Glaring down at the dead soldier, as though the guy had got himself shot on purpose merely to spite him, he bellowed, "Okay! Okay!"

He struggled inwardly to keep his voice steady. The men in his employ were not loyal to him, they were little more than hired thugs, and it wouldn't do to show them he was losing control of this situation.

Trying to make it sound as though he was being generous, he said, "Fine. You can walk away, Captain. I just want what's in that ship."

Still huddled beneath the ramp of the Predator ship, Rory touched his dad on the arm. "He's lying."

McKenna looked down at Rory looking up at him, his face trusting, open, and he gave him a brief hug. "Yes, he is. Good boy."

Another voice joined the conversation. "McKenna? McKenna?"

It was Casey. He shuffled to the edge of the ramp, peered out from under it. At first, he couldn't see her when he looked in what he thought was the direction her voice had come from, but then he saw movement in a tree on the opposite side of the crater and realized she was perched up there, waving at him.

"Why isn't the ship taking off?" she said.

It was a good question. The Upgrade was in there, so what was to stop it from firing up the engines? If it did, of course, he and Rory would have to get out from under there quick, if they didn't want to be—

His thoughts were interrupted by an astonishing sound.

It was laughter of a sort, deep and mocking, and interspersed with clicks and chirps—and it was coming from the Predator ship, through a kind of loudspeaker system!

The laughter was followed by a high-pitched warbling screech, like a radio trying to tune in to a frequency. Rory clapped his hands over his ears, his face creasing up with pain, and McKenna did the same. He suspected that Nebraska and Casey and Traeger and everyone else were reacting the same way too.

Someone must have asked a question, because as the sound died down enough for McKenna to remove his hands from his ears, he heard Traeger say, "It's the translator… It's using the translator."

After a further pause, there came the most astonishing sound of all. A voice. But not just any voice. *Emily's* voice. Or rather, a weird, almost otherworldly amalgam of Emily's voice and several others that the Upgrade must have recorded, speaking words that sounded as though they had been filtered through a machine—emotionless and robotic.

"Hell-o," the voice began incongruously. "I have enjoyed watching you kill each other. Now you are twelve only. Among you, I detect one who is a true warrior. The one called… Mac-Kenna. He will be your leader. He will be my prize."

McKenna sensed all eyes turning toward his hiding place. The Upgrade's words sent a chill through him.

Then Baxley's voice came floating across the clearing. "Hey man, who'd you fuck to get pole position?"

No one laughed. McKenna glanced at Rory and thought, *So what happens now?*

The alien loudspeaker system crackled again, and the strange, filtered voice boomed once more across the crash site: "All are targets. Targets run. I offer time advantage. Go!"

There was a pause. Then Casey called out uncertainly, "Time advantage? What's that? Like a head start?"

"We request twenty-four hours!" Nettles yelled from somewhere over to McKenna's left.

Suddenly, numbers began to appear on the big screen that the techs had been hauling across the mud of the crater before all the shit had gone down, and which was still miraculously undamaged, despite the subsequent gunfire and explosions. The numbers were distorted, jagged, but still recognizable. McKenna realized the Upgrade must be projecting them from the ship.

5:00… 4:59… 4:58…

A countdown. Their "time advantage." Their head start before the Upgrade started to come after them.

Nettles' disgusted voice drifted across the clearing again. "This guy's a dick, yo."

Traeger had already weighed up the options and come to a decision. He rose from behind the GPV, stepping out into plain view, his gun still in his hand but dangling from one finger, the barrel pointing at the ground. He stood there for maybe five seconds, waiting, and then McKenna emerged from beneath the ramp of the Predator ship, and stood up too, his weapon likewise pointing at the ground.

This was the cue for everyone else to emerge from hiding, like mice after the cat has vacated the house.

Casey climbed down from her tree, and pushed her way through the still incomplete and partially damaged perimeter fence. She walked across the clearing toward McKenna, studiously avoiding looking at the mangled and dismembered bodies strewn everywhere across the ground.

"Can I swear in front of your kid?" she asked, directing a vague smile at Rory, who was peeking out from beneath the ramp.

"No, but I can," McKenna said. "We're fucked, aren't we?"

Casey nodded. "Six ways from Sunday."

A merc padded across to them, his weapon also pointed at the ground, a makeshift ally now due to the bigger threat they were all facing. Glancing uneasily at the Predator ship, and even more uneasily at the inexorable countdown on the big screen, he said gruffly, "We split up, twelve different directions." Then, glancing at Traeger, he added, "McKenna's the one it wants."

McKenna snorted a laugh, but Traeger, ever the strategist, shook his head. "Nix. It'll take us one by one. That's the fucker's MO."

Though she hated to agree with him, Casey nodded. "He's right."

From across the clearing came the sound of an engine wheezing and grinding. They looked across at a jeep that one of the mercs was trying to start. Its headlights came on, flickered, then went out.

Another merc tried another vehicle, with the same result. Unnecessarily, he called out, "Nothing's starting. Vehicles are fried."

"Son of a bitch triggered an EMP," Traeger said.

"Range?" asked McKenna.

Baxley was approaching them now, glaring balefully at the mercs, who glared right back at him.

Rory, who had slid out from under the ramp, and was now standing quietly beside his father, pointed up at the still-blazing arc lamps. "Localized."

"Chopper should be okay," Baxley said.

"One way to find out," McKenna said. Raising his voice, he shouted, "Everyone, mount up!"

Such was the authority in his voice that even Traeger's men leaped into action. The team mobilized quickly, grabbing and priming extra weapons, stuffing ammo into their backpacks, scouring the grounded vehicles for other equipment they might need.

Casey noticed Traeger watching the scene silently, albeit with a grimly amused smile on his lips, and wondered what was cooking in that devious brain of his. A merc sidled up to him—big guy with a dyed yellow goatee and worried eyes. His voice was a boyish quaver.

"Wait. It's gonna… hunt us?"

Casey scowled at him. "Grow a dick, will you?"

"Maybe he could borrow yours," Baxley muttered under his breath.

"Fuck you, Baxley!" But she was laughing.

The group had now been joined by the rest of the Loonies, who had converged on them from a variety of directions. While Nettles gave the mostly nervous-looking mercs the stink eye, Nebraska hoisted his backpack a little higher and sparked up a cigarette.

Nodding at Rory, he said, "Any advice?"

"Yeah," said Rory. "Smoking's bad for you."

Nebraska rolled his eyes. "I mean the Predator. How do we kill it?"

Deadpan, Rory replied, "Get it to start smoking."

During the preparations, Traeger had slipped quietly away and he was now leaning into the trunk of the jeep he, Rory, and Sapir had arrived in. Casey had known he was up to something, and now she watched him out of the corner of her eye as he hauled out an army duffel bag. Clearly eager to do whatever it was he was doing without being seen, his movements were jerky, nervous, and as he yanked out the bag, items spilled from its open end onto the ground. Hastily, he scrambled to stuff them back into the bag, but not before Casey recognized some of the Predator tech she had seen displayed in glass cases at Project: Stargazer. She walked across, trying to make as little noise as possible, and stood over him. Suddenly, realizing someone was there, Traeger glanced up quickly.

He looked like a kid who'd been busted watching porn by his mom.

"Trick or treat bag?" Casey asked caustically.

She saw his brain working, trying to come up with an answer that might mollify her. He straightened up, took a couple of steps backward, and for a moment she thought he was about to turn tail and make a run for it.

But he backed into something that made his eyes jerk open in surprise, and when he turned around there was their old friend, the Predator dog with the bolt through its brain. It stood, mandibles clicking, wagging its tail, as if it wanted to play.

Casey waved her arms at it. "Go! Shoo! Go home!"

But the Predator dog simply wagged its tail harder and woofed at her. It was loving this game!

The creature's appearance had given Traeger the opportunity to divert attention away from his own devious behavior. "That thing'll give us away," he snarled. "Get it the fuck out of here."

Casey glared at him. Then she strode forward and snatched up one of the spilled items he hadn't had time to scoop back into the duffel bag—an exploding cuff, like the one she had seen the Upgrade use on a merc earlier. Marching to the edge of the crater, the Predator dog capering around her, she drew back her arm and hurled the cuff as far as she could into the jungle.

Excitedly, the creature ran after it. As soon as it did, McKenna gave the word and the rag-tag team, which comprised Loonies, mercenaries, an Army Ranger, a CIA agent, an evolutionary biologist, and a highly gifted kid, double-timed it into the jungle on the far side of the crater.

By the time the Predator dog returned, the cuff clenched in its massive, drooling jaws, the clearing was empty.

Whining, the Predator dog dropped the cuff on the muddy ground and looked around, bewildered.

23

The group had death at their heels, and they needed no further encouragement than that. They moved swiftly through the jungle, ducking and dodging around trees and plants. Under the weight of their heavy clothing, backpacks, and weapons, the men grunted with exertion, sweat streaming down their faces, but not for a moment did they think of stopping for a rest, or even slowing down.

Rory could keep up with the group purely because he was smaller and lighter, and because he wasn't carrying anything except for the invisibility ball in his pocket, which his dad had given to him. Holding Casey's hand, he was able to negotiate the thick foliage far more easily than the bulkier soldiers in front of him.

Except for his mom, Rory was usually nervous around girls and women, and he didn't like people touching him at the best of times, but he found comfort in the warmth of Casey's hand in his, and he liked the way she kept glancing at him and smiling. She was looking out for him, and not in a patronizing way. It was like she knew the two of them were kindred spirits—both science-minded, both clever, both introverted—and that therefore they had to stick together.

Just ahead of them, Traeger was fumbling in his duffel bag as he ran along. Rory wondered whether the CIA agent was looking for a weapon—but what he eventually pulled out of the bag shocked Rory far more than a Predator weapon would have. Shocked him and filled his head with bad memories.

It was the Predator mask. The one that Rory had worn while trick-or-treating. The one he'd been wearing when he—*it*—had killed that man on his porch.

He'd thrown it into the bushes close to the man's house, but he guessed it must have been recovered, and that it had found its way back into Traeger's hands, as all such Predator tech seemed to do.

Dropping back a little, Traeger pointed the mask in Rory's direction and waved it like a threat. Panting, he said, "On Halloween, this thing blew up a whole house. How do you fire it?"

Despite its bad associations, Rory guessed he was kind of glad the mask was back in their possession—it might prove useful against their pursuer—but he wished it was in the hands of pretty much anyone except Traeger.

"Um, you don't," he said. "It just… fires by itself. When it's attacked."

Traeger's lips curled into a snarl, and for a moment Rory thought the agent was going to call him a liar. But it turned out he was just frustrated. "Really?" he said.

"Fuck!" And he glared at the mask, as if demanding it give up its secrets.

Up ahead, Rory saw his dad glance back, and realized he must have heard the exchange. Allowing Coyle to take the lead, he dropped back with Nebraska to speak to them. Rory felt a sense of satisfaction at the fact that neither his dad nor Nebraska was panting and sweating half as much as Traeger was. His dad did look anxious, though, as if, having been name-checked by the alien, he felt a special responsibility to keep them all alive.

Barely giving Traeger and the mask a second look, his dad addressed Casey. "Okay, so what do we know?" He waggled the fingers of his free hand at the side of his head in an imitation of the alien's "dreadlocks." "Casey, the… uh… Marley shit?"

"I'm thinking sensory receptors," Casey said, glancing at Rory as if for affirmation. He liked that. He nodded. "Like cat whiskers. Weak spot, maybe?"

"You said it left you alone back at Stargazer," Nebraska reminded her. "How come?"

Casey shrugged. "I was unarmed and naked. Didn't pose a threat."

"No one's getting naked," Baxley shouted from up ahead.

"Speak for yourself," Nettles retorted.

Despite the situation, everyone snorted laughter, even Traeger and the mercs—it was a brief release of tension they all needed. The only people who didn't laugh were Rory, who sometimes didn't get jokes as quickly as others did, and his dad, who not only continued to look grim, but who looked a little irritated now too.

Seeing this, Nettles veered over to him. "Fuck your guilt," he said.

Now his dad looked surprised. No, more than surprised—startled. "Excuse me?"

Nettles' voice was low, but Rory still heard what he said.

"You lost men. I get it. You'll lose some today." He paused, and Rory saw his expression change, become determined, earnest, like an unspoken promise. "But you're *not* gonna lose your son."

The Upgrade stands on the far side of the crater, facing the ship. All is ready. It has ensured that there will be nothing left for the humans to use, nothing they can turn to their advantage. It glances at the screen, and sees the numbers ticking down—0:09… 0:08… 0:07…

At 0:05, it presses a button on its wrist gauntlet and the ship is annihilated in a flash of intense white light, a contained but devastating explosion that causes the trees nearby to sway and thrash, and that sends an echoing boom *rolling through the jungle like a war cry.*

As the echoes die away, the Upgrade looks again at the screen.

0:02… 0:01… 0:00…

Time to hunt.

Somewhere behind them came the sound of an explosion, and a brief column of light, which lit up the sky. Traeger wondered what the oversized crab-faced bastard was up to, and then it came to him with a pang of despair. The fucker must have blown up the ship to stop it from falling into enemy hands. *Shit, shit, shit!*

Boiling with anger, he rooted around once again in his duffel bag, thinking that if he couldn't have the ship, then he would have the son of a bitch himself. He knew there must be *something* in here he could use against it—something with easy-to-follow instructions, that didn't involve him engaging in hand-to-hand combat.

He plucked out a couple of things—a nunchucks-type device, followed by an alien throwing star, like a Japanese shuriken, that required a wrist gauntlet (and, no doubt, years of practice) to operate it effectively—but almost immediately rejected them, dropping them back into the bag. The third item he pulled out, however, was ideal. A compact shoulder cannon, connected to a tiny pad-like sensor, which you attached to the side of your head, and which responded directly to what your brain told it to do.

Although Traeger hadn't risked trying out the cannon himself, he'd been present at some of the tests, and it had proved an effective weapon. Still running, he affixed the cannon to his shoulder and pressed the sensor against his skull just below his ear. He gritted his teeth, expecting to feel a little pain as it clamped itself to his flesh, but it adhered painlessly. He swiveled his head and the barrel responded, completely in sync with his movements. Bingo!

Feeling some of his old confidence flowing back, he tossed the duffel bag to the nearest merc—it was the one with the yellow goatee and the worried eyes.

"Carry this," he ordered.

Somewhere to their left—in the darkness of the jungle it was impossible to tell how far away—a branch snapped loudly, a sound that could clearly be heard even over the tramp of their footsteps and the constant rustle-swish of the undergrowth they were running through. Flashlights turned in that direction, but there was nothing to be seen except overlapping leaves and black shadows.

Most of the group simply faced front again and picked up their pace, but Traeger saw the merc with the yellow goatee suddenly stop dead, his eyes going wide and his mouth dropping wetly open. His body shaking as he succumbed to a full-blown panic attack, he delved into the duffel bag and pulled out the shuriken that Traeger had previously rejected.

"Whoa, easy," Traeger said, but panic had the merc in a vice-like grip now, and he was too far gone to listen. As the soldier turned to face the direction that the branch-snap had come from and drew back his arm, Traeger raised his hands and his voice.

"No, no, no," he warned. "You need the wrist thing—"

Too late. The merc pistoned his arm forward and the shuriken flew from his hand and disappeared into the blackness of the jungle. Traeger looked at him, aghast, and began to back away.

By this time everyone else had not only slowed, but stopped, and they were looking back to see what was happening, some of them raising their guns, as if fearing an attack. As a couple of the mercs moved toward their goateed colleague, Traeger waved them back, as if the man was infected and should not be approached.

The merc, meanwhile, simply stood where he was, as if rooted to the spot, staring in fear at the black wall of jungle in front of him. All of them could hear the swift metallic whickering of the blade he had thrown, as it sliced its way with apparent ease through whatever was standing in its way. The sound, loud at first, grew fainter, and eventually dwindled to silence; a couple of the men started to relax. But Traeger knew it was not over, and sure enough, after three seconds' grace, they all heard it again. But this time the whickering sound, faint at first, began to grow louder. The goateed merc's eyes stretched yet wider with horror as he realized what was happening. The shuriken was coming back!

"No," he gibbered, "no, no, go away!"

He backed off, instinctively throwing up his hand to shield himself.

Traeger saw a flash of metal, and next second the merc was writhing on the ground and squealing like a stuck pig, blood spurting from the stump of his wrist. His severed hand lay a few feet away from the rest of his body, fingers curled in toward the palm. The shuriken, having effortlessly lopped off the man's hand instead of clipping back into the wrist gauntlet as it was designed to do, now rapidly lost momentum and embedded itself in a tree.

The merc continued to squeal. Traeger stomped over to him, furious.

"Shut the fuck up!"

He contemplated using the shoulder cannon on the man, silencing him for good—if McKenna and his crew hadn't been watching, he might even have done so. Instead, he bent down and slapped the man hard across the face, once, twice.

Shocked, the man swallowed his scream.

But then, as though in imitation, another merc, standing on the periphery of the group, gave a sudden startled yelp.

They all turned as one to see him rising rapidly into the trees, as though yanked upward on an elasticated rope.

When he was around ten meters from the ground, legs kicking wildly, there was a shifting in the shadows somewhere in the canopy of leaves and branches above his head, and then something detached itself from the darkness and slid down the trunk like a vast snake. The group on the ground could only watch in horror as the Upgrade descended the tree headfirst. It paused to regard them, eyes glinting, mandibles stretching to reveal pink flesh inset with jagged shark-like teeth. Then it reached out with its long arms, grabbed its prey by the shoulders, and hauled him upward.

Seconds later the real screaming began, and blood began to patter down from the tree like rain.

McKenna was the first to start shooting, blazing away at the darkness above their heads into which the Upgrade and its victim had vanished. The man immediately stopped screaming—either put out of his misery by McKenna's bullets or killed by the Upgrade—but nothing fell from above. Nebraska, Nettles, Coyle, and Baxley were all firing too, but the remaining three mercs had already turned tail and fled. The noise was tremendous, bullets causing sparks to flare in the trees like a multitude of angry sprites. After a few seconds, McKenna waved an arm to call a halt to the shooting—if the Upgrade hadn't crashed dead to the ground by now, that meant it was no longer there—and indicated that they should beat a hasty retreat.

As they lowered their weapons and began to hightail it out of there, Casey grabbed McKenna's sleeve and indicated the merc with the severed hand, who was still lying on the ground, sweating and groaning. McKenna looked anguished, but shook his head. If they were going to have *any* chance of surviving this, they couldn't allow themselves to be lumbered by anything that might slow them down. He half-expected Casey to protest, but she simply nodded, and mouthed "Sorry" at the man.

Then they cleared out, leaving him alone.

The merc's name was Bruce Willis, a handle that had proved both a blessing and a curse throughout his thirty-six years on this earth. Partly because of his namesake's reputation, he had become a tough guy almost by default, developing from an amiable fat kid from a middle-class family (his dad was a pharmacy manager, his mom a school secretary) into one who did weights, and boxed, and eventually dropped out of high school to take a job first as a nightclub doorman, and then as a prison guard. He had become a merc because a friend of his told him the money was good, but he had always felt like a phony. He felt like he was never quite as committed, or ruthless, or downright batshit-crazy as the guys around him, that one day he would be found out, and when that day came he would find himself in deep shit.

And now that day had come. Because here he was, in a jungle clearing, at night, on his own, being hunted by a monster. He had lost a hand, and a fuck of a lot of blood, and was in indescribable pain, and probably dying. There was a part of him that wished he could just pass out, slip into oblivion, but he couldn't, because he had so much adrenaline racing through his system right now that it felt like his whole body was screaming. On the other hand (ha-ha), maybe now that everyone had gone away and left him, he would be left alone too. The monster would chase after the others, and he would be free to live or die at his own leisure, depending on what God (because he *did* believe in God, despite his mom's insistence that, by choosing the path he had chosen in life, he had forsaken his faith) had in mind for him.

He was still thinking these vaguely comforting thoughts when he heard a heavy thump to his right. Although it hurt to move—funny how losing a hand could make every other part of your body bellow out in pain too—he turned his head. What he saw chased all thoughts of God's mercy from his mind. The monster was standing right beside him, its colossal legs stretching up to its equally colossal torso, and from there to its hideously ugly head.

Bruce began to whimper, to plead. With great effort, he held up his remaining hand, palm out.

"I'm unarmed…" he said. "I'm not a threat… I'm not a threat…"

The monster leaned over him. It tilted its head to one side, its weird, dreadlock-like appendages slithering across its shoulders.

His voice became a whisper. "I don't pose a threat… I don't…"

He only stopped pleading when the monster rammed a taloned hand between his lips and ripped his spine out through his mouth.

The triumphal, ululating screech of the Upgrade echoed through the woods, chilling them all even though they were sweating and panting with exertion.

"Sounds like we lost another red shirt," Coyle gasped, his pack bouncing on his back as he ran. Then he gestured to his left and shouted, "Glimmer, on your nine!"

They turned to look, saw shadowy movement in the trees. Several flashlight beams picked out a hulking, dark shape, moving at panther-like speed through the jungle. Then it vanished.

Everyone thumped to a stop. Casey looked around and knew that they were all thinking the same as she was: running was pointless; their enemy was so much faster than they were; all they were doing was expending needless energy. Yet what else could they do?

They were looking to McKenna, but for once he looked as clueless as the rest of them.

"Up ahead," Casey said, pointing. "This way." When

McKenna gave her a questioning look, she explained, "Lynch. He set some pyro to cover our back trail."

She hoped she was right—not only that Lynch *had* had time to set the pyro before the alien had got him, but also that they were where she thought they were (she had a good sense of direction, but in the darkness of the jungle it was easy to get turned around and not know it). It was a long shot—but the comfort was, she knew that McKenna also knew it was a long shot, yet he was nodding regardless.

"Fine," he said. "Let's trap the motherfucker."

He led the way along the path she had indicated. It was narrow, hemmed in by trees and brush. A choke point. Nettles passed him a detonator. Baxley squeezed past Nettles and tapped McKenna on the shoulder, and when McKenna turned he said, "Set it," then jerked his head at Coyle. "We'll draw him in."

Coyle raised his eyebrows. "What is this 'we,' kemosabe?"

But the way he said it, McKenna knew he was committed one hundred percent. Knew that Coyle—like Baxley, like all of them—would do whatever it took to protect his buddies, and most especially Rory, even if it meant risking his own life. McKenna locked eyes with both of them for a long moment, his face solemn. He didn't have the words to express the depth of his gratitude, his admiration, his love, for these two crazy men. In the end he nodded tersely, and they nodded back. It was enough.

Then he turned and hurried after the others, leaving Coyle and Baxley behind.

N N N

Alone, Coyle and Baxley looked at each other. Both were relaxed, both breathing deeply and evenly.

Then a faint rustle in the bushes nearby caused them both to jerk up their guns and spin round.

After a moment, Baxley frowned and lowered his gun. "Calm down," he said to Coyle.

Coyle looked indignant. "*Me* calm down? Sure, thanks… *twitchy*."

"Just don't shoot me, fucker," Baxley muttered.

They began to walk back along the trail. As soon as it widened out, Coyle raised his weapon and let loose a burst of gunfire, strafing the foliage in front of them, shredding leaves and branches.

"Hey, asshole!" he hollered into the darkness. "What's the difference between a golf ball and a G-spot?"

Baxley shot him an incredulous look. "You're telling it a joke?"

Coyle shrugged. "If he laughs it'll give away his position."

"That's the dumbest thing I ever—"

Before he could finish his sentence, the tree closest to him exploded. There was a blast of heat and light, and the thing simply shattered into pieces as though struck by lightning.

The two of them ducked, Baxley letting out an involuntary yelp as splinters showered over him. The echoes of the blast were still fading when another sound replaced it—a deep, booming, otherworldly laugh that reverberated through the jungle.

Baxley and Coyle looked at each other. They both

recognized that laugh. Distorted though it was, it was Traeger's laugh, mocking and without humor.

And I didn't even get to the punchline, Coyle thought.

Then, yelling in defiance, both men raised their guns and let fly, blitzing the jungle with bullets. After five seconds they stopped, and then, in silent agreement, they turned and ran as fast as they could, back along the trail, toward the choke point, jumping over logs and crashing through bushes.

"Come and get us, motherfucker! This way!" Baxley yelled gleefully.

Just ahead of him he heard Coyle shrieking with laughter.

After maybe seventy meters, the choke hole widened out into a clearing. It was here that the hunted were hoping to become the hunters. With their trap hastily set, they scrambled for cover, diving behind trees and bushes, hoping against hope that their desperate counter-attack against a creature that was faster, stronger, technologically superior, and infinitely more vicious than they were would end this nightmare once and for all.

Typically, McKenna and Nebraska were the last to seek shelter. As the whoops of Coyle and Baxley grew louder, McKenna hurried across the clearing, and Nebraska followed, though not before kicking a little more dirt over the string of claymore mines they were all hoping would turn the Upgrade into dog food. Nebraska jumped over a boulder directly opposite the arch of tree branches that formed the clearing's entrance, and crouched behind it, his shoulder pressed up against its rough stone surface. Peering over the top of the boulder, he took a last look around, like a party organizer checking the final details before the arrival of the special guest. In the darkness and the drifting jungle mist he caught glimpses of mercs and Loonies, what little light there was flashing on the barrels of their guns, and glinting in their eyes. Over to his left, he could just about make out Casey crouched next to Traeger, who seemed to be fiddling with that weird alien cannon he was wearing on his shoulder. Sensing Nebraska's gaze, Casey glanced across at him and gave him a hopeful thumbs-up. He nodded back at her.

Then he faced front again. From the sounds of it, Coyle and Baxley were almost here. The party was about to begin.

Still whooping and yelling—not only a lure for the Upgrade, but also a release of tension and a sheer primal expression of joy at still being alive—Coyle and Baxley burst into the clearing.

"*Contaaaaccct!*" Baxley yelled, then he and Coyle were leaping through the air like a pair of Olympic long jumpers, clearing the strings of explosives that had been set up across the ground in front of them and threaded into the tree branches above their heads. They hit the ground, rolled like experts, and within a split second were up on their feet again, heading for cover, arms swinging, legs pumping. They ran either side of a big tree and met up again behind it, panting and sweating.

Suddenly, Baxley started grinning, then chuckling to himself. Coyle raised his eyebrows.

"Shit, man… your joke," Baxley explained. "I just got it. A guy might actually *look* for a golf ball."

"Come on," Casey murmured, "come on."

It had only been twenty seconds, maybe less, since Baxley and Coyle had entered the arena, but in this situation twenty seconds seemed like a *loooong* time. The jungle was full of night sounds—rustles and birdcalls and the ripple of leaves in the wind. Casey could feel her heart thumping at the base of her throat, could smell Traeger's sweat, and feel the sharp edge of something in the CIA agent's duffel bag—possibly the Predator mask—pressing against her leg. She glanced up, hoping the Upgrade hadn't outmaneuvered them, that it wasn't even now up there in the blackness of the trees above their heads, lowering itself down to snatch its prey, silent as a spider on a thread of silk…

She heard someone gasp, and her eyes immediately seemed to refocus, to sharpen. *There*. A suggestion of movement at the entrance to the clearing. A shimmer. She held her breath, sensed Traeger tense beside her.

And then, just like that, the Upgrade stepped into the clearing, ducking under the archway of branches, rising to its full height.

Even now, its cloaked form a rippling, shimmering mass of forest come alive, Casey found the alien both impressively beautiful and utterly terrifying. It was like something from folklore. A demon warrior. A perfect killing machine. Relentless and unstoppable. When it moved into the kill zone and got itself blown into chunks of unrecognizable meat, she knew she'd feel a pang of genuine sorrow and regret. And yet right now she wanted that to happen more than anything else in the world.

Two more steps, she thought. *Two more steps and all this will be over*. But the Upgrade wasn't moving. Shit. Clearly it could sense something. Suspected a trap. Although it was cloaked, she could discern its movements—its head jerking bird-like as it surveyed its surroundings. Could it see the string of claymore mines in the dirt? The pack of explosives attached to tree branches above its head, wired to blow the instant it walked underneath? It was dark, but what if the alien had night vision? What if—

Abruptly, the Upgrade decloaked.

Now it stood there at the entrance to the clearing in all its glory. A defiant gesture. A *mocking* gesture. It cocked its head at them, and although its expression was impossible to read, Casey guessed it was chiding them, expressing a kind of mock-disappointment at how pathetic they were, how unworthy they were as opponents.

"No… no… no…" murmured Traeger beside her, weariness and despair in his voice.

She glanced at Nebraska. He was clutching his gun in both hands, half-raising it, and she wondered how much longer it would be before this turned into a straight-out firefight. Maybe if Traeger took the initiative, fired his shoulder cannon, caught the Upgrade by surprise—

But it was the Upgrade who took the initiative. Almost before she realized that the alien had moved, it raised a hand, fired something from its wrist gauntlet, something that flashed in the meager light. A blade.

She didn't realize what had happened until she heard a grisly sound, followed by an almost regretful sigh to her right. Turning, she saw another of Traeger's mercs fold and crumple to the ground, blood pouring from a hole in his chest. Immediately, she guessed that the Upgrade's blade had passed clean through the tree and then through the soldier, like a bullet through soft putty. The Upgrade was showing them their defenses were worthless, that there was nowhere to hide.

"He didn't buy it!" McKenna yelled. "Open fire!"

Weapons blazed from all around the clearing, and suddenly the darkness was lit up by staccato flashes of gunfire. Bullets tore up trees and bushes, the air filling with the confetti of splinters and shredded foliage. Through it all, Casey tried to keep track of the Upgrade, which had moved even before McKenna had finished giving his order. She saw it dart to its left, weave in and out between the tree trunks so swiftly she couldn't even tell whether it had reengaged its cloaking mechanism or not. Big as it was, the alien was a fleeting shadow, gone before the bullets could reach it.

Although she wasn't a soldier, it was obvious to Casey what McKenna and his guys were doing wrong. They were all concentrating their gunfire on one place, which invariably was always the place the Upgrade had just vacated, instead of strafing the entire area, which would effectively have created a barrier of bullets in front of them and given the Upgrade nowhere to hide. She moved out of hiding and waved her arms, trying to snag either Nebraska's or McKenna's attention. But they were in the zone, fully focused, and so instead she simply tried yelling at the men to spread the barrage over a wider area, but she couldn't make herself heard above the noise. She glanced back at Traeger, hoping for some help, but despite toting the only weapon that might prove useful against their enemy, he was cowering behind his tree, keeping his head down. She wondered briefly whether to risk breaking cover entirely and rush across the short stretch of open ground between her and Nebraska—but then the decision was taken out of her hands.

She was vaguely aware of something flashing past on her left-hand side and instinctively ducked, whilst at the same time following its trajectory with her eyes. She only realized it was the Upgrade's throwing blade returning when she saw the Upgrade's arm snake out from behind a tree and the blade snap neatly back into place on its wrist gauntlet. She was surprised to see the Upgrade way over to her left. Last time she'd been aware of it, it had been darting between the trees to the right of the entrance to the clearing—and indeed, that was where McKenna and his men were still concentrating their fire.

"Over there!" she yelled, pointing at the Upgrade as it moved forward, keeping to the shadows, striding with one massive step over the string of claymore mines—but no one saw her or heard her.

No one, that is, except the Upgrade itself.

Casey felt herself go cold all over as the Upgrade's head suddenly snapped round, its eyes boring into her. She saw it reach for its throwing blade again, and dived back behind her tree, but having already witnessed how easily the blade could slice through thick bark she knew she might as well have been standing out in the open. Desperately, she lunged for Traeger's duffel bag and grabbed the first thing that came to hand—the Predator mask. As the Upgrade flung out its arm, releasing the blade, she dived to one side and swung the mask out wildly in front of her, using it as a tiny makeshift shield.

She was only aware the blade had hit the mask and deflected away when she felt the mask jerked from her hand. She yelped, her fingers stinging, the force of the blow causing the mask to fly one way and she the other. She came down in a heap, which knocked the breath from her, and heard the mask land several meters away with a clanging thump. What happened next happened suddenly and without warning.

The mask came alive.

Casey heard a *whirr* and a *click*, and sitting up she saw something extending from an aperture at the side of the mask that was parallel to the eye sockets—a tube of some kind. All at once she remembered Rory telling them how the mask had instinctively responded when it or its wearer had been under attack—how it had reduced one of his neighbors to ash and obliterated the front porch of the guy's house.

Locking onto its target, the mask now fired a bolt of pure concentrated energy at its attacker. So swift and accurate was the streak of light that not even the Upgrade was quick enough to dodge out of its way. The energy bolt hit it in the center of its chest, knocking it off its feet. The creature flew backward, smoke coiling up from its body, and crashed down right in the middle of the makeshift minefield they had created.

The shooting stopped and an almost stunned silence filled the clearing. Casey rose shakily to her feet, hardly daring to hope.

Was this it? Was the thing dead?

As the alien lay there motionless, some of the men began to emerge cautiously from hiding.

Then the Upgrade stirred, flexing one of its huge hands. Seizing his chance, McKenna yelled, "Light him up!"

Whoever was closest to the remote—Casey thought it might have been Nettles—grabbed it and pressed the button. They all flinched back, shielding their eyes and ears as best they could from the colossal *BOOM!* that shook the clearing. The Upgrade's body lifted into the air and slammed back down again, orange powder—phosphorous—settling over it. If it had been a man, Casey thought, it would have been blown to smithereens twice over. But the creature, though barely conscious, still seemed to be intact.

Like piranhas around a much larger but ailing enemy, Loonies and mercs alike closed in for the kill. They opened fire from all directions, the Upgrade's body jerking as a multitude of bullets spanged off its armor, and maybe even off its alien hide.

Casey turned to her right to see Nebraska leap up onto the boulder he'd been hiding behind, a flare gun in his hand. Shouting at the men to stand clear, he pointed it at the prone body of the Upgrade and pulled the trigger. The projectile arced across the clearing, a mini blazing comet. Nebraska's aim was perfect. The flare hit the Upgrade dead center, the phosphorous on its body ignited, and suddenly the alien was engulfed from head to toe in flames.

That's it, Casey thought with a kind of wonder. *It's dead. We've killed it*. But as though it could read her mind, and wanted to prove her wrong, the Upgrade suddenly leaped to its feet, roaring and flailing, causing men to fall back before it. As it beat at the flames that had transformed it into a fire demon, McKenna kept circling it, kept firing at it—until suddenly his gun clicked empty.

"Mag," he shouted, and Rory tossed one across to him. He caught it cleanly, but even before he could load it and resume firing, Traeger was emerging from hiding, shouting across at him to stand back.

McKenna had barely done so when Trager faced the Upgrade and let loose with the shoulder cannon. *Oh, so now he wants to be a hero*, Casey thought cynically. He fired once, then again, each shot a direct hit, each shot rocking the Upgrade back on its heels.

How much more punishment can it take? Casey wondered. One thing was for sure. The Upgrade was an incredibly tough motherfucker. But it wasn't indestructible. Because *nothing* was indestruct—

All at once, glancing at Traeger, Casey noticed that the left leg of his pants had caught fire. The Upgrade's flailing had caused little fires to break out everywhere, clumps of blazing foliage flying around the clearing like dying fireworks. Most fizzled out as they landed, but one must have drifted down onto the back of Traeger's leg and set the fabric of his pants alight. Even now, flames were licking up his calf toward his knee—and he was so caught up in the assault on the Upgrade that he hadn't even noticed.

"Hey! Traeger!" she yelled, gesturing at his burning pants.

Distracted, he jerked his head around, saw the flames, and panicked.

Big mistake.

As his head swiveled round, so did the shoulder cannon, in sync with his movements. Only now it was pointing at the back of his skull, and the sudden surge of adrenaline in his brain was enough to trigger it. There was a *whoosh!* as the cannon fired, and suddenly Traeger's head was nothing but flying offal. As the merc standing closest to him was splattered with blood and shards of bone and porridgey lumps of brain matter, Traeger's headless body staggered sideways a couple of paces, and then tumbled forward, hitting the ground with a graceless thump.

"Fuck me!" Casey blurted, and clapped a hand to her mouth. Traeger had been a ruthless fucker with a rotten black soul, but she still felt guiltily responsible for his death. If she hadn't pointed out that his pants were on fire…

If she hadn't pointed it out, he'd have burned to death anyway, she told herself firmly.

She still felt bad—though it was perhaps a good thing that she didn't have the luxury of wallowing in remorse for long. With a bellow of rage, the Upgrade, still burning, rallied again, surging to its feet like a boxer on the ropes who refuses to go down, and swinging one vast, burning arm in the direction of a merc who had ventured too close to it. The merc leaped back with a yell, the Upgrade's clawed hand missing his face by mere inches and smashing into a tree. Sturdy as it was, the tree splintered in a shower of sparks, several of its branches shaking loose and crashing to the ground. One of them embedded itself into the soft earth and toppled sideways, its torn end coming to rest against the thicker branch of another tree that jutted out from the trunk at an almost perfect right angle. Now the fallen branch, canted sideways, resembled a ladder leaning against the side of a house. And suddenly Casey saw Baxley leaping onto that ladder and scaling it like a monkey, his face twisted demonically, nothing in his eyes but the raging desire to bring their enemy down.

No! she thought as Baxley reached the top of the leaning branch and launched himself, screaming, through the air. He looked just like Bruce Lee, or Charlie Chan, arms and legs pinwheeling as he hurtled toward the still-burning Upgrade.

She cried out as he landed on its back and scrabbled for purchase, throwing an arm around its neck. In his other hand, Casey saw, he was holding a knife, which he used to stab the Upgrade savagely in the face, burying the blade deep into its right eye.

The Upgrade howled, and thrashed from side to side, but Baxley, his own clothes and hair burning now, held on. Then the Upgrade reached round with its left arm and plucked him from its shoulder. It held him in the air for a moment, dangling and kicking, and then it hurled him away from itself as hard as it could. Baxley flew through the air, only to hit the jutting javelin of a tree branch, which went clean through his body. It entered his back and burst out through his chest, like a metal skewer through a piece of barbecued meat.

As he hung there, pinned like a burning butterfly, twenty feet up in the air, Casey let out a gasp, too horrified even to scream. She'd known Baxley only a very short time, but due to the sheer intensity of what they'd shared, and the fact they'd put their lives on the line for each other time and again, she'd grown to think of him—as she thought of all the Loonies—as a brother. They'd been under sentence of death pretty much since they met, but it was still impossible to believe that, suddenly and violently, he was gone.

McKenna was far more used to death than Casey was, but even he stared up at Baxley with horror. Then he became aware of movement to his left, and turned to see Coyle stumbling forward, eyes wide, staring up at his friend in disbelief. "*Help him!*" Coyle screamed. "*Someone help him!*"

The Upgrade took advantage of the distraction to show that, despite being consumed by fire and half-blinded, it was not yet beyond fighting back. It flicked out its wrist once again, and a split second later its lethal throwing blade was whistling across the clearing. Before McKenna, or anyone else, knew what was happening, the blade had sliced through Coyle's left leg like a laser beam, severing it cleanly from his body. With a spray of blood, the leg toppled one way and Coyle the other. McKenna heard Casey scream, and then Rory.

Spinning round, he saw the Upgrade turn and stumble away into the jungle. Despite its injuries, it moved fast, its burning shape flickering in and out between the blackness of the trees. Accompanied by Nebraska and Nettles, he gave chase. The thing was probably three-quarters dead already, but he wanted to finish the job if he could.

Lying on the ground, feeling the life drain out of him, Coyle looked up at his friend. Baxley was still burning, his body still twitching. Could he still feel pain? Coyle didn't know, but he wasn't taking any chances.

He groped for his gun, which lay on the ground next to his right hand. His arm felt like lead, and the gun was ridiculously heavy, but through sheer force of will he gripped it, lifted it, leveled it, pulled the trigger.

His aim was true. He saw Baxley's head snap back and his body slump forward, relaxed now. No more pain.

Don't say I never do nothing for you, he thought fuzzily. *Goodbye, old friend.*

Then he died.

Casey might have been with Coyle at the moment of his death if she hadn't been trying to save her own hide. As she was moving across the clearing toward him, and saw him groping for his gun, she heard a whistling sound from the far side of the clearing, faint at first but getting rapidly louder.

She knew what it was immediately. The Upgrade's throwing blade, having taken off Coyle's leg and kept on going, had now reached the end of its piece of invisible elastic and was heading back home. It was only the shock of seeing Baxley and Coyle die so horrifically, one after the other, that had made her forget all about it. Now she shouted a warning and threw herself to the ground.

She only just made it. Another second, and the blade would have gone through her without pause, smashing ribs and vertebrae and punching through her internal organs as if they weren't even there.

Lying on the ground, she saw it flash above her head and fly into the blackness of the jungle, following the route taken not only by the fleeing Upgrade, but also by his pursuers.

McKenna and Nebraska.

Crashing through the undergrowth, rifles held diagonally across their chests, McKenna and Nebraska pursued their quarry with grim determination. The Upgrade was a constant flicker of flame through the trees ahead, and although it was still moving fast, it was clearly hampered by its injuries, which meant that both men could keep up with it easily.

McKenna wondered what would happen once the Upgrade was dead. With Traeger gone too, would the trumped-up charges against him melt away? And what about Casey and Nebraska and Nettles? Would they be free to resume whatever life they'd been living before they'd found themselves in a fight between a maverick offshoot of the US government and a couple of alien hunters? They were heroes now, after all. Heroes who may have helped save the world from—

Then the still-burning body of the Upgrade abruptly disappeared, interrupting his thoughts.

What had happened? Had the flames on the alien's body finally petered out? Had it collapsed? He and Nebraska halted, a questioning look passing between them. After a moment, Nebraska gave a single nod, whose meaning McKenna understood without a word needing to be exchanged: *Proceed with caution.*

They resumed their pursuit, but slowly now, McKenna thinking that if he could wish for anything at that moment it would be a pair of night goggles. He kept his senses attuned, but there was no sound, aside from the usual rustle of leaves and foliage stirred by the warm night breeze, and no sign of a flame ahead or even above them.

They had been moving for maybe a couple of minutes when Nebraska suddenly drew in a sharp breath and grabbed McKenna's arm. McKenna looked at him, thinking he must have spotted a movement or a flicker of flame, but instead he pointed at the ground directly ahead.

McKenna looked at where he was pointing—and as his eyes adjusted, a vertiginous dizziness swept over him.

The blackness in front of him was not the jungle floor, as he'd thought, but the edge of a steep ravine. Another couple of seconds and he'd have stepped right off it and plunged into the depths below.

Unslinging his pack, he extracted a flashlight. He hadn't wanted to draw attention to their position by using it before, but now he switched it on and shone the beam over the edge of the precipice.

Some thirty or forty meters below them was a creek bed, the water glistening blackly in the torchlight. And rising from the creek bed, though dispersing before it reached the lip of the ravine on which they were standing, was a pall of thick, gray smoke—as though something large, something that had been on fire, had crashed down into the water.

McKenna and Nebraska looked at each other again. This was it, then. The end of the road. The Upgrade had fallen over the precipice, and into the creek, and was almost certainly dead. But there was no way of checking, no way of clambering down the side of the ravine to make sure, especially in the dark.

McKenna opened his mouth to say they might as well head back, when Nebraska suddenly reached out a hand and shoved him to one side. As he fell to his right and Nebraska dived to his left, McKenna heard a high-pitched whistling sound, and then something flashed between them and arced down into the ravine.

What the hell, McKenna thought, then all at once he realized. It was the Upgrade's throwing star, the one that had taken Coyle's leg, and almost certainly his life. It was returning to its point of origin, the alien's wrist gauntlet, which was hopefully, at this moment, being washed downstream, strapped to the charred corpse of an alien killer.

Reacting to a powerful electronic homing signal, the throwing star plunged over the side of the ravine and hurtled down toward the black thread of water below. Suddenly, as though in response, a huge arm, blackened and steaming but intact, thrust up through the surface of the water, taloned fingers clawing at the air.

The throwing star attached itself to the metal gauntlet encasing the wrist with a metallic snap. The hand flexed again, and then the water beside it surged and boiled as the rest of the body broke the surface.

24

It was dawn. They were running.

Again.

They had had at least a couple hours' respite after their victory, a time to rest and recuperate, to eat a little food and bury their fallen comrades. When McKenna and Nebraska had returned to the clearing to announce that they *thought* the Upgrade was dead, there had been tired cheers—but only from the couple of Traeger's mercs who had survived the encounter. For the rest of them, the price had been too high for them to feel they could celebrate their enemy's downfall—and when Nettles had glared at the mercs for daring to express their joy and relief, they had shut up quickly, and then had slunk away soon afterward, like funeral attendees who had suddenly realized they were in the wrong church.

McKenna had thought it was tempting fate to hang around too long, and so as soon as they were ready they were back on the move again. With Rory on his shoulders, he led the way through the jungle toward the helicopter, which they had landed on a plateau at the jungle's edge, a couple of miles to the south. They had covered around half that distance, maybe a little more, when Casey voiced her suspicion that they were being followed.

McKenna wanted to tell her that they were fine, that it was nothing but her imagination, but he would just have been fooling himself. Casey was smart, levelheaded, and eminently capable, and he had grown to trust her instincts implicitly. Besides which, as soon as she spoke up, both Nebraska and Nettles admitted that they had been thinking the same thing—and even McKenna himself, much as he hated to say so in front of Rory, told them that his own Spidey-senses had been tingling for a little while too.

The question was, was their pursuer—or pursuers— human or alien? McKenna hoped they would never need to find out. They doubled their pace, and covered the last mile of jungle in less than eight minutes. It was a relief when they finally burst from the tangle of trees and undergrowth to see the ludicrous pink helicopter still standing where they had left it, like a loyal pet awaiting their return.

As they broke cover and started running for the chopper, McKenna glanced back—and just for an instant he thought he saw movement in the jungle behind them. But it was too swift, too fleeting, for him to be sure, and the next instant his eyes were dazzled by the dawn sun rising over the distant hills. He faced front again, jogging toward the chopper, Rory bouncing on his shoulders.

Nettles was already in the pilot's seat, Nebraska and Casey climbing in beside him. The engine coughed into life and the rotors started to turn.

"Come on!" Nettles shouted.

Another minute, McKenna thought. Another minute and they would be up in the air, flying away from this place. Eight of them had arrived here, and five would be leaving. It wasn't great odds, but it could have been worse.

He was a dozen steps from the chopper when a blazing streak of energy erupted from the edge of the jungle and hit the machine like a thunderbolt. Nettles, Casey, and Nebraska were blasted clean out of the still-open door of the cockpit, which crumpled like a deflating balloon as the rotors warped out of shape and stuttered to a halt.

The shock wave of the blast knocked McKenna off his feet, Rory tumbling from his shoulders. As he lay dazed, he saw Casey stagger upright and beckon to Rory, who ran across to her, bent low to make himself less of a target. McKenna watched as the scientist and his son took refuge behind the only cover available to them— the still-smoking ruins of the helicopter—and then, pushing himself groggily to his knees, he glanced over his shoulder.

He was not surprised by what he saw, but it still sent a weary shudder of horror and dismay through him.

From the trees at the edge of the jungle, its huge body shimmering as it decloaked, stepped the Upgrade. It was battered and blackened, its right eye a suppurating mass of gore, but even now it still looked more than capable of ripping them apart with its bare hands.

It looked mightily pissed off too—but then it always did. McKenna wondered what it would be like to be born in a rage, and to stay that way your entire life.

The Upgrade's gaze swept over him, and then it turned its attention to Nebraska and Nettles, who were clambering to their feet, and to Casey and Rory, sheltering behind the wrecked helicopter. Remembering the declaration the creature had made back at the crash site as to who its real target was, and all the people who had died since, McKenna decided that enough was enough. If the alien wanted him, it could have him. He didn't want to have to see anyone else die because of him today.

Rising to his feet, he spread his arms and walked toward the alien. "Okay," he said. "I'm over here. I'm the one you want. Leave them alone."

The Upgrade snapped its head back round to regard him. McKenna braced himself as the creature strode forward, wrapped one huge hand around his throat and lifted him off his feet. For a second he hung there, staring into the creature's one good eye—and then, to his amazement, he felt himself flying through the air, having been tossed aside like yesterday's fish.

He hit the ground, rolled, and by the time he had managed to prop himself up on one knee, the Upgrade was striding toward the helicopter. McKenna saw Nettles and Nebraska racing to retrieve their guns, which were lying some distance away, having been flung out like shrapnel when the energy bolt had hit the chopper. Then he saw Casey run out from hiding, her hands held up in front of her, as if that could halt the progress of the colossal brute bearing down on her.

"Please…" he heard her say, but before she could utter another word the Upgrade swung an arm, swatting her aside like a troublesome fly.

McKenna felt cold prickling terror sweep through him as the Upgrade shoved aside the ruined helicopter, exposing Rory's cowering form. Reaching down, it swept the boy up as though he was a puppy, and then it turned and headed for a rising slope of rock, topped with trees, that fringed the far side of the natural plateau on which they had landed the helicopter. Beyond those trees, McKenna remembered from their approach, was a quarry—a vast natural bowl of pale rock and baked earth. He saw the Upgrade reach the top of the slope and disappear into the trees, still carrying his son.

As a soldier, McKenna was used to staying calm under pressure, but now his body was sizzling with panic. "No," he shouted, his voice raw and ragged. "*No!*" He tried to get to his feet, to run after the Upgrade, but he had hit the ground with such force when the Upgrade had tossed him aside that his legs were still throbbing with numbness, and no sooner was he on his feet than they crumpled beneath him again. He slapped the ground, spat blood on the dry earth—he had bitten his tongue when he landed—and started to crawl toward his gun, for all the good that would do.

Then Casey was beside him, her elbow grazed and bleeding, dirt streaking her face.

"He lied," McKenna almost sobbed. "Said he wanted me…"

Casey shook her head, grabbed his arm to support him as he made another attempt to stand. "No, he didn't. He said he wanted *McKenna*."

Suddenly, the penny dropped. McKenna looked at her with horror.

"He wants an upgrade," Casey went on. "Get it? Not you, your son. The next step on the evolutionary chain."

He let out a roar of rage and despair, using the adrenaline of it to rise to his feet with Casey's help, to stamp the feeling back into his numb legs. He began to run toward the trees into which the Upgrade had disappeared with Rory, Casey running alongside him, and Nebraska and Nettles, having now retrieved their weapons, bringing up the rear.

They reached the tree line within ten seconds, and in another ten had burst through the trees to the other side. When they had passed over the quarry in the helicopter yesterday, it had looked empty, but now McKenna realized it had not been empty at all. They arrived just in time to see a glassy shimmer, and next moment the stark, brutal lines of a Predator ship—larger and sturdier than the damaged escape pod at the crash site—materialized before their eyes.

There was no sign of the Upgrade itself—which probably meant that he and Rory were already inside. As the rumble of engines filled their ears, McKenna once again felt panic sluice through him.

We're too late, he thought.

N N N

Rory couldn't decide which was the worst option—dying right now, or being taken to the Predator's planet. Like everyone else, he had thought his dad was the alien's target, but as soon as the Upgrade had thrown his dad aside and turned its attention to him, he had realized what its true intentions were.

It thought he was smart. Smart enough that his intelligence would enhance its own race. But how would they extract that intelligence and apply it to themselves? He thought it best not to think about that for now.

When the Upgrade had lifted Rory up, he had curled into a ball and stayed quiet. He hadn't struggled, hadn't protested, hadn't tried to communicate with the alien in any way, because he knew it would be pointless. He didn't like looking at the Upgrade's mangled face, because it was scary and also gruesome enough to make him feel sick, so he had kept his eyes tightly shut during the short journey to its ship. The alien smelled of overdone barbecue and its flesh was rough and hot. As it descended the rocky slope of the quarry and marched to its ship, he had heard its heart beating, a regular, rapid boom, strong and somehow ominous, like a war drum.

He only opened his eyes once they were inside the Upgrade's ship—because how could he not? Terrified as he was, this was an alien spacecraft, and therefore it was automatically awesome.

It was a lot different to the ships he had seen on TV and in movies—darker, and full of weird angles, and more functional somehow, and yet at the same time more real and more... well, *alien*. There was a command deck of sorts, but it contained machinery whose function he couldn't even begin to hazard a guess at. And there were bewildering displays of jagged, ever-changing alien symbols flickering across seemingly every surface. There were organic-looking pods set into alcoves along one wall too, like giant moth cocoons made from dark crystalline material, similar to the ones in the craft that the smaller Predator had arrived in.

Rory was peering at the pods, trying to work out their function, when the Upgrade tossed him into one of them, as carelessly as he himself might toss a ball of crumpled paper into a wastepaper basket. He cowered in there, not daring to move, as the Upgrade moved across to the command deck and busied itself with various controls. Moments later there was a whooshing hiss, followed by a deep rumble, which could only mean one thing. The Upgrade was firing up the engines.

Rory's heart started to beat very fast indeed. Was this it? Were these his last minutes on Earth? Would he see his mom and dad ever again? Would he ever see another human being?

Where would he be this time tomorrow? In space? On another planet?

As the rumbling of the engines rose in pitch and power, becoming a screech as savage as the war cry of the Upgrade itself, he clung to the sides of the pod and tried not to cry.

"Dad," he whispered

25

McKenna, Casey, Nebraska, and Nettles watched, aghast, as the Predator ship, its engines screaming, slowly began to rise. Dust blew up from the quarry and blasted over them, stinging their skin, making them screw up their eyes.

Casey pointed at a rising outcrop of rock a little further along the rim, which jutted out over the quarry like a natural viewing platform.

"I'll go low, you go high!" she yelled above the din of the engines.

McKenna nodded, then he, Nebraska, and Nettles turned and sprinted up the hill toward the outcrop, attempting to get above the ship, which was now rising from the ground, plasma exhaust spewing beneath it.

McKenna reached the outcrop first, his concern for Rory causing adrenaline to pump through his system, overcoming his tiredness. The ship kept rising; it was fifteen feet below the outcrop now. As McKenna bolted up the hill, it continued to rise, blowing exhaust, preparing for departure.

McKenna reached the top of the outcrop. Without hesitation, he jumped…

…and landed on top of the ship, yelping in pain as his ankle twisted and he went sprawling across the smooth, alien metal surface. He scrambled to his feet, aware of the pain in his ankle but sublimating it. He turned to see that Nebraska and Nettles had waited for the ship to rise until it was exactly level with the outcrop. Now they stepped onto its surface as if they were getting onto an elevator.

McKenna shot them a withering glare.

"Shoot it down!" he called over the wind that began to whip around them as the ship took on speed. "Aim for the engines!"

Nebraska and Nettles traded shrugs, then all three of them opened fire. Bullets spat from their weapons, raking the ship's roof, then ricocheted off with nary a dent. Even so, McKenna kept pulling his trigger with grim determination, trying to quell the thought of just how fucked they would be, standing on top of a rising spacecraft, if they couldn't force it to land.

And then, as if things couldn't get any worse, the ship abruptly turned, tilted, and all three of them fell. McKenna hit the hull, sliding, scrambling to find a handhold, seconds away from having nothing but open sky beneath him.

Casey had managed to find a place with a gentle gradient where she could scramble down into the quarry without mishap. Unslinging the M4 from her shoulder, which she had picked up in the clearing after the firefight with the Upgrade, she ran across the dusty surface of the quarry floor until she was standing directly beneath the rising ship.

From below, she couldn't see any part of the ship that looked particularly vulnerable. Everything looked shielded, armored, the outer skin of the craft—knowing the Predators as she now did—seemingly as tough and uncompromising as everything else about them. She knew that for several reasons it was probably a very bad idea to stand beneath the ship and fire up at it—but she did it anyway. Gritting her teeth, she fired a full clip at the ship's underbelly, hearing her bullets whine and clatter as they ricocheted.

When the ship tilted to one side, she was astonished, then elated, then alarmed. *She'd done it!* Or at least one of them had. But she quickly realized that wasn't the case, that the ship's pilot was simply either taking evasive action or adjusting the ship's trajectory as part of its normal take-off routine. Next moment, as if to confirm this, the roar of the engines abruptly increased, and the jet-wash knocked Casey off her feet.

"…ohshitohshitohshit…" Nettles chanted like it was a prayer to God. Maybe it was, McKenna thought, as in, *oh-shit-please-God-don't-let-me-die.*

McKenna knew how he felt. He clung to the roof of the ship, the wind whipping around him. He could see Nettles and Nebraska in his peripheral vision, but he dared not look at them. It required all his focus just to hang on. The ship kept ascending. Their perch was precarious. At any second, he figured the ship would zip further skyward, moving faster, tilting backward, breaking through the atmosphere. All three of them would take a long, long fall to their deaths… and Rory would still be aboard the alien craft, where he'd suffer at the hands of the Upgrade Predator. It would tap his spine for his DNA, tear him apart. He'd scream in pain.

His boy.

McKenna needed to focus. He had to hold on. But if he, Nettles, and Nebraska had any chance to survive— and to save Rory—then he couldn't wait another second. It was all or nothing, now.

Back in the clearing he'd given Rory one of the earwig comms units he'd brought with him from the RV, so that, if for any reason they got separated, they could still communicate with each other. Now he cupped one hand to his ear, and, hoping the comms unit was still working, shouted over the rushing wind.

"Rory, I'm on top of the ship! Are you okay?"

For a few seconds, he heard no reply. But then there came muffled static, and Rory's shocked reply.

"Mom was right. You *are* crazy."

Rory knew there were two things keeping him alive. The first was that the Predator wanted something from him. The second was that the monstrosity didn't consider him a physical threat. He peered from the open pod, or hibernation chamber, or whatever this thing was, watching, waiting for an opportunity to do something that would save him, or his father, or by some miracle both of them.

He'd just told his dad he was crazy when he saw the Upgrade press a series of buttons, and next second something started happening on one of the monitors. The screen showed an outline, like a blueprint, of the ship and all its systems... and then a blinking dotted line began to form, surrounding the ship. Rory's eyes widened as he realized what it meant, and tucking himself back into the pod, he frantically tapped the comms unit his father had given him.

"Dad? There's a force field going online—automatic!"

Static. Then: "Uh... say again?"

"Look out!" Rory hissed.

McKenna saw the air shimmer around him. He felt a prickle of static around his legs. Whipping around, the import of what Rory had reported hit him, and he had time to shout only a single word. He screamed at his men to jump, even as he did so himself... or tried. The instant he attempted to launch himself upward, the pain from his injured ankle flared up again and his leg buckled. He stumbled to one side like a drunk, then fell flat on his back on top of the ship.

Nebraska must have felt the tingling too—either that, or he trusted McKenna implicitly—because he jumped without hesitation.

Nettles, on the other hand... hesitated. Maybe, McKenna thought, his mind was racing and he just needed a moment to process. Unfortunately, he didn't get that moment. He was still standing on the surface of the ship when the force field blasted on with an ionized sizzling noise—a force field that, although invisible, still sheared neatly through Nettles' legs at knee-level.

McKenna lay beneath the field, which was just above him, and watched a lock of his hair feathering down, clipped, to rest on the invisible barrier before being carried away by the wind. He also saw Nettles' foreshortened body falling away, his blood running in a dozen trickling lines across the outer surface of the force field.

Nebraska, meanwhile, came down boots first on top of the force shield. It looked surreal, as if he was standing in midair. He threw himself onto his belly, legs splayed, palms flat, eyes wide with terror as he held on, separated from McKenna only by a meter or so of invisible energy.

Breathless but protected, McKenna lay beneath the shield, and looked helplessly up at his friend. They locked eyes through the barrier, inches apart—then, as the ship rose higher, increasing speed, Nebraska's hands began to slip. For a second he looked anguished, desperate, and then all at once he seemed to accept his fate and his face relaxed. He looked again at McKenna through the invisible shield, gave him a wry smile and shrugged his shoulders. He mouthed something—McKenna couldn't quite make it out, but what he thought Nebraska said was: *It's been fun.*

Then Nebraska's body slid away, over the curve of the ship's surface, and he was gone.

McKenna wanted to mourn him, knew that the memory of Nebraska's last moments would be seared into his mind forever. But he didn't have the luxury to grieve now. Nebraska and Nettles had just died trying to help him save his son, and his best tribute to them would be to try to complete the mission.

But how? Desperation mounting, McKenna drew the pistol he still carried. He gripped it tight, steeled himself, and then rolled toward the edge of the ship. Every survival instinct told him to stop, screamed at him that this was lunacy, that it was suicide.

But he kept going.

He rolled right over the curving edge of the ship, and fell.

But not very far.

He hit the inside of the force field and tumbled down an invisible slide, slewing and twisting in what seemed to be midair until he came to a stop, underneath the alien craft. Where his hands touched, where his knees touched, there appeared to be only air. The utter wrongness of that made his brain reject what he saw and caused his guts to churn, so he flopped over and focused on what was above him.

The ship's underbelly.

He looked around, and a spark of hope ignited in him. Only feet away, he saw the yawning shadow of an empty port, where an escape pod had once nestled. Taking a breath, he rolled again, then crawled on elbows and knees until he reached the opening, before clambering inside. Clinging to a strut inside the opening, he glanced around and spotted a keypad.

"Rory!" he shouted over their commlink. "What's the sequence? I watched you put it in. Tell me!"

Static, and then: "To the pod? I... I can't remember!"

McKenna took a deep breath. "Okay, do this. *Try*."

"I can't think! It's all mixed up in my head!"

"Damn it, son! I watched you! It was one, two, then over three, up two..."

McKenna's words trailed off. He blinked, staring at the keypad, and realized he didn't need Rory to remember. "Holy shit," he murmured. "I fucking know it!" Frantically, he stabbed a finger at the pad, tapping buttons.

"Rory?" he continued. "You know how I always said be a big boy?"

"Yeah?"

"Screw it. Make yourself small, kid." He tapped the last digits of the sequence into the keypad. "Down! Now!"

The hatch slid open. McKenna lunged inside, gun comfortable in his hand. He unloaded all the grief and fear that he had felt for his men, and for his son. Teeth bared, he targeted every blinking light he saw, blazing away with shot after shot.

Sparks flew from consoles, and the whole ship shuddered. Whatever McKenna had hit, the alien craft was taking it personally.

Shrouded in the gray gloom of the command deck, the massive Predator whipped around, faux-dreadlocks flying. It spotted McKenna, saw the open hatch where the escape pod should have been, and a trilling series of clicks issued from its mandibles as it lifted an arm and fired.

It wasn't an energy beam that erupted from its wrist

gauntlet this time, though. It was a metal cable, which spat through the air like a whirling bolo. One end of the cable embedded itself in a wall panel, while the bolo part wrapped itself around McKenna's left leg, below the knee, and cinched tight. Jerked off his feet by the Upgrade, he yelled out in pain as the ship dipped and veered, plummeting toward the tree line. He smelled smoke and glanced at Rory, who was clinging for dear life to the walls of the pod he was crouched in. He had disabled the ship, as planned, but at what cost? Had he saved Rory from torture and death at the hands of an alien hunter, only for them both to now die in a devastating explosion when the spaceship crashed?

Alarms wailed as the tops of trees started to rush up fast in the forward view screen. Under other circumstances, the Upgrade might have moved in for the kill, but right now it clearly had other things on its mind. It detached the other end of the metal rope from its wrist gauntlet with the stab of a button and turned back toward the main control panel. As it busied itself at the controls, trying to correct the damage that McKenna had done, McKenna himself picked at the wire wrapped around his leg, trying to work himself loose. Unable to do so, he scooped up his dropped gun and fired at the wall panel that the other end of the cable was attached to. The panel buckled, part of it tearing loose from the wall. McKenna raised his gun again, thinking one more shot might do it, when the ship impacted with something—the top of a tree, maybe—and tilted vertiginously to one side.

Rory yelled out as McKenna started to slide toward the

still-open hatchway. The metal cable between his leg and the wall panel went taut, held for a moment... and then the damaged wall panel tore itself loose from the wall!

Now McKenna was yelling too, and clawing at the smooth floor, but he couldn't halt his slide toward oblivion. He thought of Nebraska sliding off the edge of the ship. Was he going to go the same way? Then he was out of the hatch and falling through space, wind buffeting him as he plunged toward certain death.

The wall panel with the clawed end of the metal cable still firmly embedded in it clattered after McKenna's falling body—and became jammed in the narrow hatchway. McKenna slammed to a stop, the loops of cable tightening yet further, cutting into his leg, drawing blood. Now he was dangling upside down beneath the ship like the weirdest car ornament imaginable. He swung to and fro, and then to his horror saw the tree line rising to meet him. Next moment he had covered his head with his arms and was trying to protect himself as best he could, as his body was dragged through a mass of branches and leaves.

If the Upgrade's ship had continued to increase speed, McKenna would almost certainly have been ripped to shreds before the craft reached the ground. However, to avoid crashing, the alien must have employed the forward thrusters, because almost as soon as McKenna's body dipped beneath the tree line he felt his forward momentum slowing down. Instead of punctured flesh and broken bones, therefore, he received only superficial injuries—scratches and bruises. Now that he'd avoided being shredded, though, his main problem was how he'd avoid hitting the ground first, and then the ship landing on top of him—but at that moment Fate intervened.

The wall panel stuck in the escape pod hatchway snapped in half, and suddenly McKenna was tumbling straight down between the trees. It was still a long way to the ground, but luckily the chunk of panel, which tumbled after him, was big enough to slow his progress. He dropped in increments, *oof*ing and *ouch*ing as his body thumped against branches and was slashed by twigs. He was still four or five meters from the ground when the panel stuck in the crook of a branch and jammed tight, leaving him dangling, groaning, bleeding, bruised, and fighting desperately to stay conscious.

Although it was slowing all the while, the ship still hit the tops of the trees with a mighty *WHUMPH!* and ricocheted upward like a flat stone bouncing off the surface of a lake. Beyond the quarry and the trees was a huge area of swampland, and it was into this that the ship eventually crashed, skimming across an oily expanse of brackish water before hurtling headfirst into a tangle of fallen, moss-covered trees.

The impact caused the viewing port at the front of the ship to explode inward, and the Upgrade, which had been standing at the main control panel, to be ejected like a cork from a pop gun. It flew through the air, limbs pinwheeling, splashed down into the boggy water and was instantly submerged.

The crumpled, battered ship subsided, sinking a little further into the primordial ooze before coming to rest.

For several seconds the echoes of the bellowing chaos that for the last few minutes had disturbed this ancient stretch of land seemed to thrum in the twisted trees, to ripple across the water.

Then the echoes subsided, and all was silent once more.

McKenna came to, upside down, his side thudding with pain, his arms and legs scraped and bloody, and his clothing torn in too many places to count. Taking stock, he looked ahead of him, and through a thin layer of trees saw a green and brown spread of swamp below. The Upgrade's ship sat half-submerged, canted at an angle, shattered trees downed around it. Something shifted beneath the mossy surface of the water, cutting a V-line toward him, and McKenna thought his luck had gone from astonishingly bad to astonishingly good and then to eaten-by-an-alligator.

But it wasn't an alligator at all.

What rose from the swamp, huge and hunched over, was the Upgrade. Somehow, the gigantic Predator had been thrown from its ship. Where Rory might be, McKenna had no idea, but he knew that if this monster still lived, he needed to take every advantage he could find to try to kill it.

Thankful that his sidearm hadn't been shaken loose by his plunge through the trees, he drew it and shot the Upgrade twice in the chest.

Caught off guard, it bellowed as it staggered backward and collided with its own ship. Shooting out a hand, it clutched at the ship, steadying itself.

Which turned out to be a mistake.

Bruised and aching, more than a little disoriented, Rory saw it all unfold on the ship's monitors. When the bullets hit the Upgrade and it staggered back against its own spacecraft, he leaped for the control console and pounded it with his fist.

Just like that, the force shield flickered on.

McKenna bared his teeth as he saw the air sizzle and the force field zap into place. The Predator bellowed in rage and pain, then jerked away from the ship as if stung. McKenna watched it slowly raise its arm in front of its face, then stare down with what could only be interpreted as astonishment at the neatly cauterized stump where its hand and forearm had been only a moment before. He knew he wasn't safe yet, and neither was Rory, but that didn't stop the grin from spreading across his face.

Although his body was a throbbing mass of pain, he somehow managed to untangle himself from the branches and the metal cable wrapped around his leg and let himself drop. He hit a small hillock at the edge of the swamp, rolled down it a little way, then clambered to his feet. Denying his blazing ribs, his throbbing back, and his aching legs, he started running toward the Upgrade, which had forged its way to the edge of the swamp now, over to his left. As it used an overhanging tree to haul itself from the bog, he leveled his weapon and fired several more shots, then dove behind a tree before it could retaliate. He breathed through his teeth as the pain flared, head swimming.

Then he blinked, wondering if he had started hallucinating. Because right in front of him, incongruous as hell, just lying there as if it was the most ordinary thing in the world, was a motorcycle.

Overhead, something shifted in the trees. He snapped his head back, stared up into the branches, taking aim at nothing—and then the nothing shimmered and materialized into Dr. Casey Brackett. She was wearing the wrist gauntlet from the original Predator, the one she must have appropriated from Traeger's duffel bag. Sweating, strands of hair sticking to her face, she looked like a savage up there in the trees.

But Casey's unexpected appearance had distracted him from the Upgrade. Suddenly, it unleashed a war cry as it splashed into view, moving around the tree to get to McKenna.

Snarling, unleashing a war cry of her own, Casey launched herself from the branches onto the Upgrade's shoulders. She grabbed a fistful of its dreadlocks, whipped back her gauntleted hand, and used the blades attached to the gauntlet to slice the dreadlocks clean off.

Roaring, the Upgrade staggered and weaved, clawing blindly at the air.

Once again sublimating his pain, McKenna rushed

forward, and took aim at the Upgrade's chest. Point blank. The huge Predator twisted, putting Casey in McKenna's sights, and he hesitated. In the same moment, the monster whipped her off his back and sent her spinning away through the air, to splash down in the swamp. McKenna got off a single shot before the Upgrade twisted back around, impossibly fast, and knocked him sprawling.

He hit the sodden ground, barely holding onto his gun. Mossy trees stood before him and he knew he had to get to cover, knew he needed a few seconds to breathe, and knew too that if the Upgrade had anything to do with it, he wouldn't get those seconds.

Casey had a mouthful of stinking mud. She choked it up, vomited a pint of filthy water, and dragged herself to her hands and knees. Her head spun and she knew she must have a concussion, but she didn't worry too much about the injury. Dead women didn't need to have their wits about them.

She managed to pull herself onto firmer ground and take cover behind a tree, thinking that if she could just have a minute or so to recover she'd be fit enough to rejoin the fray. But almost immediately she heard a heavy panting above her and she squinted, painfully raising her head.

She was stunned by what she saw. It was the Predator dog, the stupid mutt who'd had a bolt shot through his head and become their faithful hound. They'd been bred to track any prey, so it wasn't that he'd tracked her that seemed a miracle, but the fact he'd wanted to. The dog had been bred to kill what it tracked, but this adorably ugly son of a bitch gazed at her with loving eyes.

He had something in his mandibles, and as she rose to her feet he dropped it with a *plop*.

The bomb cuff from Traeger's bag. The one she'd tossed away earlier, back at the crash site. The crazy mutt had fetched it back and found her, just so it could continue the game.

Casey picked it up, staggered out from behind the tree, and spotted the Upgrade. It was wading through the swamp in pursuit of McKenna. He was running toward the ship, presumably to find cover or rescue Rory. But she could see he'd never make it. The Upgrade would catch him and kill him. And then it would kill her, then Rory.

McKenna heard his name shouted, and glanced round to see Casey holding something in her raised hand. It took him less than a second to recognize the bomb cuff. Still running, he shouted, "Toss it!"

Casey slung the bomb cuff across the swamp and McKenna caught it on the run, snatched it from the air and then dove. An ion blast seared the air over his head and tore through the swamp, incinerating trees and rocks and moss.

McKenna rolled, reached into the shallow muck beneath the ship, and came up with the Upgrade's severed arm.

The gauntlet on the arm had double-pronged projectiles, like hellish crossbow bolts. He looped the destruct collar over the prongs, pivoted, and took aim. He shouted Casey's name, hoping she could see him, hoping she understood exactly what he needed her to do. She still wore the original Predator's wrist gauntlet, and she knew the arming code. Would she—?

The light on the destruct collar started blinking red, quickening.

The Upgrade thundered toward him. It unleashed another war cry. McKenna nearly stumbled as he pulled the trigger, but his aim was good enough. The bolt took the alien in the leg, imbedding itself in the flesh and bone—

McKenna shouted for Casey to get down, even as he dove for cover. The explosion ripped his words from the air, shook the earth beneath them as flames erupted. A fireball swept over their heads and buffeted the ship, and it felt like the world had cracked in half.

It took long seconds this time before McKenna managed to stagger to his feet. When he did, he spotted Casey on one knee. She hoisted herself up by holding onto a tree. The flames were subsiding, the thick air holding onto the smoke, cloaking the swamp in it, but they pushed themselves toward the edge of a massive, scorched crater, swamp muck and other debris spilling down over its edges...

Down inside it lay the bloodied green mess of the Upgrade. It writhed in pain, burnt and broken, barely alive.

McKenna looked at Casey and felt as if they mirrored one another. He saw a grim determination in her face that he knew reflected his own.

"Dad!"

McKenna watched as Rory stepped tentatively out of

the open hatch of the ship. He rushed across the boggy ground and McKenna opened his arms and embraced his son—but his eyes never left the Predator, down in that smoking crater.

The Upgrade, its chest rising and falling rapidly, stared right back at him.

"Who are you?" McKenna asked it. "What are you?"

He didn't really expect an answer, and he didn't get one. Instead, as the swamp muck continued to pour down into the crater, the wounded alien's one good eye flickered to regard Rory. For a moment, it almost seemed to McKenna that the dying Predator was favoring the boy with a look approaching fondness or admiration, or both.

Then it lurched and hurled itself out of the crater, talons bared, lashing out for Rory.

McKenna spun Rory out of its reach, and in the same moment raised his gun and put two bullets through its left eye.

The Predator slumped, sliding back down into the muck, its last breath wheezing out of it as it finally died.

McKenna turned to study Rory, both of them spattered in the creature's green blood.

"Sorry."

"That's okay," Rory replied. "You can shoot him again if you want."

McKenna shook his head and grinned. "I'm good."

26

Trudging back through the clump of jungle that was sandwiched by the swampland on one side and the quarry on the other, Rory came to a sudden halt. McKenna halted too and looked at his son. All three of them were exhausted, filthy, and pretty banged up, and he wondered whether Rory had finally reached his limit, whether he was about to break down and crumple into tears.

He didn't, though. Instead, he took something from his pocket and placed it almost reverently on the ground beside him. And then he started to dig a hole in the soft earth with his hands.

McKenna knelt on one side of his son, and Casey knelt on the other.

"Whatcha got there?" he asked softly.

"Stuff from the guys," Rory replied.

McKenna and Casey exchanged a look. McKenna's raised eyebrows said it all: *He's been collecting mementoes? All this time? And I didn't know?*

He looked more closely at what Rory had spread out on the ground beside him—a bandana, which he guessed must have belonged to one of the guys, its corners turned up to create a little parcel. He glanced a question at his son—*May I?*—and Rory nodded. McKenna reached out and carefully peeled back the four corners of material.

Inside was a crumpled cigarette packet, which had belonged to Nebraska, an equally crumpled Tootsie Roll, fortunately still in its wrapper, which Coyle must have given to Rory from the stock he'd acquired back at the Iron Horse Motel, and one of Lynch's pornographic playing cards.

McKenna swallowed hard. He looked again at Casey, and saw her eyes shimmer with tears. Gently, he wrapped the items up again and said, "Son, these are the forgotten ones. The ones no one's gonna remember." He gestured at the three of them. "Just us."

Rory finished digging his hole. His hands were caked with dirt.

As if handling some ancient and invaluable artifact, McKenna pinched the four corners of the bandana together with his fingers and lifted it. "What say we lay 'em to rest, huh?"

Rory nodded, and McKenna gently lowered the bandana into the hole. Rory was about to start scooping dirt over the little package of treasures when Casey told him to hang on, and unslung her backpack from her shoulders. She opened it, rooted inside, and with trembling fingers withdrew the small foil unicorn that Nettles had left at her bedside back at the motel—it seemed a thousand years ago now. She sighed, and placed the unicorn on top of the bandana, then nodded to Rory to cover everything up.

When he had done so, they all rose wearily, McKenna groaning as he stretched his stiff limbs.

Looking up at the dawn sky, a swirl of pink and purple streaked with yellow, stars still flecking it like diamonds, Casey said, "So… what's next?"

McKenna and Rory looked up too. After a moment McKenna said, "Hey, you on the left…" He pointed. "I see you. We're still here. Come and get us, motherfuckers."

Rory gave him an admonishing look. "Language, Dad."

They all laughed.

Then Casey hoisted her backpack onto her shoulders once again, and they trudged wearily away.

ACKNOWLEDGEMENTS

The Predator toybox is such a fun one to play in, and we'd like to thank everyone at Fox for allowing us to do so – and, in particular, Nicole Spiegel for sending us reams of cool reference material. We'd also like to thank our agent Howard Morhaim, and our editors at Titan, Steve Saffel and Gary Budden, for smoothing the process. And in a more general vein, we'd like to thank our fabulous wives, Connie and Nel, and our equally fabulous children, Nicholas, Daniel, Lily Grace, David, and Polly.

Christopher Golden is the *New York Times* bestselling author of *Snowblind*, *Ararat*, *Of Saints and Shadows*, and many other novels. As editor, his anthologies include *Seize the Night*, *Dark Cities*, and *The New Dead*, among others. Golden has also written screenplays, radio plays, an animated web series, short stories, non-fiction, and video games. He is one-third of the popular pop culture podcast Three Guys with Beards.

Mark Morris has written over twenty-five novels, including the *Obsidian Heart* trilogy and four books in the popular *Doctor Who* range. He is also the author of two short story collections and several novellas. His short fiction, articles, and reviews have appeared in a wide variety of anthologies and magazines, and he is editor of *Cinema Macabre*, a book of horror movie essays for which he won the 2007 British Fantasy Award.

LET THE HUNTING BEGIN!

PREDATOR COMICS AND GRAPHIC NOVELS AVAILABLE NOW.

AVAILABLE AT YOUR LOCAL COMICS SHOP
To find a comics shop in your area, visit comicshoplocator.com
For more information or to order direct visit DarkHorse.com or call 1-800-862-0052

Predator™ & © 2018 Twentieth Century Fox Film Corporation. All rights reserved. TM indicates a trademark
of Twentieth Century Fox Film Cor poration. Dark Horse Comics® and the Dark Horse logo are trademarks
of Dark Horse Comics, Inc., registered in various categories and countries. All rights reserved.

THE PREDATOR
OFFICIAL
FAN APP

EXCLUSIVE SER

EMOJIS

FAN FORUM

OFFICIAL NEWS

STICKERS

JOIN THE HUNT

ULTIMATE WEAPON

Chris Ryan was born near Newcastle in 1961. He joined the SAS in 1984. During his ten years he was involved in overt and covert operations and was also Sniper team commander of the anti-terrorist team. During the Gulf War, Chris was the only member of an eight-man team to escape from Iraq, of which three colleagues were killed and four captured. It was the longest escape and evasion in the history of the SAS. For this he was awarded the Military Medal. For his last two years he was selecting and training potential recruits for the SAS.

He wrote about his experiences in the bestseller *The One That Got Away* which was also adapted for screen. He is also the author of the bestsellers, *Stand By, Stand By, Zero Option, The Kremlin Device, Tenth Man Down, The Hit List, The Watchman, Land of Fire, Greed, The Increment, Blackout, Ultimate Weapon, Strike Back* and *Firefight. Chris Ryan's SAS Fitness Book* and *Chris Ryan's Ultimate Survival Guide* are published by Century.

He lectures in business motivation and security and is currently working as a bodyguard in America.

Also available by CHRIS RYAN

Fiction
Stand By, Stand By
Zero Option
The Kremlin Device
Tenth Man Down
The Hit List
The Watchman
Land of Fire
Greed
The Increment
Blackout
Ultimate Weapon
Strike Back
Firefight

Non-fiction
The One That Got Away
Chris Ryan's SAS Fitness Book
Chris Ryan's Ultimate Survival Guide